FLIRTING WITH MURDER

A totally gripping British crime mystery

BRIAN BATTISON

Detective Jim Ashworth Book 3

Originally published as *Crisis of Conscience*

JOFFE BOOKS

Revised edition 2021
Joffe Books, London
www.joffebooks.com

First published in Great Britain in 1995
as *Crisis of Conscience*

Cover art by Nina Kicul

ISBN: 978-1-78931-692-6

To my sister
Shirley Francis
for happy memories of long ago

PROLOGUE

As the man edged closer to the couple locked in the act of copulation every breath he took seemed to roar in his ears, and despite all efforts at stealth, his every step seemed to crash and vibrate in the still air of the late March evening.

Any second now he expected them to become aware of his approach, pause in their fervour, challenge him. But as he crawled through the bracken which would take him to within yards of the lovers, the only sounds in Bluebell Wood were of mounting passion.

He held his breath, the trapped dank air foul in his mouth, and stifled a curse as blackberry thorns tore at his cheek.

Then he was in position; his crouching stance afforded him a perfect view of the lovemaking. Breathing more easily he watched the couple begin their long climb towards a crescendo, the woman urging her partner on.

And as he watched a strange mixture of emotions churned within him. His eyes took in the woman's long white legs, willingly open as her partner lifted and lowered, lifted and lowered himself upon her; and he heard her raking sobs of sheer delight as feelings of anger and excitement engulfed him.

But then their joy in climax brought back the tortured voices inside his head; and the pain of betrayal within his heart was so real, it was as if a dagger had been thrust into it.

After a while the man rolled off, lay on his back, and although their desires had been quenched it was obvious they had not been fully extinguished, for as the woman kissed her partner's lips, they each toyed intimately with the other's body.

It was the woman who broke the embrace. 'I'd better be going,' she said in a hushed voice.

'Oh, come on,' the man urged, 'he won't miss you for another half an hour.'

'He might,' the woman insisted. 'He's getting a bit suspicious lately, and I'm supposed to be at my mum's.'

'All right, but I'll see you again, won't I?'

'You know you will,' she smiled. 'I can't do without it now.'

They stood and, as the man picked up his raincoat which had served as a lovers' bed, the woman smoothed down her crumpled skirt.

As they made arrangements for later in the week the watcher closed his eyes. His voices had risen to screaming pitch, reverberating around his skull, pulling him first one way, then the other. He wanted to cradle his head in his hands but dared not move.

When he opened his eyes he saw that the couple had parted: the man heading for open fields; the woman setting off on a fifteen-minute walk in the opposite direction which would lead her to a back lane in Bridgetown close to her house.

She hurried along, pulling on her thick, quilted anorak, eager to be home, for her pleasure could not be fully savoured until the fear of possible discovery had been removed.

He began to stalk her, moving quickly, keeping to cover, but making just enough sound to betray his presence.

The woman became agitated, glanced over her shoulder, called, 'Who's there? Is that you, Terry?'

She stopped, hoping her lover would appear and she could chastise him for giving her a fright. When he did not, she turned and ran; the gloom, the almost total silence of the wood fuelling her panic.

But her high-heeled shoes slowed her down and the man caught up with her easily.

'It's all right, Margaret,' he said as he drew level.

She stopped. 'Oh, God.' Her voice was shaking with emotion. 'You scared me half to death. What are you doing here?'

'Just walking.'

Her laughter was interlaced with relief. 'You gave me a turn, you did.'

'I followed you, Margaret.' His tone was now low and even.

Shock registered on the woman's face. 'You've got no right to do that.'

She tried to edge away but, menacingly, he cut off every avenue of escape. 'What do you want?'

'You're never that nice to me, Margaret.' His voice was quiet and calm, which made it all the more chilling.

'Leave me alone.'

Her eyes were wide with panic as she searched for some path around him. She broke to the right, stumbling and crashing through thick undergrowth, crying out in fear.

Unhurriedly the man followed, certain of catching her, certain that his own sexual demons would have to be exorcised.

CHAPTER 1

The ringing of the telephone sliced through Dr Gwen Anthony's thoughts. As she tripped down the stairs of the cottage to answer it, her usual effervescent nature was somewhat subdued. Indeed her present mood matched exactly, in both severity and colour, the plain black dress which was her working attire.

She was a tall woman, past her mid-forties, yet her well-preserved body still curved in the right places; and her black hair, severely tied back, highlighted rather than detracted from the blue eyes, that usually flashed humour and devilment, set in her flawless face.

Standing in the hall with its ceiling beams she lifted the receiver. Her full lips were pursed as she listened attentively for a few moments before saying, 'Right, I'll be there as soon as I can.'

She replaced the receiver, made a few scribbled notes on a pad beside the telephone then, sighing resignedly, made her way to the kitchen.

Gwen and her doctor husband, Nigel, shared a general practice in Bridgetown, where Gwen also served as a locum pathologist to the town's police force.

In common with many cottage-dwellers, they had taken great pains to preserve original features: beamed ceilings and walls; inglenook fireplaces; window seats; but practicality and convenience had been their first considerations when designing the kitchen.

Gwen entered the large square room with its professionally-installed oak units, its oven, hob, and ceramic tiling. Her husband was reading the *Daily Telegraph* and drinking coffee at the breakfast bar.

'That was the police station,' she announced. 'A woman's body has been discovered in Bluebell Wood—'

'And they want you to attend to it,' her husband cut in.

'Yes, that's right.' Gwen poured coffee for herself.

'Leaving me to cope with morning surgery again,' Nigel Anthony remarked haughtily.

'Don't be so bloody silly,' Gwen flared. 'It's only eight thirty. I'll be through well before surgery.'

In the silence that followed, Gwen studied the newspaper concealing her husband's face and wondered why she had married him. True, the joint practice was financially rewarding, allowing them to enjoy an extremely comfortable lifestyle — one which Gwen would be loath to give up; and until the last few months she had been relatively happy with her marriage, always having the freedom she required. But of late that had changed.

She held her breath as Nigel lowered the newspaper and looked at her. The boyish good looks he had retained throughout his thirties had faded, helped on their way by his fondness for brandy. And although his dark pin-striped suit, white shirt and regimental tie lent him an air of distinguished ease, his face was lined, the skin dark and puffy beneath his hazel eyes; and his brown hair, flecked with grey, was beginning to recede at the temples.

Finally he spoke. 'At least it'll give you a chance to see your friend, Ashworth, again. Won't it?'

Gwen felt the flush of guilt spread over her face. 'Oh, for God's sake, don't start that again. It's getting pathetic.'

'Pathetic? That's what I am now, is it? Well, your friend's not the only one capable of doing a little detective work . . .'

His tone implied that this was ground they had covered many times before. '. . . and it seems that you went for a drink with your friend to pass on some post-mortem findings.'

'That's right.' Gwen slammed her coffee cup onto the breakfast bar. 'We've been over this until I'm sick of it. I've told you—'

'Yes, but what you haven't told me is what you were doing in the quite long period which elapsed between leaving the pub and arriving home.'

'I keep telling you—'

'Ah, that's just what you don't do,' Nigel insisted.

'What do you think I am?' Gwen asked heatedly.

'Well, what can we try for size? A whore?'

Gwen felt tears bubbling in her eyes. 'Nigel, I can't stand much more of this. I'm a doctor and pathologist . . . I meet a lot of people just going about my daily business. Why the hell have you developed this thing about Jim Ashworth?'

But she knew only too well why.

Her husband's voice followed her into the hall. 'Maybe I should have a word with the man.'

'Yes, you do that,' she called back angrily, collecting her coat and doctor's bag before slamming out of the cottage into the pale sunlight of an early spring morning.

Her step was heavy as she walked down the garden path, edged with colourful spring flowers, and climbed into the Land Rover.

The mile of rutted track which must be negotiated before reaching the main road was the penance she had to pay for the privilege of living in total solitude.

As she drove along, most of her anger was directed towards herself. Although she had never thought of herself as morally lax, Gwen had always regarded monogamy as something which society tried to impose on people, and it was an imposition she had always resisted.

Throughout her twenty years of married life it had worked out very well, mostly because she had never allowed her indiscretions away from the marital bed to lead to Nigel being neglected; indeed, the combination of guilt and the need for subterfuge had always ensured the exact opposite.

But one night, just over two months ago, she had dawdled briefly with one Chief Inspector Jim Ashworth of Bridgetown CID. Her car was now passing the small lay-by, completely shielded from the road by a high hedge, where the encounter had taken place; and in spite of the trouble it had caused, Gwen found herself smiling at the memory. That night, not only had the earth moved, but all the planets in the galaxy had been somewhat rearranged.

Unfortunately this had caused her to behave in what she now termed as 'post-first-orgasm-manner.' She had made several foolish telephone calls to Ashworth, one of which her husband overheard; and although it had contained nothing really damning, she had used a lot of rather silly double meanings. And as always in matters of adultery, a probing partner had little difficulty in unearthing some incriminating evidence for the imagination to distort and magnify.

But now, away from the oppressive atmosphere of the cottage and her husband's presence, Gwen's mood lightened. Surely, she reasoned as the Land Rover bumped and rattled over the last twenty yards of track, if she could just keep a check on her amorous, flirtatious nature, keep denying anything had happened, and get Jim to do the same, then the storm clouds would pass as quickly as they had gathered. But she knew a lot of self-discipline would be needed on her part for Ashworth still made her feel like a love-sick schoolgirl.

'Another day, another body,' she remarked cheerfully as the tyres gripped the tarmac of the road.

* * *

Jim Ashworth parked his Sierra behind the line of police vehicles which filled up the lane. He was a large, thickset man; and although a combination of diet and exercise had trimmed fifteen pounds from his frame, bringing him down to thirteen and a half stone, his sheer size, his rugged face and hostile brown eyes beneath black hair peppered with grey, made him a formidable sight.

His was an ageless face which had never been young and would probably never be old. Even as he approached his mid-fifties, most would have found it difficult to believe he was expecting his fifth grandchild; an experience — he never tired of telling his wife, Sarah — he was finding relatively painless.

As he climbed from the car, the poet within him — whom most would have doubted existed — marvelled at the wood with its mixture of evergreens, oaks and ashes, under which clumps of bluebells abounded. Beyond the centuries-old stile an erratic path weaved through the trees.

The uniformed officer, whose job it was to stop enquiring members of the public from entering the wood, clicked his heels and stood to attention on becoming aware of Ashworth's approach.

'Good morning, sir.'

Despite his fierce appearance, and apart from occasional displays of bad temper, Ashworth was, more often than not, reasonable, calm and courteous.

He smiled warmly at the officer. 'Good morning.'

'Area's sealed off, sir. DS Bedford, Dr Anthony, and the Forensic team are in attendance. They're about ten minutes' walk along the path.'

'Good man,' Ashworth said as he climbed the stile.

On any other morning the wooded walk with shafts of sunlight filtering through the trees would have been enjoyable, but as every step took him nearer to a corpse, the beauty of nature was pushed to the back of Ashworth's mind.

He saw the white police tent, erected where the body lay and quickened his step, eager to get the viewing of the victim over with and the investigation under way.

Newly promoted Detective Sergeant Holly Bedford was waiting outside the tent. Twenty-six years old, she was tall, gawky, and her dated page-boy hairstyle did little to alleviate the plainness of her face.

'Good morning, sir,' she said.

'Morning, Holly. What have we got then?'

'Female, sir. Reported missing by her husband at ten last night. A man walking his dog found the body at eight this morning.'

'Right. Is Dr Anthony inside?' He indicated the tent, now delaying for as long as possible the moment when he would have to pull the flap aside and enter.

'She is, sir.' Holly made no attempt to conceal her dislike for the doctor from either her tone or her expression.

Ashworth stared down at the red mass of bloodied pulp which some fourteen hours before had been a human face. Blonde hair surrounded it, but it was impossible to tell whether the owner of that hair had been pretty or plain for every feature had been destroyed.

Gwen Anthony looked up. 'Nasty one, Jim.'

'Yes, I'd agree with that.'

Without prompting she launched into the information as she got to her feet. 'Right then. Female, obviously. Around thirty-five years old. I believe your people know who she is — a Margaret Johnson apparently. Quite simply beaten to death. Every one of her ribs is cracked so God knows what internal injuries she's got. Most probably dead before her assailant started on the head. No weapon used as such . . . she was simply kicked to death.'

'What time was this?'

'About seven thirty last night, I'd say. No sign of sexual assault but, although her clothing is intact, sexual intercourse did take place, and I'd say immediately prior to death.'

'Thanks, Gwen.' Ashworth turned to leave.

'Jim, I need to see you,' she said, her tone less brisk.

'Gwen . . .' Ashworth began.

He was eager to be outside the tent, mainly because Gwen had been his one deviation from the straight and narrow in thirty years of marriage — and it was a mistake he had no intention of repeating — but also because, even though he had spent over thirty years in the police service, the hardness of heart and strength of stomach required for viewing the dead still evaded him.

'I must talk to you, Jim,' Gwen whispered urgently. 'My husband has found out about us.'

'Oh, God,' Ashworth mumbled. 'I'll see you before you leave.'

He left the tent, wondering how long his recently consumed breakfast would have tenure inside his stomach.

Next, Holly filled him in on what the Forensic team had gleaned so far. It would seem that the woman had met her death some minutes after leaving the spot where she had lain with another for some considerable time; the grass was still flattened over a fairly large area. There was also evidence to suggest the presence of a third party concealed in the bushes. The woman must have left and then walked to the spot where she was killed.

Although the ground was very dry, the woman's slim high heels had left clear indentations in the path, whereas the flat shoes of her male companion and those of the onlooker left no marks. It seemed that the woman had run part of the way, then stopped and struggled a considerable amount before moving to the fateful spot.

As Ashworth listened only half of his mind took in what Holly was relaying, for he was worrying about possible recriminations that could ensue now that his fling with Gwen had been discovered.

'Well, let's just hope it's an open and shut case,' he said. 'The husband found out she was having an affair and killed her. Has he been informed yet?'

Holly, puzzled by her superior's preoccupation, replied, 'No, sir. We'll need him to identify the body—'

'Yes, of course,' Ashworth snapped. 'You go back to the station and make arrangements for that. I need to have a word with the doctor.'

'Yes, sir,' Holly said, pointedly eyeing the tent. 'Will you be coming with me to see the husband?'

'Yes, as soon as I'm through here.'

As Ashworth watched Holly's retreating back, Gwen appeared from the tent. Removing her rubber gloves, she dropped them into a polythene bag and sealed it, all the while watching the Scene of Crime officers and Forensic team as they scoured the wood.

'Somewhere quiet,' she suggested.

Ashworth nodded and fell in beside her as she took the path towards the road.

'How much does he know?' Ashworth asked.

'Nothing really, he just suspects. But he's making my life hell. He's talking about coming to see you.'

'Really,' Ashworth commented, his tone implying that he was not relishing the encounter.

'I'm denying it, Jim. If you do the same he'll just have to forget it.'

'I hope so.'

'He will.'

'Is he causing you any trouble?'

Gwen smiled, touched by his concern. 'No, not really, he's getting sexually demanding but it's not a problem.'

The stile came into sight as Ashworth said, 'I'd have though it would have had the opposite effect on him.'

'No, Jim, you see he's got all these conflicting emotions inside him and they find an outlet in sex—'

'Gwen, this is not the day for a lecture on psychology,' Ashworth said abruptly.

'Of course not,' she conceded, slightly abashed. 'I think I'd better pass all the post-mortem details to one of your officers . . . just to be on the safe side.'

'Yes, I agree. I'll ask Holly to deal with it.'

The corners of Gwen's mouth turned down. 'The girl doesn't like me.'

'That won't affect the information.'

Gwen stopped well short of the stile and the inquisitive ear of the policeman guarding it.

'I shall hate not seeing you, Jim,' she said with candour, watching his face closely for a reaction.

Ashworth looked away, studying the wood. 'I think you must enjoy playing with fire,' he said eventually.

Gwen's giggle was mischievous. 'Don't you?'

'Not when I start to get burnt.'

'I'm not finished with you yet, Jim. When this has died down we'll work something out.'

She touched his sleeve and Ashworth's eyes instinctively went to the policeman at the stile. The young man was standing with his back to them, a lighted cigarette in his cupped hand, blissfully unaware of their presence.

'No, Gwen,' Ashworth said resolutely, 'we're in enough trouble as it is.'

Undeterred, Gwen asked, 'Do you want a telephone number where it'll be safe to contact me?'

Maybe an older man's fancy also turns to love in the spring, or perhaps any red-blooded male would find difficulty in resisting a proposition from Gwen Anthony.

Whatever the reason, Ashworth said, 'Yes,' while telling himself he would need to check that she was all right from time to time.

Scribbling a number, she said, 'It's the surgery. Just ask to be put through to me.'

* * *

Holly Bedford picked her way through the traffic in Bridgetown High Street. Her ten-year-old mini was performing better now that warmer weather had arrived, but she still contemplated investing her increase in salary on a more recent model.

Holly, widowed at the early age of twenty-three, had moved to Bridgetown with her mother-in-law, Emily, just a few months ago. It was while she was enjoying a fling with a flamboyant detective constable named Mike Whitworth who had since returned to Manchester, that Holly had arrived home one evening to find Emily dead after suffering a heart attack in her armchair.

Now her small three-bedroomed semi was shared with the third member of CID: Josh Abraham. This had caused more than a few raised eyebrows among members of the force not yet aware of Josh's homosexuality, but the arrangement suited Holly; Josh's board money helped with the mortgage, and their brother/sister relationship was easy and undemanding.

She pulled into the crowded station carpark and sat waiting as a panda car vacated a space.

The CID office was on the top floor of the modern building; its glass walls ensuring that the occupants were afforded a perfect view of the town.

Josh was sitting at the computer, his brown suede bomber jacket draped over the back of his chair.

'Is it the missing woman?' he asked, dividing his attention between Holly and the computer screen.

'Yes, looks like it. Seems likely she was in the wood for a bit of hanky-panky and got herself beaten to death.'

'Where's Ashworth?'

'Huh, talking of hanky-panky . . .' Holly said deliberately, hanging her duffle coat behind the door. 'He's with his very good friend, Gwen Anthony.'

'I'm sure you're wrong about those two,' Josh said evenly.

Holly sat at her desk. 'Am I? That's not the way it looked when our Chief Inspector dismissed me so they could be alone together in the wood . . .'

Josh laughed. 'Alone? With a dead body, Scene of Crime officers, Forensic, and half of Bridgetown nick?'

Josh's name had recently been added to a rather exclusive list of people to whom Ashworth had been forced to apologize after being proved wrong.

The extraction of that apology and being asked to stay on in CID by the truculent Ashworth had proved to Josh that miracles do happen, and he had absolutely no intention of finding out if a second was in the offing by meddling in his superior's private life.

'You know what I mean,' Holly said sulkily.

'None of our business, Holly.'

Further discussion was curtailed by the man himself. Ashworth closed the door briskly and stood with hands dug deep into the pockets of his battered waxed cotton jacket.

'Right, what's the dead woman's address?'

'It's on Cherry Tree Estate, sir,' Holly offered.

'Let's go and break the news to her husband then.'

'Would you rather I took a WPC and did it myself, sir?' Holly asked.

Ashworth fixed her with a stare. 'I'm quite capable of breaking news of death, young lady.'

Holly stood her ground. 'I know that, sir, it's just that the man's bound to be distraught and I thought female officers might be more appropriate.'

'Huh, don't let's forget, the man's a suspect. It's either him or the boyfriend — open and shut case.'

Holly exchanged a look with Josh as the telephone on her desk began to ring. 'Hello, Bridgetown CID,' she said automatically. 'It's Dr Anthony for you, sir.'

Ashworth looked slightly flustered as he took the receiver. 'Hello, Gwen.'

'It's not Gwen,' a male voice informed him. 'This is her husband.'

There was a pause and Ashworth could feel perspiration in the palm of his hand. 'What can I do for you?' he asked.

'I think we should meet. There's something I want to discuss with you.'

'And where would you like to do that?'

Nigel Anthony gave a humourless chuckle. 'I could visit your home, or the police station . . . or we could meet for a drink.'

'The latter, I think.'

Anthony chuckled again. 'Now I thought you'd say that. Make it the Bull and Butcher at eight this evening.'

There was a click and the line went dead.

Ashworth forcefully replaced the receiver. 'Right,' he barked, 'we haven't got all day, Holly.' Then he stormed out of the office, leaving the door open behind him.

'I'd say something's upset him, wouldn't you?' Josh remarked.

'And I know what it is.' Holly pointed to the telephone as she grabbed her coat from the peg. 'That was Dr Anthony, as in . . . husband.'

'Ah,' Josh intoned with a good deal of meaning.

CHAPTER 2

Not one word passed Ashworth's lips on the drive to Cherry Tree Estate.

Ordinarily he would have been lamenting the decline of Bridgetown since all the modern estates had been built around it, leaving it little more than a village trapped inside a town. He was forever asking how anyone could have done such a dreadful thing to his Bridgetown with its quaint thatched cottages.

Holly never knew how to answer, so was pleased the discussion was not taking place on this particular journey.

Ashworth's expression was grim as he fixed his eyes on the road ahead.

Cherry Tree Estate was made up of middle-of-the-range houses: four-bedroomed semis, all remarkably similar, set well back from the road. Young laburnum and blossom trees lined the pavements; their trunks no thicker than a man's wrist.

Becket Brook Close stood on the perimeter of the town, ensuring its occupants had wonderful views over open countryside to the rear.

Ashworth stopped the Sierra outside number 33 and turned to Holly. 'What's the husband's name?'

'Ian,' Holly replied shortly.

He saw the net curtain at the bay window move as they got out of the car. 'Looks like we're expected,' he said heavily. 'Let's get this over with.'

As they approached the house, the front door was opened by a man whose creased shirt and grey trousers suggested he had been sitting up all night; his brown hair was dishevelled, a day's growth of stubble showed on his clean-cut face.

'Have you found Margaret?' he asked before they reached the step.

'Mr Ian Johnson?' Ashworth asked.

'Yes. Have you found Margaret?'

Ashworth produced his warrant card. 'Bridgetown Police, sir. Could we come inside?'

'Just tell me if you've found her,' Johnson said, his voice rising.

A woman appeared behind him.

'They won't tell you nothing on the step, Ian,' she said, her tone suggesting there was little she did not know. 'Come back in the lounge, Ian,' she coaxed. Then to the officers, 'You'd better come in.'

Ashworth watched as she closed the door. A typical middle-aged housewife, her blue leisure suit appeared at odds with her tartan slippers; her hair was tightly curled, its blonde shade not her natural colour. Ashworth ruefully thought that any money she might have spent on face creams over the years had been wasted and guessed that those small blue eyes would miss very little.

'And you are?' he asked.

'Mrs Leabon. I'm the neighbour . . . here to help out.' She glanced towards the lounge door. 'Margaret's mother's in there,' she whispered, 'so just break the news gently. Though, goodness knows, they must be the only two that haven't heard it yet.'

They were ushered into the lounge, an L-shaped room with a dining-set at one end, and a light green suite almost filling the rest of it.

Ian Johnson stood expectantly in front of the fireplace. The woman Ashworth took to be Margaret Johnson's mother perched uncomfortably on the edge of an easy chair.

'Have you found her?' Johnson asked again.

'I think you'd better sit down, sir.'

Ashworth's doom-laden voice told Margaret's mother that the news was not good. She rose resignedly from her chair and went to her son-in-law. 'Come on, Ian, come and sit down.'

Ashworth continued gravely, 'I'm afraid I've some bad news for you, Mr Johnson . . . your wife is dead.'

Johnson sank into the chair, clutching the woman's hand. 'Dead?' he repeated. 'How? When?'

'Her body was discovered this morning in Bluebell Wood,' Ashworth told him gently, 'and we've reason to believe foul play was involved.'

Ashworth was all too aware of the devastation his words were causing to the dead woman's relatives, but there was never any easy way to break such news.

Johnson shook his head in disbelief. 'Are you saying Margaret was murdered?'

'Yes, sir, I'm afraid that's what I am saying.'

Johnson turned confused eyes to his distraught mother-in-law. 'But what was she doing in Bluebell Wood?'

'I was hoping you might be able to throw some light on that for us, sir,' Ashworth said as he studied the man, trying to decide if these first symptoms of shock were real.

The woman looked up at Ashworth then. 'I'm Margaret's mother — Mrs Thomas — and I don't think now is the time, do you?' she said quietly. 'I think the best thing for Ian to do is take a sleeping-pill and try to get some rest.'

The mother's grief was evident and real. Her eyes, already hollow from lack of sleep, filled with tears but she bravely attempted to fight them back for, in common with many other women, she saw herself as the backbone of the family and her duty now was to hold together what was left of it.

'Yes, of course,' Ashworth concurred. 'We'll come back some other time.'

'Then let me show you out,' Mrs Thomas managed to say firmly. 'And perhaps you'd better go too, Jessie.'

Mrs Leabon was affronted. 'Well, if I can't be of any help.'

'No, dear, I don't think so.'

Mrs Thomas led them to the front door. In the hall Ashworth resisted the shepherding guidance of the woman's arm, and said, 'Mrs Thomas, I'm afraid there's one thing that won't wait, and that's identification of the body.'

'Oh, yes.' She sighed heavily. 'Either my husband or I will take care of that. We'll both be staying here . . .' It was then she came close to breaking down.

Ashworth quickly opened the front door. 'I'll send a car for you.'

Holly glanced at the barometer to the right of the door; it read 'fair,' and she thought how inappropriate that was, given the circumstances.

Once outside it was obvious their visit had attracted a lot of attention. Quite a few of the residents had deemed it necessary to clean windows, sweep drives or tidy front gardens.

Jessie Leabon was undoubtedly enjoying her moment of notoriety. With arms folded across her sagging bosom, she said, 'I should have stayed to help. I'm good in an emergency.'

And not very happy when you think you might be missing something, Holly thought drily. 'Did you know the deceased woman well?' she asked.

'Margaret?' she said, turning to Holly. 'The deceased woman . . . it sends a shiver down your spine doesn't it?' And to emphasize the point she did indeed shiver. 'Yes, I knew her very well. I went to school with her mother.'

'Can you think of anything that might help us with our enquiries?' Ashworth said gruffly.

Mrs Leabon shook her head. 'It's not for me to speak ill of the dead.'

'Helping to find her murderer wouldn't be doing that,' Holly jumped in quickly, afraid that Ashworth's brisk manner might alienate this woman who could prove a valuable source of information.

'Well, put like that, I don't suppose it is gossip.'

'Of course it isn't,' Holly smiled reassuringly.

Mrs Leabon glanced up and down the close. 'Just look at them . . . all minding everybody's business. You'll have to come in for a cup of tea. This lot' — she indicated the watching neighbours — 'are making me feel naked.'

They followed her into the next house as she asked them not to look at how untidy the place was — beds unmade upstairs, washing-up still in the sink, yesterday's dust still on the carpet . . . but as they must understand, today was not an ordinary day.

Holly made sympathetic noises as they sat at the kitchen table, and Ashworth remained uncharacteristically silent throughout the making of the tea.

'I'm not that surprised,' Mrs Leabon said ominously as she placed a plateful of mixed biscuits in the centre of the table.

'Do you know much about Margaret's private life?' Holly quizzed.

'Not really,' the woman replied unhelpfully as she fetched the tea, 'but she's a . . . I mean was a very outgoing girl; friendly . . . you know. But Ian's just the opposite. He'd sit there in front of the telly all day, he would, left to himself.'

Ashworth sipped tea from a mug decorated with bold red stripes. 'Do you know if they argued, had fights, that sort of thing?' he asked casually.

'No more than most.' There was a trace of bitterness in Mrs Leabon's reply which suggested her own union might be less than tranquil. 'But it was Margaret who did most of the shouting and laying down the law. Ian's a nice, quiet lad.'

'What were these rows about?' Ashworth probed.

'I didn't say they were rows,' Mrs Leabon said sharply with an offended look. 'I wasn't a witness to them so it's not for me to comment, is it?'

'No, no, of course not,' Ashworth agreed. He guessed that if he appeared reluctant to pursue the point, the woman would be all the more eager to do so.

Mrs Leabon did not disappoint. She went on, 'But if you ask me, most of it would have been to do with money.'

'The old evil,' Ashworth mused before biting into a bourbon biscuit.

'Yes, that's right. Margaret lost her job, see . . .' She had lowered her voice as if fearful that her words might travel through the bricks of her home and reach the ears of those bereaved next door. 'And she was nearing the end of her time on the dole; another few weeks and she wouldn't have been eligible for anything.'

Ashworth's delicate stomach condition of earlier in the day seemed to have resolved itself, and he took a custard cream from the plate as he asked, 'How's that?'

'Well, you're only entitled to the dole for so long,' Mrs Leabon explained. 'Then you have to go on Income Support . . . and that's means-tested. So, with Ian working, they wouldn't have got anything.'

'Ah,' Ashworth said. His mood was beginning to lighten considerably as he dwelt less on his own problems. 'And that would have caused them difficulties?'

Mrs Leabon's expression indicated that it would. 'Like a good many others they'd overstretched themselves,' she confided, 'with the mortgage and what have you. It was all right when they were both working and while Margaret was getting her benefit.'

'But without it they'd have been in a mess,' Ashworth said as he eyed the biscuits before remembering his waistline and resisting. 'Did Margaret go out much?'

'Hardly at all.' Then a thought struck her. 'Except . . .' She stopped to think.

'Go on,' Ashworth urged. 'Except what?'

'It's just that when you asked that question you jogged my memory.'

'Yes.'

‘I’m not one to pry, you understand,’ Mrs Leabon said defensively.

‘No, of course not.’

Holly had to hide a smile as she caught the note of exasperation in Ashworth’s voice.

‘Well you see, I went round one evening a few days ago. I didn’t stay very long — Ian was watching football on the telly and he made it very plain I was disturbing him. Anyway, he did say that Margaret had started going to her mum’s a lot during the last couple of weeks . . .’

She dropped her voice to a conspiratorial note. ‘But this morning when I was in their kitchen, making a pot of tea, I heard them talking about it, and it seems that Margaret hadn’t been anywhere near her mum’s.’

‘I see. Where did Margaret work?’ Ashworth asked.

‘Before she went on the dole?’

‘Yes,’ Ashworth said flatly, resisting the urge to raise his eyes to the ceiling in irritation.

‘Giles Insurance, in the High Street. She worked on the counter, giving quotes and what not.’

‘Mrs Leabon,’ Ashworth said cordially as he left his seat, ‘you’ve been a great help, and thank you for the tea and biscuits.’

‘Well I don’t know how,’ she said, clearly pleased, as she showed them to the door.

Ashworth thanked the woman again and they stood on the step as the door was closed behind them.

Holly gave him an uneasy look. ‘Sorry, sir, that wasn’t a lot of use to us, was it?’

‘On the contrary, it was invaluable,’ Ashworth assured her, heading for the car.

He was back to his old self again and Holly warmed to him, for when Ashworth was in a good temper he possessed a charm which made most people forgive him almost anything.

‘But I hoped it would lead us to the boyfriend,’ she said, trying to match his step.

‘It has, Holly.’

He said no more until they were installed in the Sierra. As he struggled into his seat-belt, Ashworth turned to her. 'We know the woman went out very little, so the only contacts she could have had would have been the people she worked with.'

'But that was a long time ago, sir,' Holly pointed out, 'and Mrs Leabon said Margaret had only been going out for a couple of weeks.'

Ashworth started the engine. 'Maybe she'd rekindled an old flame. We'll find lover boy at Giles Insurance, Holly, you can count on that.'

* * *

Jenny Chambers sat in the armless chair, her backside numbing uncomfortably on the hard plastic-covered upholstery. She gazed around the large third-floor office with a feeling of hostility, noting that all male eyes were upon her.

Jenny's looks ensured that she was always a focal point for masculine attention. Her hair was thick, auburn and cut in the latest style. She wore black ski-pants and a tight white sweater; clothes which highlighted her long legs, trim waist and full breasts. And as if those attributes were not enough, she also possessed classic features: large long-lashed blue eyes, a strong nose, perfectly formed lips.

She stubbed out her cigarette irritably in the large ashtray on the table beside her. The local Job Centre was not her favourite place and as she was ten minutes past her interview time and still had not been called, she was becoming more and more annoyed.

Jenny was twenty-five years old and until four months ago had worked as a typist for a company in Bridgenorton, a small town not far away. But the firm went into receivership and Jenny was forced to join the ranks of the unemployed.

At first she was devastated but soon came to realize that unemployment benefit supplemented by various cash-in-hand excursions into the black economy meant she was in fact better off than when she was working full-time and paying taxes.

What she could not stand, however, was the way in which the employment staff continually harassed her, forever wanting to send her to job clubs where she could learn — with twenty others in the same position — how to write letters, and fill in job applications for positions which, by and large, did not exist.

Suddenly a female voice called, 'Mrs Chambers?'

'Yes,' Jenny said thankfully, making her way to the woman.

'Take a seat,' the woman said as she fussed around the desk, a smile on her plump, middle-aged face. 'Well,' she beamed, finally sitting down, 'this interview is to see if we can help you in any way. How's your search for work going?'

'Not very well, I'm afraid,' Jenny sighed. 'It's so depressing.'

'Yes, I know.' The woman's professional feigned concern was obvious. 'You have been looking for work, of course?' she questioned keenly.

'Of course,' Jenny gushed, 'that's all I ever do.'

Reaching into her handbag, she pulled out a sheet of paper. 'I've got a list of all the job applications I've made since the last interview.'

Jenny passed it to the woman. Most of the applications on the list were fictitious, compiled from the Situations Vacant pages in the local newspaper.

'You have been busy,' the woman said, scanning the list. 'And you've had no positive replies from any of these?' Her tone held suspicion.

'Oh, yes,' Jenny said brightly, 'some of them didn't even bother to answer, but I did get two interviews. I've got the letters somewhere in my bag.' She foraged about for them, saying, 'I didn't get either of them, though.'

This, at least, was true for Jenny had evolved a ploy which she considered to be almost foolproof. By only applying for jobs where the boss was a woman — who would take into account the effect Jenny might have on male staff, and who would probably be a little jealous of her anyway — she was more likely to receive a pleasantly worded, 'Thank you for your interest, but unfortunately . . .'

'Oh, here they are.' Jenny passed the letters across the desk and could not resist a slight grin as the woman studied them.

'Bad luck,' she commented; then leaning forward, 'I don't know if you're aware of the package of measures we have to help people in your position . . .' Her smile was patronizing. 'There's the Job Club . . . now that gives you access to stationery, postage stamps, and our trained staff who are on hand to help you in applying for jobs.'

'I know,' Jenny said doubtfully, 'but I like to get the first edition of the evening paper and write off straight away. If I attended the Job Club I'd have to wait until the next day.'

'Yes,' the woman agreed reluctantly, 'there is that.' After a pause, 'Have you thought of training for additional skills?'

'No.' Jenny was resolute, feeling now was the time to toughen her attitude. 'I've got good typing skills and computer experience, and I've only been out of work for four months so I still feel fairly confident about finding a job.'

'All right,' the woman said in a businesslike fashion. 'If there's nothing else I can help you with I'll just sign the papers to say I've seen you.'

'Thank you,' Jenny said, relieved it was over. She rose to leave. 'I'll go downstairs and look through the vacancies while I'm here.'

'Hold on a minute, Mrs Chambers, one of our managers wants to have a word with you.'

Jenny sank back into the chair, fearing her fraudulent claims had been exposed. Trying to keep her voice light and even, she asked, 'What about?'

'Just procedure,' the woman assured her. 'Would you like to follow me?'

Picking up her coat from the back of the chair, Jenny obeyed, and for once she was oblivious to the male reactions all around her.

As she followed the woman down a long thin corridor Jenny reasoned that they couldn't know anything — they might suspect but they couldn't know. If they did she would have heard by now. She presumed they were simply trying to frighten her into taking a job, that was all. But despite all attempts to reassure herself, Jenny could still feel the frantic beating of her heart.

They stopped at a door. The woman knocked briskly, then entered. 'Mrs Chambers,' she announced.

With some trepidation Jenny stepped into the office. The man sitting behind the desk did not look up. Jenny heard the door close firmly behind her.

The office was sparsely furnished in usual governmental department fashion, yet even with just a desk, two chairs and a dull grey metal filing cabinet, it seemed full to capacity.

The distant sound of a pneumatic drill filtered in through the open window.

'Sit down, Mrs Chambers,' he said, without looking up.

Jenny sat, noting with unease that the man seemed to know her name without having to refer to a file.

The man's name, printed in white letters against the dark background of a nameplate on the front of his desk, was: G. Fox.

Gerald Fox was a young man — about twenty-nine — but extremely old-fashioned. His Harris tweed sports jacket, grey flannel trousers and brogue shoes were as far removed from trendy as it was possible to be.

His greasy skin bore a porous sheen, his mousy brown hair was already losing the lustre of youth, yet his brown eyes had a gentle refined quality about them.

He finally put down the pen and looked up. 'Thank you for coming in to see me, Mrs Chambers.'

His voice was so soft that Jenny had to concentrate to catch the words over the drone of the pneumatic drill.

Glancing at a file before him, he said, 'You've been unemployed for four months now, I see.'

Jenny met his eyes and held his gaze. 'That's right.'

'And in that time you haven't done any work?'

'Of course not. If I had, I'd have signed off, wouldn't I?'

'Yes, of course you would.'

At any moment Jenny expected him to produce some damning evidence against her. Instead he smiled.

'You do understand that if you take any work, even if it's voluntary, you have to declare it.'

'I do, yes.'

His smile remained shy and constant. 'You'd be surprised how many people get themselves into trouble just because they don't understand the rules.'

'I won't let that happen to me,' Jenny said adamantly.

The interview was over almost before it had begun and Jenny was negotiating her way along the maze of corridors back to the main office.

She knew they were onto her; everything about Fox's manner said that he suspected something but did not have enough proof.

Pushing through the swing doors Jenny entered the main office, stopping at the first desk which was tenanted by a man.

'Excuse me,' she said, using her most disarming smile. 'Mr Fox . . . what is he exactly?'

The man's eyes took a route around her body before settling on her face. Jenny smiled inwardly; she could imagine the lecherous thoughts going through his mind, but with his middle-aged appearance, receding hair and thickening waistline, memory and imagination were probably all that was left for him in that department.

'Investigator. Fraud,' he said.

Those words enforced Jenny's fears. 'He looks into people who are working and drawing the dole at the same time then.'

'That's it, love. New policy see — if we can't persuade the jobless to go on the sick to bring the total down . . . we lock them up,' he joked.

But as Jenny descended the stairs to the Job Centre below, his humour was lost on her.

Perhaps she should try for a job after all . . . get herself off the unemployment register.

* * *

During the walk to the offices of Giles Insurance, Holly was once again subjected to Ashworth's set piece on The Real Bridgetown: how the County Council planning department had all but destroyed it by granting permission for the monstrous housing estates which now surrounded it.

'People have to live somewhere, sir,' she said briskly, 'and it all helps the local economy to grow.'

Ashworth gave her a sideways glance, well aware that his DS was developing a tendency to wind him up. He decided to leave it there.

They reached the offices and Ashworth's quest for the identity of Margaret Johnson's clandestine lover proved far easier than either of them had anticipated.

The old boards of the winding staircase creaked and groaned beneath their feet as a member of the counter staff showed them to the office of Terry Giles. The man looked up nervously as they entered.

Ashworth glanced around, finding the room, with its 200-year-old oak beams, much to his liking. He noticed several golf trophies on the top shelf of a built-in cupboard, along with bottles of spirits and mixers.

Rising from his seat, Giles offered Ashworth his outstretched hand. 'Hello, I'm Terry Giles,' he said, his voice strong, confident.

The man's handshake was not so confident, Ashworth observed, as he said, 'I'm Chief Inspector Ashworth and this—'

'Yes, I'm aware of who you are,' Giles said glibly, 'and I must say, you're very thorough. I didn't expect you to trace me so quickly. In fact I was contemplating contacting you.'

'I'm glad we saved you the trouble,' Ashworth smiled.

'Please sit down,' Giles said expansively.

They sat in the plain wooden-backed chairs as Ashworth made a study of Terry Giles, whose thick black hair and smooth skin belied his forty-five years.

'We're making enquiries into the death of Margaret Johnson,' Ashworth began.

'Yes, dreadful business,' Giles intoned. 'I've only just heard. It still hasn't sunk in yet.'

'Am I to take it, by what you've just said, that you have some information which could assist us?'

Giles looked from one to the other, fingering the knot of his expensive tie. 'Yes,' he said boldly. 'The fact is, I was with Margaret in Bluebell Wood last night.'

'What time was that, sir?' Holly interjected.

'Oh, I don't know . . . about six until quarter to seven, I think.'

'You were lovers?' Ashworth asked.

'Yes, we were,' Giles admitted frankly. 'We had been for a couple of weeks.'

Ashworth noted that this fitted in with what Mrs Leabon had said about Margaret only going out during the last two weeks, but something still bothered him about it.

'And she was alive when you left her?' he asked.

'Oh yes, very much so, Chief Inspector.'

Despite the man's outward show of confidence, Ashworth sensed he was nervous.

Holly asked, 'Did you and Margaret Johnson leave the wood together?'

Giles gave her the assured smile of a man who knows he is attractive to women, and replied, 'No, we didn't. We had no desire to be seen together.'

Ashworth remained silent, allowing Holly to explore her line of questioning.

'Were you aware of anyone else being present in the wood?'

Giles shook his head.

'We believe, sir,' Holly went on, 'that a third party was close to you and Mrs Johnson when you were . . . lying on the ground.'

Giles was visibly shocked by this disclosure. He said, 'What? While we were actually . . .? Watching us, you mean?'

'So we believe,' Holly said, pleased to have penetrated his ladies' man veneer. 'Have you any idea who that person might have been?'

'No. None.'

'Did Mrs Johnson ever seem worried that her husband might be suspicious?'

'No.' Giles paused. 'Hold on, she did say something last night.'

Putting his hand to his forehead, he leant back in his chair. 'I wanted her to stay longer, and she said something about her husband starting to suspect, and she was only supposed to be at her mother's.'

Holly jotted that down, then said, 'You left Mrs Johnson where exactly?'

'Where we'd . . .' His voice trailed off. 'She went off towards the stile and I went home in the opposite direction, across the fields.'

'You're a bachelor, are you, sir?' Holly asked, looking at the ring finger of his left hand.

'Yes, I am.'

'And is there anyone who can verify your movements after seven p.m. last night?'

'Will that be necessary?'

'It may well be, sir,' Ashworth cut in. 'What did you do after leaving Mrs Johnson?'

'I went home, prepared a meal, then had a few drinks while I watched the golf on television. Look, where is all this heading?'

Ashworth scrutinized the man. 'You were one of the last people to see Margaret Johnson alive, so naturally we're interested in your movements.'

'Does that make me a suspect?' Giles asked, his confidence peeling away.

Ashworth did not answer.

Giles, clearly agitated, said, 'Look, I'd better remind you, I was going to come forward. Doesn't that mean I've got nothing to hide?'

'But you didn't come forward,' Ashworth replied firmly. 'We've only a few more questions so we won't take up much more of your time.'

Giles sighed. 'Ask away.'

'You said you were having an affair with Margaret Johnson for the last two weeks.'

'Yes, that's right.'

'And she worked for you for how long?'

'Three years.'

'And did you have a relationship with her during that time?'

Giles shook his head. 'No.'

'So, almost twelve months after she left your employ, you started having an affair.'

'Yes, that's right,' Giles confirmed.

'That's not very clear to me,' Ashworth mused. 'I mean, how did you meet her again? Why did nothing happen during the three years she worked for you?'

Giles's eyes darted from Ashworth to Holly and back again. He looked peeved as he said, 'Because neither of us wanted anything to happen during that time.'

'So you bumped into each other a year after she'd left her job and it just came over you both, did it?' Ashworth said evenly.

'That's offensive. It wasn't like that.'

'How was it then?'

'Margaret was getting desperate for work. She called in a few times to see if I had any vacancies and we went for a drink. That was it, really.'

'Thank you, sir. That's cleared that up,' Ashworth said, sounding anything but happy with the explanation. 'We'll leave you in peace.'

They had left the building and were walking along the High Street before Ashworth spoke again.

He said, 'Before we'd been to see Mr Smarty Pants, I'd have put my money on the husband. Now I'm not so sure.'

'He does think he's the cat's whiskers, doesn't he?' Holly remarked.

She glanced over her shoulder and saw Giles was watching them from the first-floor window. 'What's bothering you about him, sir? He seemed very frank to me.'

'Yes,' Ashworth agreed, 'and it's his frankness that bothers me.'

Although Holly was beginning to understand the workings of Ashworth's mind, she was still puzzled.

'I'm not following you, sir.'

'Well, if the affair started when Margaret Johnson went to him looking for a job, why didn't he give her one?'

Holly almost laughed at Ashworth's unintended double meaning. 'So you think he's lying about when the affair started?'

They stopped at the Sierra.

'No, I don't. As you observed, he was very open and frank about that. If it had been going on for years I'm sure he would have admitted it. No reason not to. What he's lying about is the reason Margaret Johnson went to see him. I'm fairly certain it wasn't about a job.'

'Well, it didn't strike me, I must admit, but I suppose it is odd.' She laughed. 'You don't miss much, do you?'

'Very little.' And as if to demonstrate the point, he added, 'And I didn't mean 'give her one' in that sense.'

This time Holly did laugh.

Ashworth opened the passenger door. 'Get in,' he ordered good-naturedly.

CHAPTER 3

There could not be many who considered that a trip to their local Tesco supermarket possessed the same therapeutic qualities as a long relaxing holiday.

But Gladys Smart did.

She leisurely pushed her trolley along every aisle, pausing repeatedly to inspect products she would never have contemplated buying.

When she had reached the 'Special Offer Leg of Lamb — £1.99 lb' freezer for the third time, Gladys knew her little excursion was almost over.

Feeling every one of her seventy-six years she trundled towards the checkout; the 2lb bag of sugar, packet of Cuppa Soup, and one thin-sliced white loaf looking lost in the deep belly of the trolley.

No one, not even the checkout girl, gave her a second glance. She was just an old lady in a fawn mackintosh. No one noticed the cross she had to bear; but it was there for all to see, etched into her tired lined face, her watery faded eyes.

Once through the checkout, Gladys transferred the goods to her brown plastic shopping bag. She was eager now to be home, for her son would be waiting.

Her son. The very thought of him brought bitterness coursing through her.

With reluctance, she trudged slowly towards the exit.

* * *

Ashworth and Holly arrived back at CID to find Josh lunching on spam rolls. He looked up as they entered.

'Mrs Ashworth phoned, sir,' he said, hurriedly swallowing his mouthful of meat and bread as he picked up a note pad beside the VDU.

'What did she say?' Ashworth asked, knowing that the meticulous constable would have written down every word.

'Could you ring her, sir? She said it's not urgent, but could you make it as soon as possible?' He replaced the pad. 'That's all, sir.'

'Right,' Ashworth said, hanging up his coat. 'I'll make the call from the other office.'

He was gone for ten minutes. Finally he emerged and, looking hungrily at Josh's empty plate, he said abruptly, 'I'm off to the canteen for lunch.'

'He doesn't look very happy, does he?' Holly remarked as soon as the door was closed. 'How did Mrs Ashworth sound?'

Josh shrugged. 'A little worried, I suppose. You know how she usually asks how you are, whether you've settled in? Well, she didn't this time. She just said, Get Jim to ring me, will you?'

'Perhaps the past is catching up with the great man,' Holly suggested shrewdly as she settled in behind her desk.

'I'm sure you're wrong,' Josh said.

And then, feeling that Holly was beginning to take an almost obsessive interest in Ashworth's private life, he changed the subject. 'What did you find out about the case?'

'We saw the husband and interviewed the boyfriend. He's Terry Giles of Giles Insurance Brokers. Margaret Johnson used to work for him.'

'And?'

'Ashworth seems to think it's one or the other, but I don't agree.'

Josh's look of interest urged her on.

She said, 'The way I see it, if it was the husband, would he have hidden in the bushes and watched while another man was making love to his wife? I mean, would you do that?'

'Me? With a wife? I'll never know, dear, will I?' Josh replied, attempting a camp act.

'You know what I mean, you bloody fool,' Holly laughed, as Josh returned his attention to the computer. 'No, I think he'd have gone berserk on the spot. Probably would have damaged both of them.'

She sat watching Josh's back, listening to the tapping of the computer keys for a few moments, then asked, 'And why should the boyfriend kill her? What motive could he have had?'

Josh sat back. 'Could have been madly in love with the woman and she wanted to end the affair,' he speculated.

'No, Terry Giles didn't seem the type of man who'd fall in love. He probably regards the female sex organ in the same way as a bus . . . if he misses one, there'll always be another along soon.'

Josh snorted at the well-worn joke, then drained his coffee.

Crushing the plastic cup, he tossed it into the wastepaper basket, saying, 'Actually, Holly, I agree with you about the case. That's why I've been doing some checking on the data file.'

'And what have you come up with?'

He pressed a button and studied the information which appeared on the screen. 'Eighteen months ago,' he said, turning to face her, 'there were four unsolved murders in Bradford — three women and a male. Now during the investigation it came to light that the common thread running through all the cases was that the victims had been committing adultery.'

'Josh, I know you're clever,' Holly said with deliberate condescension, 'but what has this got to do with our case?

We're in Bridgetown not Bradford, and we've only got one body.'

'At the moment,' Josh said darkly. He was used to having his ideas ridiculed so paid little attention to Holly's mocking tone. 'But the Bradford police went through all the motions we're going through now, and they came up with one big nothing.'

'Any ideas then?'

'Yes, one . . . but it really is way out. I'll tell you about it tonight.'

* * *

The flat which Jenny Chambers shared with her husband, David, smelt of cigarette smoke.

Jenny was standing in the tiny hall, speaking urgently into the telephone. 'Russ, I can't, the employment people are onto me.'

She listened for a moment, then laughed. 'Of course the money's handy . . . but it won't be if they catch me, will it? No, I'm sorry, but I can't,' she insisted.

Even so, her resistance was crumbling and when she spoke again it was with resignation. 'Yes, okay then, eight a.m. . . . but this is the last time, Russ.'

She replaced the receiver, lit another cigarette and wandered into the living room.

'How the hell did I get into this?' she asked herself miserably.

* * *

Ashworth had been dreading the confrontation with Gwen Anthony's husband but, typical of the man, the thought of trying to avoid or delay it had never entered his mind; he simply wanted it dealt with and done.

He realized Nigel Anthony had chosen a location in which he would suffer the maximum amount of embarrassment. The Bull and Butcher was a public house situated in the High Street, where Ashworth, being a public figure, was well known to both the landlord and his patrons. He also realized the rendezvous had been planned for eight p.m. because at that time the place was certain to be packed.

The rich aroma of hops, the sounds of cheerful debate and lively conversation usually warmed him, but tonight, as Ashworth made his way to the bar, he was oblivious to it all.

He spotted Anthony sitting alone at a corner table, a large brandy in front of him. The doctor raised his hand in recognition but Ashworth chose to ignore him and carried on to the bar.

Although he did not want a drink, Ashworth felt that not to order one would only draw attention to himself. He paid for the half pint of non-alcoholic lager, chatted to the landlord for a few minutes, then wandered over to join Anthony.

Ashworth had already decided that a bombastic approach would not be advisable; after all, he was the one in the wrong.

'Anthony,' he said, sitting down to face the man. 'What can I do for you?'

'Not a great deal.' Anthony's sneer indicated that he was not in a conciliatory mood. 'Actually, Ashworth, you've already told me what I want to know.'

Ashworth, sensing he could be dealing with a volatile situation, kept his voice even. 'You'll have to refresh my memory . . . I can't remember telling you anything.'

It was plain to see that Anthony had consumed quite an amount of brandy; his movements were clumsy as he took a sip from his drink.

'Your problem is you're not intelligent enough to know you're thick.'

Ashworth raised his eyebrows but did not speak.

Anthony, his voice threatening, went on, 'When I rang you today, you gave yourself away. If you had asked me why I wanted to meet you . . . if you had asked what all this was about . . . well . . . that's how an innocent man would have reacted.'

He was hitting the tabletop with his forefinger, emphasizing the words, as he said, 'But all you wanted to do was get rid of me. Thinking, no doubt, that you could sweep your sleazy little affair with my wife under the carpet in private.'

'I knew what you wanted,' Ashworth admitted quietly. 'I saw your wife this morning, in the course of our work. And, yes, I did think this matter would be better sorted out in private,' he glanced around the crowded bar, 'although that's hardly how I'd describe this place.'

'Do you deny there's something between you and my wife?' Anthony asked bluntly.

'Of course I do.'

Ashworth had to look away; he was not a man who lied easily.

The doctor appeared not to have heard. A peevish note crept into his voice as he said, 'You're not the first, oh no. If my wife sold cornflakes she'd give it away with every box . . .'

'Anthony, if I could suggest—'

'It's all over town, you know. I'm surprised your wife hasn't heard about it, what with her Church connections, and the Women's Institute.'

'If I could suggest that you don't have any more to drink . . .'

Anthony's eyes narrowed as he glared at Ashworth. 'You think I'm going to cause a scene, don't you? That's what you'd do, isn't it? Offer to take the man outside for a fight?'

Ashworth sighed.

Anthony leant forward. 'But I'm more subtle than that. I'm going to hurt you, Ashworth . . . at home, and in your job.'

He laughed at Ashworth's worried expression. 'People respect you, don't they? Chief Inspector Ashworth . . . pillar of the community. But they're not going to think that when I'm done with you.'

He fell back in his seat, pointed a finger with disdain. 'Where it hurts, Ashworth . . . where it hurts.'

Ashworth rose and looked down at the doctor. 'You're a drunken bore,' he said. 'Pull yourself together, man.'

He turned to leave. 'Oh, and don't drive home in that state. Take a taxi,' he said, with an authority he did not feel.

Reaching the door, he looked back. Anthony was smiling.

In the car park Ashworth was greeted by warm spring air; a half moon showed in a clear sky freckled with stars.

And he felt regret flood over him.

* * *

Regret for her double-deception was not uppermost in Jenny Chambers's mind as she made her way to the Save U Supermarket on the edge of Bridgetown's council estate. Only the discovery of those deceptions bothered her.

She continually checked that no one was following, scrutinized every parked car along the road, all the time telling herself she was being silly. The Department of Employment doesn't spy on people; well, at any rate, not by following them about.

And David wasn't showing any signs of suspicion; she'd have recognized them by now. God knows, she'd had enough experience and near-misses in that department.

The supermarket was closed and in total darkness when she reached it, but the automatic doors slid open at her approach. Jenny had a final look around, took a deep breath, and walked in.

'Hi, Jen,' Russ Evans, the store manager, greeted her warmly. 'I didn't think you were coming.'

'I had a job to get away.'

'I'd better lock the doors now,' he whispered.

'I can't stay long . . . and I definitely can't do what we usually do,' she said without conviction.

'But, Jen, why not?'

'Because . . .' she began coyly; but as always the sight of Russ weakened her resolve.

He was tall, rugged and handsome, with blond hair and blue eyes; a combination which guaranteed that Jenny would need little persuasion before saying yes.

'Come through to the back,' he urged.

The atmosphere in the empty, darkened supermarket was eerie. Street lights threw their shadows against the walls as they moved between the racks. But even the dimness of the store could not prepare their eyes for the total blackness of the storeroom.

'That's better,' Russ said, taking her into his arms and kissing her, his hand working around her breasts.

'No, Russ,' Jenny complained, struggling to get free, 'I've told you I've got to stop coming here. The employment people are onto me.'

'Didn't I say I'd take care of that?'

His words floated into her ear on warm breath; she could smell his aftershave, could feel her nipples hardening under his caress.

'Look, I'll bring the typing to your place. That'll kill two birds with one stone.'

'God, Russ,' she breathed, clinging to him.

'That's more like it.' His hand worked up between her thighs, pulling her skirt along with it. 'Now let's get these off, shall we?'

Suddenly Jenny stiffened, her hand clamped on his, stopping it. 'I can hear something outside,' she whispered urgently.

'For God's sake, Jen, you're getting paranoid.'

He crossed reluctantly to a small, barred window and peered out. 'There's only the loading bay and the yard out there; nobody can get into it. It must have been a cat or something.'

'I'm sorry,' Jenny said. 'Did you mean it about bringing the typing round?'

'Yes, 'course I did. Nobody'll ever find out about it. And if I come to your flat twice a week . . .' he went back to her '. . . well, it's nice in here . . . but it'll be even better in a bed.'

'That's all you think about,' Jenny said, smiling.

'Yes,' he admitted. 'Now let's get these off, shall we?'

Once again his hand probed between her legs, and this time Jenny did not resist.

* * *

Holly was finding many advantages in living with Josh. For a start she did not feel sexually threatened in any way; but she did sometimes wonder why our Creator had forged him in a manner so attractive to women, and then made him completely indifferent to them. Still, it was nice to know he wouldn't simply use her body and offer nothing in return.

This evening Josh had prepared the meal: ham omelette, served with chips and peas. Holly ate it down to the last morsel; not only because Josh was an excellent cook, but also because she was attempting to fill out her boyish figure. So far the attempt had proved futile for it seemed that however much food she consumed, her weight remained steady at eight stone; and at five foot ten, this meant there was precious little flesh on her frame.

A comfortable silence prevailed as they ate at the kitchen table.

'That was great, Josh,' Holly said, finishing the last of the omelette.

'It was fair,' he replied modestly. 'I'll wash up and then we'll have a beer.'

Holly gathered the plates and took them to the sink. 'No, I'll do the washing-up, and then I'll have my drink in here if you want to watch TV.'

Josh considered her for a moment, then said quietly, 'You'll have to face it sooner or later, Holly . . . the only alternative is to move.'

Holly busily turned on the tap, holding her fingers under the flow, waiting for the water to warm.

'I don't know what you mean,' she said, too brightly. 'I just feel more comfortable in here, that's all.'

She heard Josh's chair scrape on the floor as he got up. 'The lounge has unhappy associations for you, doesn't it? Because of your mother-in-law, I mean. Well, that won't change until you use the room and create a different atmosphere.'

Holly knew he was right. It was now two months since Emily's death but the memory of it was still as stark as when it had happened; and the fact that she felt very little grief — only a deep sense of shock — meant that as the days went by, guilt piled onto guilt.

She suddenly felt awkward and embarrassed by the fact that Josh could read her so easily. 'I can't get used to living with a man who has so much sensitivity,' she smiled.

'We're all girls together,' Josh said lightly.

'Don't put yourself down,' she scolded, turning to face him.

'I think it's warm enough now.' He nodded towards the steaming water gurgling away down the sink.

'Come on,' he said, picking up the tea towel, 'let's do this together, eh? The washing-up . . . and the lounge.'

Holly gave him a grateful smile and filled the bowl with hot water.

Later on, settled in front of the television, they watched the news reports. Margaret Johnson's murder had not attracted nationwide attention, but the local station gave the story prominent coverage.

As the image of Bluebell Wood faded, replaced by the drawing of a proposed motorway link which could bring 400 jobs to the area, Holly said, 'What was that theory you had about the murder? You said you'd tell me tonight.'

Josh was sprawled across his chair, drinking lager straight from the can. He looked across at her and said seriously, 'Ley lines.'

'Ley lines? What are they?'

'They're patterns of invisible underground lines that have complex powers and violent energy charges. It's believed they were first discovered by prehistoric ley hunters; they're people who mapped the countryside to find power spots for sacred constructions and astronomical sites. Stonehenge, for one.'

Holly took a long drink of lager and said, 'I'm not really following any of this, Josh.'

'Sometimes, when these lines cross, they can generate enormous power. Now if that power can be harnessed by witchcraft . . .'

He had been speaking earnestly, his expression suggesting that this explanation was quite rational.

Holly was watching him with amazement, her mouth gaping open. 'Witchcraft?' she repeated incredulously.

'Yes,' Josh said, refusing to be put off. 'There are numerous documented cases of murders, rapes, people being violently ill for no apparent reason. And in all these cases the common denominator was that ley lines crossed near to where the victims lived.'

'Are you really thinking of putting this to Jim Ashworth?' Holly laughed.

'Yes, I am, I think it's valid. Don't you?'

Holly thought of Ashworth's no-nonsense, down-to-earth approach to all things and she said, a touch doubtfully, 'I'd wait till he's having a good day, if I were you.'

* * *

Jenny Chambers, lost in the throes of illicit passion inside the darkened storeroom, had forgotten all about the passing of time. And consequently she was late leaving the supermarket.

Heavy rain had fallen and the pavements glistened and shone as she hurried along the deserted streets, her footsteps echoing in the stillness. Under the light of a street lamp she glanced at her watch: ten p.m. Her husband would be finishing his match at the snooker club about now.

Jenny silently prayed he would stay for a drink afterwards and arrive home at ten thirty to find her sitting in the armchair as if she had never left it.

But she could not quash her niggling worries. What if he didn't stay for a drink? What if he went straight home after the match? His key could be turning in the lock before she was even halfway there. How would she explain her absence?

She told herself to stop being ridiculous. He always stayed for a drink; he was a creature of habit. He always stayed for one drink, then came home and bored her to death with a blow-by-blow account of the match.

Everything about him — including his lovemaking — was predictable . . . monotonous. Even so, the thought that he might, just once, break the pattern quickened her footsteps.

Jenny reached the perimeter of the recreation ground; she could just pick out silhouettes of children's slides and swings against the night sky.

Should she cut across? A shudder ran down her spine at the thought. However, it persisted; she could save ten minutes by running across that dimly lit area. It would take what . . . five minutes to cross it? Then another five and she would be home. And the central path was lit so there was nothing to worry about.

She stopped to consider it. Mist was swirling in the glow from street lamps and the whole area appeared to be deserted.

Taking a deep breath Jenny hastened along the path with a courage born of desperation for her watch now told her it was ten fifteen.

Tension and her hurried gait began to affect her breathing. When she was halfway across and could clearly see the other side she slowed a little, drawing air into her aching lungs. Safety beckoned and drew her.

It started as she passed a heavily landscaped area by a large pond.

At first she thought it was her own breathing she could hear. Stopping, she looked around, held her breath. But it was still there: the slow steady rasping sound which seemed to be almost beside her.

With a small cry she ran towards the comparative safety of the road.

Footsteps rang out behind her, so close her bladder threatened to overflow.

If anyone heard the screams, they did not bother to investigate.

CHAPTER 4

Ashworth was restless. Even three good measures of malt whisky had failed to anaesthetize his brain cells to the point where sleep was inevitable.

He looked across at Sarah, his wife, sleeping peacefully, her face half concealed by the dip in her pillow.

The trouble-free sleep of the righteous, he thought enviously.

For fear of waking Sarah, Ashworth resisted the urge to toss and turn and lay on his back, staring at the ceiling; his mind focused on the problem that was preventing his own rest.

Margaret Johnson's murder? The questions he would be asking her husband the following day? These were the issues that should have been robbing him of sleep, but he felt unable to bring them into his mind for the required meticulous examination.

It was Nigel Anthony, looming large and frightening in his imagination, who was causing Ashworth's insomnia.

Over and over again his mind tormented him with images so vivid, he could see Anthony telephoning Sarah, could hear the words . . .

'Ah, Mrs Ashworth, this is Dr Nigel Anthony.'

'Yes? What can I do for you?' Then, with concern edging into her voice, 'It's not about Jim, is it?'

'Well, yes, Mrs Ashworth, it is. You see, your husband and my wife are having an affair.'

'If this is a joke, Dr Anthony, I don't think it's very funny.'

'I wish it were a joke, but the fact is, your husband and my wife are having a sordid dirty little affair. If you don't believe me, why don't you ask around? It's all over town. It seems you and I are the last to hear about it.'

Ashworth could imagine Sarah slamming down the telephone, anxiously murmuring, 'No, not Jim . . . he wouldn't . . . not my Jim.'

This awful scenario threatened not only to continue, but also to widen its destructive passage throughout his life, for the full impact of Anthony's drunken tirade had not registered until Ashworth was driving home.

The man had forcefully stated he would harm Ashworth's home life . . . and his career.

Sarah startled him by suddenly laughing and turning over; her dream was obviously a happy one.

As he lay in the darkened room, Ashworth speculated as to what would happen to the peace and stability he had enjoyed throughout the last thirty years if the stalwart anchor which had kept it all in place were to be removed.

Then, sighing wretchedly, he began to take deep breaths, concentrating on the air moving in and out of his lungs, in an effort to empty his mind and induce sleep.

* * *

The following morning finally heralded the arrival of spring. Crocuses and primroses in Ashworth's large front garden were beginning to fade before the splendour of tulips and daffodils. The vibrant clumps of yellows, reds and pinks suggested that Sarah's artistic flair was responsible for their arrangement.

The sky was a clear blue, and warmth from the early morning sun promised a 'shirt sleeves' day lay ahead.

Ashworth stomped up the steps of the station. He realized he was stomping and made a conscious effort to control his body language.

As he reached the double doors he was greeted by a mass exodus of uniformed officers; more than a dozen noisily erupted from the building, adjusting caps, buttoning tunics.

Apart from Sergeant Martin Dutton, and Bobby Adams, the new recruit who seemed to be growing in both stature and confidence daily, Ashworth had little to do with the uniformed branch, most of whom he regarded as too young, too short; and a growing proportion — to his mind — were entirely the wrong shape, given the number of women now attracted to the police force.

Ashworth held steady to the rather dated view that females should be cosseted, protected, not sent out on the streets to face violent criminals.

Sergeant Dutton, his bald head resplendently pink beneath the fluorescent lighting, was manning reception. His face broke into a friendly smile when Ashworth marched in.

'Morning, Jim.'

'Martin.' Ashworth nodded towards the retreating officers. 'Is it just that they don't like me, or has someone called the cavalry out?'

'One for you, Jim, I'm afraid,' Dutton reported sombrely. 'Another body's turned up. Young woman. Lumbertub Park.'

'Oh, God,' Ashworth groaned.

'Sorry, Jim, I would have rung you when it came through to control, but Holly Bedford was in and she said you'd be on your way in any case.'

'It's all right, Martin.' Ashworth leant on the reception desk and exhaled with some venom.

'You all right, Jim? You look a bit peaky.'

'I think it's something to do with coming to work every day to find a body waiting for me.'

'Yes, I know what you mean,' Dutton sympathized. 'Sign of the times, I suppose.'

'I think you're right,' Ashworth agreed before heading for the stairs, which he took two at a time.

Holly was at her desk, hands deep in the pockets of her anorak.

'Morning, sir. Have you heard the news?'

'Some of it,' Ashworth grunted. 'Fill me in on the details.'

'We believe the victim's name is Jenny Chambers. The husband reported her missing at eleven thirty last night. Her body was found in Lumbertub Park this morning by a jogger.'

Ashworth paced the office as he listened. 'What leads you to believe it's this Chambers woman?' he asked shortly.

'The description of the victim fits that of the missing woman,' Holly said, frowning.

'And you've set everything in motion, I take it?'

'Yes, sir,' Holly replied pointedly. 'Scene of Crime have been secured. The police surgeon and pathologist have been informed, as have Forensic.'

Ashworth glanced at Josh's empty chair, the silent computer.

'And Josh is there too, sir,' Holly added.

She was on the point of asking if her handling of the affair was in order, when Ashworth snapped, 'Right, we'd better get there then.'

* * *

Ashworth stared down at his second body in as many days. This time the features were still recognizable. Pretty, very pretty, but slightly marred by the fact that someone had caved in the side of her skull.

Gwen Anthony moved close to him. Alone with a corpse in the confines of the small tent, neither was fully concentrating on professional matters.

'There are similarities, Jim.'

'Such as?'

Ordinarily Ashworth would have averted his eyes from the body, but today he just stared morosely at it.

'Both viciously attacked. Far more violence used than was necessary to bring about death. Both had taken part in sexual intercourse shortly before death, but no signs of sexual assault.'

As Ashworth squatted down, the smell of death was pungent in his nostrils. 'So, if that wasn't what he was after, and we know robbery wasn't a factor, they both have to be crimes of passion.'

'Errant wives, found out by their husbands, you mean?' Her voice held a trace of bitterness.

'Yes, more or less.'

'No, Jim,' she said, shaking her head. 'The odds against this occurring twice in two days must be a million to one.'

'Why not?' Ashworth desperately wanted a simple solution to these murders.

'Well, *we* know that all husbands who catch their wives at it don't kill them,' she said heavily. 'It's a course perhaps one in a million would take. For it to happen twice in two days, and for the attacks to be so violent, I'd say was very unlikely.'

'But not impossible?'

'No, but improbable. And there's something else that adds weight to that — both women had sex shortly before death. Now that indicates their killers could have been following them, and I think human nature dictates that if the husbands had been responsible then, surely, at least one of them would have attacked the lover.'

'Has anyone ever told you, you've got a marvellous talent for destroying watertight cases?'

As Gwen laughed, a lot of the worry disappeared from her face. 'We go well together, Jim.' She touched his sleeve tenderly. 'Think about that . . . because I can't stand living with Nigel for much longer.'

Ashworth broached what was on his mind. 'He threatened to tell Sarah about us. Do you think he'd do it?'

'In his present frame of mind, I think he's capable of doing anything.'

That wasn't what Ashworth had wanted to hear.

He looked gloomily down at the corpse, aware for the first time that they were holding an intimate discussion in its presence. Still, they were safe; Jenny Chambers wasn't going to pass on any secrets.

'Somewhere around ten thirty,' Gwen said.

'Eh?' Ashworth responded blankly.

'Time of death . . . ten thirty, or thereabouts. You forgot to ask.'

'So I did.' He slowly stood up. 'I must be slipping.'

Outside, in the warm sunlight, they imagined every pair of eyes was upon them, whereas all were simply going about their business and — with the exception of Holly — assumed that the Chief Inspector and the doctor were doing the same.

They strode along a winding path which led to a large pond in a hollow.

'What else did he say, Jim?'

'Just that he knew we were having an affair, and that he intended to cause me as much trouble as he could. Most of the rest was just drunken talk.'

At the pond they stopped. Fish attracted to the sun-warmed water dimpled the surface.

'Was he that drunk?'

'Not paralytic, but he'd have needed an act of divine intervention to pass the breathalyser. Was he drunk when he got home?'

'No. He said he went and sat in the surgery to sober up. It was after eleven when he came in, but then he started knocking it back again.'

'Did he cause you any problems?'

Once again she was touched by Ashworth's evident concern. 'No. He went through the usual three stages: maudlin;

aggressive; through to threatening violence. Just after that he slipped into stage four . . . fell asleep in the chair.'

'You seem to be taking all this in your stride, Gwen.'

She laughed; a very infectious laugh. 'It does have its lighter moments to sustain me. Last night when Nigel came in he had mud all over him. Apparently he'd fallen over after leaving the pub. When he started raving later on, I kept picturing him staggering to the surgery, covered in the stuff.'

As Ashworth gave a polite laugh he was struck by an absurd thought: did Anthony go to the surgery, or did he collect the mud here as he murdered the girl? No, the idea was preposterous . . .

'Anyway, we'd better get back, Jim,' Gwen said with finality, 'your keeper is watching you.'

'My keeper?'

'Holly Bedford. She probably thinks I'm going to lure you into the bushes to play Doctors and Policemen.' They began the walk back. 'I'm sure she fancies you.'

'Nonsense,' Ashworth snorted.

'I can't think of any other reason why she should behave like a mother hen every time I go near you.'

They passed the tent which housed the body; inside flash bulbs burst with regularity as the Scene of Crime officers got their photographs.

'Tell me, Gwen, would there have been much blood on the killer's clothing?'

She considered this for a while. 'Not necessarily. The woman's brain was all but caved in, but as this was done with a hammer it's possible there was very little blood on the killer.'

'Thanks, Gwen, I'll be in touch.'

'Make sure of that, Jim.' Her eyes held their flirtatious message.

At the top of the slight rise, Holly joined them.

'Bye, Jim.' She nodded briskly at Holly. 'Sergeant.'

'Bye,' Holly said coolly.

As Gwen made for her Land Rover, Ashworth glanced around the park. A small knot of onlookers had gathered beyond the police cordon.

'Why is it that people are attracted to dead bodies?' Ashworth asked dismally.

Holly made no reply, so he said, 'Right, have you got everything from Forensic?'

'All they can give us at the moment.'

'Good. The pond will have to be dragged . . . we're looking for a hammer. Let's get back to the station and sift through what we've got.'

* * *

Although death had been an unwelcome visitor to Margaret Johnson and Jenny Chambers, if its presence were to be felt at 22 Elinham Road, it would be fêted as a visiting hero.

And, as if not to impede its entry, Gladys Smart opened wide the upstairs window.

'I'll catch cold,' her husband weakly called from the bed. 'The doctor said the next bout of pneumonia will likely kill me. Huh, but I reckon you'd like that.'

Yes, Gladys said under her breath, adding aloud, 'It's a lovely spring morning, Cliff. The fresh air should do you good.'

'Nothing can do me good now,' the old man moaned, 'I'm done for.'

Gladys crossed to the old-fashioned wooden bed, her footsteps muffled by a large rug covering the linoleum.

'Now we'll have none of that talk,' she chided. 'Here, let me prop you up.'

Gladys fussed with the pillows, helped her husband to a sitting position. He groaned with pain, and by the time the operation was completed, he was breathless.

Screwing up his eyes, Clifford Smart stated feebly, 'I can't stand this pain much longer.'

Weight loss had caused the skin to hang in folds on his once robust frame; and the chemotherapy to which he had been subjected in an attempt to halt the advance of the cancer which now ravaged his body had deprived him of what little hair he'd had left.

'Shall I get your painkillers?' Gladys asked with dutiful but unfelt kindness.

'Yes,' he sobbed, 'give me the lot, for God's sake, and let me die in peace.'

'Don't talk like that, Cliff,' she scolded, but in an automatic, unthinking manner.

Her husband had made that request so often, Gladys no longer listened. When the pain had first become unbearable, she had taken to leaving the full phial of painkillers beside his bed, but he never attempted to take more than the prescribed dosage.

As she trudged, exhausted, down the stairs to make a pot of tea, she could hear the happy sounds of children on their way to school.

And suddenly Gladys felt old, trapped, and so utterly alone.

* * *

Back at the CID office Ashworth's attention was only half on what was being said. The thought that Nigel Anthony might be involved in the murders was too absurd to consider, and yet he could not dismiss it.

But Ashworth knew he could not voice these thoughts so, as he sat facing Holly and Josh, he began the task of recounting the similarities in the two cases; the prime one being that both victims had engaged in sexual intercourse shortly before death, but this act seemed not to have been part of the attack.

'What's the SP on Jenny Chambers?' he asked. 'What time was her husband expecting her home? And where had he been led to believe she'd be spending the evening?'

Holly consulted her notebook. 'All we've got at the moment is that he arrived home from a snooker match to find the house empty. His wife hadn't informed him that she intended going out.'

'So,' Ashworth mused, 'the lady was playing an away-match . . . just as Margaret Johnson was.'

'Therefore adultery is another connecting factor in both cases,' Josh said.

'What makes you say that?' Ashworth asked sharply.

'Because it is, sir,' Josh answered, slightly bemused. 'Both women—'

'Yes, yes,' Ashworth snapped, irritably, 'but it could simply be coincidental.'

Josh threw a what-have-I-done? look at Holly.

'Anything else?' Ashworth barked.

Unperturbed by his superior's abruptness, Josh said in an even voice, 'Yes, there is. Forensic haven't released any of the women's belongings yet, but it does appear that both were unemployed and both had attended interviews at the Employment Office in the past week.'

Ashworth tilted back his chair and gazed up at the ceiling. 'I don't see how that's relevant either.'

'Well, I do, sir,' Holly said firmly. 'Both women had interviews with a fraud investigator named Gerald Fox—'

'We're not interested in whether or not they were making fraudulent claims.'

Holly's patience was beginning to dissipate. 'I disagree, sir,' she said. 'In my opinion, Margaret Johnson was doing some work for Giles Insurance, and if we can find out where Jenny Chambers was suspected of working, that could lead us to her lover.'

Ashworth, even in his current black mood, knew that what Holly was proposing made complete sense.

'All right,' he conceded. 'Go with Josh to break the news to Mr Chambers and then follow up on the Employment office lead. I'll take Margaret Johnson's husband.'

Ashworth collected his coat and struggled into it as he left the office. Walking along the corridor he caught the beep-beep sound as Josh's computer was switched on. It annoyed him immensely.

As he strode along, Nigel Anthony once again entered his mind. Josh had picked up on the adultery theme which had bothered Ashworth since staring down at the body of Jenny Chambers in the oppressive confines of the tent. If they were looking for someone derailed by the discovery of his partner's adultery perhaps they should look no further than him. The man was, after all, behaving strangely, consuming far too much alcohol; and he had promised to hurt Ashworth at home and in his job. No, it was far too ridiculous to consider. But the man had arrived home covered in mud. Even so, how many highly educated doctors resort to murder? Dr Crippen, for one . . .

Ashworth quickly closed the door on these thoughts for now he was anxious to be away. With two dead bodies, the Chief Constable would soon be requesting his presence. And with that prospect firmly in mind, he wanted to be away and stay away for as long as possible.

After Ashworth's departure, and although they were engaged in a double-murder investigation, the detectives brightened considerably.

Josh tapped away at the computer keys. 'Look, Holly,' he exclaimed excitedly, 'the pattern's the same.'

Holly leant over to stare at the screen.

'See?' Josh pointed. 'These are the murders in Bradford. The first two women were killed on consecutive days. Then there was a week before the next murder, and two days after that the man was killed. It's the same.'

'No, it's not,' Holly replied. 'Only half of it's the same pattern.'

She was standing close to him, could smell his manly scent, and she wondered how anyone, so outwardly masculine, could possess so many female hormones.

'Oh ye of little faith,' Josh commented lightly.

'Come on, lover, we've got work to do.'

As Holly spoke the telephone rang. She picked it up. 'DS Bedford.'

'Hello, Holly, it's Sarah Ashworth. Is Jim there?'

'No, I'm afraid he's out at the moment. Can I take a message?'

'Oh dear.' Sarah sounded distinctly perplexed. 'I did need to speak to him.' She was silent for a few seconds, then said, 'Look, will you tell him I've had a telephone call.'

'A telephone call,' Holly repeated blankly. 'He'll know what that means, will he?'

'Oh yes, he'll know.'

They said goodbye, and Holly replaced the receiver with a shrug. The way Ashworth was behaving at the moment she would have hated passing on a message he could not fully comprehend.

CHAPTER 5

Ashworth parked the Sierra some distance from Becket Brook Close. He left his waxed cotton jacket inside the car and set off for the home of Ian Johnson.

The day was warmed by brilliant sunshine which seemed to bring out the brighter side of everyone. During his walk, Ashworth was greeted with cheery good-mornings from a postman, several women with small children, and a senior citizen out walking her grossly overweight dachshund.

Ashworth responded in kind but, with morale flagging, his thoughts were gloomy. He secretly feared that the husbands and lovers of the deceased women would not stand up as suspects under scrutiny.

He also realized with dismay that he could not voice his opinion as to what might have taken place; all he could do was follow procedure and hope, for the first time in his career, that something would turn up to prove his theory wrong.

In his more mellow moments, Ashworth would admit to himself that he was a difficult man; a combination of life, his job and his obvious leadership qualities had made him so. But he now felt a strong twinge of guilt regarding his attitude towards his two detectives. They were good officers and there was no reason why they should suffer simply because he had said yes when he should have said no.

His firm knock was answered by movement inside the house and the door was opened by Mrs Thomas, Margaret Johnson's mother.

She was plainly dressed: dark trousers, blue sweater. The countless tears she had shed since yesterday had left her eyes red, puffy; and her hair, although tidy, appeared dry and uncared for.

'You'd better come in,' she said without preamble.

'Thank you.'

Ashworth followed her through to the lounge.

Ian Johnson was sitting on the settee. He was still unshaven, the stubble now extremely prominent; his hair still hung untidily over his forehead. But at least he had changed his clothes; his green sports shirt and brown cord jeans looked fresh and clean.

Ashworth noted the cup of cold coffee — a thick skin forming on its surface — on the table before the man.

He decided to get straight to the point. 'Mr Johnson, I'm sorry to have to bother you again, but there are questions I must ask.'

'Yes, I know. Sit down.'

'I'll make this as quick as possible,' he said, settling into an armchair, while Mrs Thomas hovered by the settee.

Ashworth felt a distinct air of hostility as he asked, 'When was the last time you saw your wife, sir?'

'She went out about six p.m. on the day she vanished, and that was the last I saw of her,' Johnson replied blankly.

'And she told you she was going to see her mother, I believe?' He studied his notebook. 'That's . . . Mrs Thomas . . . ?'

'Yes, that's right, Inspector,' Margaret's mother confirmed.

'Good. Now we know on this occasion your wife was not being truthful, and we also believe there were a number of other times when she misled you . . .'

Johnson glanced at his mother-in-law.

'Did you at any time suspect that your wife was not telling the truth?'

Johnson shook his head.

'What are you insinuating?' Mrs Thomas jumped in.

'Nothing,' Ashworth said slowly, 'but it does seem to me that using you as a long-term alibi was pretty dangerous. Any time you and Mr Johnson were together . . . well, just one slip of the tongue and Mrs Johnson's lies would be found out. Or he could so easily have telephoned to speak to his wife . . .'

'Ian never phoned, and we saw very little of each other before this happened. There was hardly any chance of him finding out from me,' Mrs Thomas said sharply.

'I see.' He returned his attention to the husband. 'Did you and your wife row a lot, Mr Johnson?'

'It's that busybody, Jessie,' Mrs Thomas said, her tone acidic.

She moved to the window and stared out at the road, no doubt sticking pins into the mental effigy of Jessie Leabon next door.

Ashworth remained silent; he had no intention of disclosing the fact that Mrs Leabon had told him precious little.

'Margaret and Ian did have rows . . . it's just the stress of modern living—'

'Mrs Thomas,' Ashworth said, remaining polite but firm, 'I'd much rather Mr Johnson answered the questions, if you don't mind.'

The woman gave an exaggerated sigh and turned back to the window.

Ian Johnson said, 'Maggie and I had rows. Money was tight, and there's the mortgage on this place. We just couldn't afford to live.'

'And that was causing friction?'

'Well, what do you think?' Johnson flared. 'Would you like to work all hours God sends to find everything about to be taken away from you?'

'What is it you do for a living, sir?'

'I'm a driver.'

'Lorry? Van?'

'Van. I work for Belreeds, the electrical people, in the High Street.'

'Were you aware that your wife knew Terry Giles, the insurance broker?'

'Yes, she used to work for him, didn't she?'

At this point Ashworth felt there was something very wrong; it was a combination of the questions Ian Johnson and his mother-in-law were not asking, and the frantic eye-contact which was going on between them.

Sensing he was onto something, Ashworth decided to plough on in a far more brutal fashion than he would ordinarily have done. 'Did you know that your wife was having an affair, Mr Johnson?'

'No,' he said, staring down at the carpet.

'And you were at home the night your wife was murdered?'

Johnson's head came up suddenly. He looked to Mrs Thomas for help.

Her expression advised caution. 'Ian was—'

'No,' Johnson cut in, 'I wasn't at home, no. I came in about eight thirty and found Margaret wasn't here.'

'So what did you do then, sir?'

'How do you mean, what did I do then?' Johnson buried his face in his hands.

'You said you came home to find your wife wasn't here,' Ashworth said calmly, 'which indicates that you expected her to be here.'

He paused, allowing time for his words to sink in. 'Did you phone her mother to see if she was there?'

'Of course he did,' Mrs Thomas said quickly. 'I object to these questions, Inspector. Ian's very upset, and you seem determined to trap him.'

'That's not my intention,' Ashworth assured her. 'I'm merely trying to establish what happened.' He turned back to Johnson. 'So at eight thirty you found that your wife was not where she told you she'd be. In fact she hadn't been there at any time during the evening, and yet you didn't phone the police . . .' He consulted his notebook again. '. . . until ten p.m.'

'I didn't want to bother the police,' Johnson replied feebly.

'Very commendable, sir,' Ashworth said as he got to his feet. 'I don't think I need bother you any longer. We'll need a formal statement, of course,' he added ominously.

As a relieved Mrs Thomas opened the lounge door for him, Ashworth held back and asked the question he had purposefully saved until last. 'You said you came in at eight thirty. Where had you been?'

'Just out walking.'

'Just out walking,' Ashworth repeated.

'Yes.'

'Do you remember where you went when you were . . . just out walking?'

Johnson closed his eyes. 'No. I was so depressed about money. I just walked about, trying to clear my head.'

'Fine.' Ashworth nodded, then left the house.

They watched him from the window. Neither spoke until he was across the road.

Johnson, close to tears, said, 'I should have told him.'

Mrs Thomas cradled his shoulders, tried to comfort him. 'That would have been a silly thing to do. There's no way they can suspect you of killing Margaret.'

'Oh God,' Johnson sobbed.

'Ian, I know she was my own flesh and blood, but she was a wicked girl. You working all those hours, trying to keep this place going, and she was messing about with that Terry Giles. God forgive me, but she deserved what she got.'

And as Mrs Thomas held the sobbing Johnson in her arms, she too began to cry.

* * *

Watching the laying to waste of all happiness and security in the life of David Chambers; knowing it was their news which had caused this total devastation did little to brighten the day for Holly and Josh.

The fact that David Chambers was a huge man, who worked on motorway maintenance, made the tears and incoherent ramblings all the more poignant.

Holly had telephoned his works depot and within ten minutes two of his workmates — both equally huge — had arrived to take care of him.

The only information they had been able to derive was supplied by one of the two men. It seemed they had attended a snooker match the previous evening, had hired a van for the occasion, and Chambers had been dropped off at his home at ten thirty.

If that was indeed the case, then David Chambers had a watertight alibi.

* * *

Josh skipped lightly down the steps of the Working Men's Club and climbed into the passenger seat beside Holly.

'Checks out so far,' he told her. 'Chambers was in the club all evening. He left about ten fifteen with the rest of the team. We'll have to check it out right the way through, but it seems kosher.' He reached for the seat-belt.

'Have you noticed how much time we spend checking things that don't need checking, just so the paperwork's right?' Holly remarked. 'What now?'

'I could murder a cup of tea.'

'Me too,' Holly said, starting the engine, 'but we ought to be doing something about the case, sweetie.'

'Oh, yes. Look, let's go to the mobile café in the Bridgenorton Road lay-by, then we can carry on to the Employment Offices.'

Holly eased out into the traffic, crashing the gears as she changed up into third. 'To see Fox, you mean?'

'Yes, I think that's our next logical step.'

She crashed the gears again. 'Oh, this bloody car.'

'The clutch's going, Holly. I think it'd be wise to use mine from now on.'

Holly, aiming a string of well-chosen words at the dashboard, finally got the car running smoothly.

Josh said, 'Fox, as you pointed out to Ashworth, had interviewed both women, and whatever title they give him, he's still a fraud officer, so we've a right to ask him questions.'

'Clever,' Holly acknowledged, 'and it'll give us a chance to see what he's like.'

'That too,' Josh agreed.

She drove on in silence for a while, and then asked. 'How long do you think this clutch will last?'

'Not long, the way it's going. Are you still thinking of trading it in?'

'Yes.' She slowed as they approached a roundabout. 'I've been looking at a Nissan Micra — four years old.'

'How much?'

'Four thousand.'

She took advantage of a gap in the incoming traffic and pulled out. The clutch slipped again, and the car behind honked its driver's impatience.

'Oh, shut up,' Holly muttered, finally getting the car into gear, 'or I'll pull you over and ram my warrant card up your nostrils.'

'Four grand,' Josh said, pursing his lips. 'That's a bit pricey.'

'There's only twenty thousand on the clock.'

Holly indicated left, turned into a large lay-by, and pulled up behind the mobile café.

Josh fetched two teas in plastic-lidded containers.

Settling back in his seat, he asked, 'Have you got the money?'

'I have, but I was going to buy it on HP. The garage said they'd give me a hundred-pound trade-in for the mini.'

Josh took a sip; the tea was lukewarm. 'You'd be better off scrapping the mini . . . you'd get twenty-five quid for it. If you go to the garage with cash you should get a ten per cent discount, probably more if you haggle.'

'Josh,' Holly said hesitantly, 'will you come to the garage with me and do the talking?'

'Yes, of course.' He finished his tea.

Holly stared into her own cup reflectively; Josh's company was so enjoyable, she realized it could easily interfere with the efficient discharge of her duties.

Putting the lid back on the cup, she said firmly, 'We'd better go and see Fox.'

She drove off, and the way in which the mini shuddered and rattled suggested the ailing clutch might well outlive other parts of its mechanism.

* * *

Sarah Ashworth paced the lounge.

'Ring, Jim,' she muttered.

Peanuts, their Jack Russell terrier, followed in her wake, whining and crying.

'Oh, shut up,' Sarah said with unaccustomed bad temper.

She entered the hall and sat on the bottom stair, all the time watching the telephone expectantly. The dog lay across her feet, staring up with huge, puzzled eyes.

Sarah simply sat, willing the telephone to ring.

* * *

Gwen Anthony was finishing morning surgery. As the last patient departed she felt a huge sense of relief. But then, remembering how she would be spending the afternoon, she gave out a laugh.

Gwen, she thought, if you'd rather cut up the remains of Jenny Chambers than be with Nigel, it might be time to wonder whether you've got a matrimonial problem.

The door opened and Nigel Anthony entered her surgery. 'Do you fancy a drink?'

'No.' She tidied the patient files on her desk. 'I've got a post-mortem.'

'Oh yes, I forgot . . . the second murder. Will you be back for evening surgery?'

Automatically she glanced at her watch. 'I should be.'

'Well, if you're not, I can handle it,' he said amiably.

Nigel's conduct was beginning to concern Gwen. The erratic way in which he alternated between perfectly reasonable and rational behaviour and those unpredictable brooding moods which often threatened to explode into violence was unnerving, frightening.

A lot of it could be put down to his increasing consumption of brandy, but Gwen now had to admit there was something very wrong with his mental stability.

'Right, I'm off,' she said, pulling on her coat.

'Be careful,' he called after her.

* * *

If Ashworth had not deviated from his usually rigid approach to work, he would not have known about Sarah's telephone call until much later.

As it was, he saw that very little could be done with the investigation for the time being and, wishing to stay out of the chief constable's way for as long as possible, he decided a cup of tea would be a good idea; and where better to enjoy one than in the comfort of one's home. So, on his way back to the station he made a diversion.

As he pulled into the driveway, Sarah's concerned face appeared at the lounge window.

He climbed out of the car just as the front door opened.

'What's wrong, Sarah?' he called, worried by her anxious expression.

'I've had a telephone call, Jim.'

Those who saw Ashworth as a tower of strength, an immovable object, would have been surprised to see him abandon all attempts to lock the car door because his hand was shaking so much.

CHAPTER 6

Holly parked behind the Department of Employment offices; and the shudder that ran through the mini as she switched off the engine caused Josh to wonder if this was to be its final resting place.

The building was of grey stone and, in common with the police station, glass had been used wherever possible.

They strolled to the front entrance, past office workers eating snack lunches, taking advantage of the unseasonably warm weather.

Inside, with its grey cord carpet and white walls, the building had an official, unfriendly atmosphere.

Stairs leading to the first floor were littered with crushed cigarette ends and other debris.

They pushed through swing doors and entered the main office. A large number of people were queuing to sign on, and they shouldered through these to the reception desk.

'Hi,' Josh said to the pretty Asian girl.

As Josh was tall, good-looking, with soft grey eyes, women seemed to relate to him comfortably, and his friendly manner always put them at ease. For the moment, Holly was quite happy to let him do the talking.

The girl smiled up at him. 'Hello, can I help you?'

Josh flashed his warrant card. 'Bridgetown CID.'

Holly held out her own, but the girl was too busy eyeing Josh to notice, so she flung it back into her bag with annoyance.

'We'd like to see Mr Gerald Fox, please,' Josh continued smoothly.

'I don't know if he's back from lunch yet.' The girl consulted a list on her desk. 'Yes, he is.' She turned back to Josh. 'What's he done then?'

'Nothing that we know of.' He placed his hands on the desk and leant forward. 'What's he like?'

The girl shrugged. 'I dunno. Doesn't have much to do with anybody. He hasn't been here long.'

'Not over-friendly then,' Josh ventured.

'No, he's not. Most of the men here won't leave you alone—'

'Understandable in your case,' Josh interrupted.

Blushing, the girl laughed at the compliment.

'You said he hasn't been here long . . . where did he come from?'

'Dunno. He was transferred from somewhere up north, I think. Come on, he must have done something for you to be asking all these questions.'

'No,' Josh smiled. 'I'm just enjoying talking to you.'

This caused more blushing and the girl turned away, embarrassed. 'I'll see if he's free.'

'Now, Josh,' Holly whispered, 'don't promise what you can't deliver.'

'Ouch!' Josh tossed his head as if recoiling from a blow. 'That was bitchy.'

The girl was back. 'It's through that door at the end of the office, along the corridor, and Mr Fox will meet you.'

Josh winked at her. 'Thanks.'

If Gerald Fox was in any way apprehensive about a visit from the police, it did not show in his manner. He seemed completely at ease as he watched the two officers approach.

'Mr Gerald Fox?' Holly asked, producing her warrant card.

'Yes,' Fox replied quietly.

'DS Bedford, Bridgetown CID, and this is DC Abraham. We'd like to ask you a few questions,' she informed him crisply.

'Come into the office.' He ushered them in. 'Excuse me while I get another chair from next door.'

As they listened to Fox moving about in the next room, Josh said, 'Holly, can I ask the questions?'

'All right.' She pulled a rueful face. 'I don't know, since I've been promoted I haven't got a word in edgeways.'

'You're the pretty one,' Josh winked.

'Keep lying . . . I like it.'

Any further banter was cut short by the reappearance of Gerald Fox carrying a chair.

'Sorry about that,' he said.

Inviting them to sit, Fox skirted round the desk to his own seat.

Josh said, 'We won't take up any more of your time than we have to, Mr Fox, but as you probably know there have been two women murdered in the last couple of days, and we've reason to believe you've interviewed both of them quite recently.'

'Two?' Fox appeared puzzled. 'I know one woman has been murdered, but I haven't heard anything about a second.'

Josh tutted. 'Sorry, sir, it happened last night. The media haven't picked up on the story yet.'

The pneumatic drill sounded louder today; as the road works moved ever closer the noise seemed to fill the room.

Fox got up and closed the window. 'Sorry,' he said, 'I smoke, so I like to keep the window open. Right, what's the name of the other woman?'

'Jennifer Chambers.' Josh watched Fox closely as he spoke.

'My God,' Fox exclaimed. 'I saw her yesterday morning.'

'Yes, we know that, sir,' Josh said. 'Can you tell us the reason for the interview?'

Metal grated on metal as Fox opened the filing cabinet and removed two folders. 'The same reason I interview all the other people . . . we had cause to believe that Mrs Chambers was working and drawing benefit.'

He sat down and flicked open one of the files. 'Margaret Johnson, for instance, was spending a lot of time at Giles Insurance Brokers, so we assumed she was doing some work there.'

'I think your assumption may have been correct, sir,' Josh said thoughtfully. 'What about Mrs Chambers?'

Fox turned to the other file. 'The Save U Supermarket. She often went there . . . let me see . . . between six and nine in the evenings.'

'How did you determine that?' Holly asked.

Fox, ignoring her, directed the answer at Josh. 'By surveillance mostly . . . like you people.'

'You actually watch claimants?' Holly laughed.

Fox gave her a cursory glance and nodded. 'That's right, but you'd never get anyone to admit it officially. If it was made public knowledge we'd be accused of playing Big Brother.'

Josh, aware that Fox was showing a great deal of interest in him, asked, 'So what do you do with the data once you've compiled it?'

'We have the people in for interviews and try to frighten them, without actually saying we know anything.'

Fox smiled, displaying uneven nicotine-stained teeth. 'Every so often the department calls an amnesty . . . people can sign off the dole with no questions asked. Sometimes I wonder whether I'm wasting my time.'

'I'll bet,' Josh sympathized. 'You're not from around here, are you?'

'No, I was transferred from Bradford. It seems there's no one with enough experience to deal with this sort of thing here.'

'Well, I think we can leave you to deal with it now, sir,' Josh smiled. 'Thank you. You've been a great help.'

'If I can be of any further assistance, just call in.'

Somehow, Holly had the distinct feeling she was excluded from that invitation.

As they left the building, Holly chided herself. By allowing Josh to take centre stage, she had undermined her own position; and as much as she liked her DC she was determined to make her presence felt in the police force.

Josh paused on the pavement, gazing at a café opposite. 'I could do with another cup of tea,' he said with feeling.

'Josh, we can't keep taking tea breaks,' Holly said irritably.

'Oh, come on, Holly,' he coaxed. 'Just ten minutes . . . and we'll be exchanging opinions about Fox.'

'Okay,' she said, but with reluctance.

Inside, the self-service café was almost empty. Josh got two teas and they sat on stools facing a wide shelf which served as a table.

'Well, we've unearthed someone from Bradford who's just moved here,' he remarked.

'Fox?' Holly laughed. 'You must be joking. He wouldn't be capable of murdering anybody. He's a wimp.'

'Maybe. But he was watching both women . . . he knew their movements,' he countered.

'No, Josh, it just doesn't hold water.'

'Perhaps not . . .' He smiled expansively. 'But it's got to be better than my ley lines theory.'

When Holly did not laugh at this, did not even smile, Josh said, 'Are you all right, Holly?'

'Yes . . . well, no, I'm not really.'

'Sorry I'm always wasting time drinking tea and developing crazy theories—'

'It's not that, Josh . . .'

'And you're right, it doesn't hold water . . . because Gerald Fox is gay.'

'Gay? Are you sure?'

'I should know. He's as bent as an eleven bob note, as my dad used to say.'

So Fox was gay, and Holly had thought he was a chauvinist, passing her over as a woman in a man's world.

'But surely that doesn't rule him out. I mean . . .' She toyed with her spoon, searching for words.

'Gays,' Josh prompted, exaggerating the enunciation. 'It's ever so easy to say.'

'Yes, all right, I haven't got a hang-up about the word. What I mean is, if a gay has been hurt by a straying partner, wouldn't that amount to the same as with a straight?'

'Yes.' Josh sounded far from sure. 'But if that were the case, I'd expect him to direct his anger towards other gays, rather than heterosexuals. Anyway, why the interest? A few minutes ago you thought the idea was absurd.'

Holly pushed aside the weak tea. 'I was hasty, and I don't happen to agree with Ashworth on this one. We're not looking for an enraged spouse or lover, but someone who goes out of his head when he sees people committing adultery. Gerald Fox is worth looking at,' she said firmly. 'Now, come on, let's get out of here before it's time for your next break.'

Josh gulped down the remainder of his tea and followed her out.

* * *

Although Ashworth climbed the station steps with a heavy heart, he felt that a great burden had been lifted from his mind.

Martin Dutton and Bobby Adams were manning front reception, and as Ashworth pushed through the swing doors, Dutton pointed an ominous finger towards the ceiling, indicating that Ashworth had received a summons from on high.

Catching sight of his worried expression, Dutton asked, 'Everything all right, Jim?'

'Not really, Martin,' he replied wearily. 'Sarah's had to go to Norfolk. Our daughter, Samantha, is expecting her third child and it looks as if it's going to arrive two months early.'

Dutton made all the right sympathetic noises.

'We knew it was likely to happen,' Ashworth went on. 'We've been expecting a telephone call for weeks, but it's still a shock when it comes.' He pointed towards the ceiling. 'What does he want?'

'He's a bit worried about the two dead bodies,' Dutton replied lightly, 'and he's having problems with a group of vigilantes.'

'Vigilantes?' Ashworth echoed.

'Yes.' Dutton made no attempt to suppress his smile. 'A neighbourhood watch scheme that's got out of hand apparently. Nothing serious . . . he just wants someone to read them the riot act.'

'And no prizes for guessing who's been nominated for that honour.' Ashworth glanced reluctantly towards the stairs. 'Well, I'd better get up there, I suppose.'

'Jim,' Dutton called, 'if I can do anything — about your daughter, I mean — just let me know.'

'Thanks, Martin.'

As he was in no hurry to reach his destination, Ashworth took the stairs one at a time.

* * *

The body of Jenny Chambers had been dissected, specimens bottled and labelled, and Gwen Anthony's report of her findings written out.

Gwen was crossing the hospital car park. Carrying out a post-mortem was not her favourite way of passing an afternoon and, as this had been the second in as many days, her feelings of pity and despair were deeper than usual, so she was now looking forward to the luxury of a drink.

The warm air smelt of blossom as her high heels clicked on the tarmac.

As she approached the rear of the car park, rummaging in her handbag for her keys, Gwen experienced a sensation of acute disquiet, was aware of hostile eyes on her back.

Turning quickly, she expected to find someone following but, apart from a few vehicles, the place was deserted.

Hurriedly, she unlocked the Land Rover and climbed in, surprised to find herself trembling. The tyres screeched as she did a wide circle turn and headed for the exit.

Turning into the road, Gwen glanced into her rear-view mirror and laughed. The light blue Jaguar waiting to leave the car park explained everything: it was Nigel's car. So, he was keeping an eye on her.

'You've been cutting up too many women who've been putting it about, my girl,' Gwen told herself with a relieved grin, 'and now you've started thinking your turn's come.'

She checked the mirror again. He was still there.

'Follow me home, you bastard,' she laughed.

* * *

Ashworth was outside the office of Chief Constable Ken Savage, and realizing he could put it off no longer, he knocked sharply.

'Come,' Savage commanded frostily.

Ashworth unwillingly entered.

'Jim' Savage said heartily, 'take a seat.'

He was drawing unsatisfactorily on one of the low-tar cigarettes to which he had recently changed in the hope that these would take longer to kill him.

Savage, a tall, gaunt man, had a liverish complexion with a network of broken capillaries on his hooked nose and hollow cheeks.

Ashworth sat facing him.

'What's the news on the murders then?' Savage asked, straight to the point.

'Not much to report. Early days yet,' Ashworth answered evasively.

'Yes, of course.' Savage cleared his throat. 'Jim, I've got another problem,' he began tactfully. 'A neighbourhood watch scheme that's getting out of hand.'

Ashworth chuckled. 'Whatever next?'

Savage's expression was grave. 'It's no laughing matter, Jim. The coordinator of the group's a bolshie bugger. There's a council nature reserve on his estate and he keeps ringing in every time lads use it for motorbike scrambling, or when gangs of youngsters are making a noise on it.'

'I see,' Ashworth reflected. 'If my memory serves me correctly, riding a motorbike on public land is an insurance offence and making a lot of noise is covered by disturbing the peace.'

'You haven't been talking to this Frederick chap, have you?' Savage snapped, stubbing out his cigarette. 'That's precisely the patter he gives me.'

He looked pleadingly at Ashworth. 'Jim, you know our lads can't respond immediately to that sort of thing . . . it's way down our list of priorities. Often, when we're really busy, the problem's gone away by the time we get there.'

'Yes?'

'Well, surely any normal, reasonable person would leave it there' — although Savage had only moments ago finished his cigarette, he reached for the packet on his desk — 'but not our Mr Frederick; he informs us that the residents are sick to death of having their lives made a misery, and he wants these people prosecuted . . . can you believe it?'

He threw down the cigarette packet unopened. 'And do you know what he had the gall to say? He understands my problems with shortage of manpower, so he and his friends are willing to apprehend the offenders and hold them till we can get there.'

With great difficulty, Ashworth suppressed a laugh. Anyone who did not agree with Savage immediately ruffled his feathers; and the persistent Mr Frederick seemed to have ruffled them more than most.

'We're always asking the public to help us,' Ashworth said, more out of devilment than anything else.

'Not in this way, Jim, it could lead to public disorder. I'm not going to tolerate a vigilante element on my patch.'

'Sorry, Ken, but I admire these people. I just wish we had the powers to do what they do.'

Savage relented a little. 'Yes, Jim, we all give three silent cheers when a young car thief gets a belting, but that's not the way we want Joe Public to see it. Help me out on this one, Jim. Go along and talk to these people . . . the iron fist/velvet glove technique.'

'Can't do it, Ken,' Ashworth said flatly.

Savage hardly seemed to be listening as Ashworth explained about his daughter, and how he needed to spend his off-duty hours close to the telephone.

'Right, Jim,' Savage said briskly, 'fair enough. I'm thinking now that perhaps this might not require the attention of a senior officer.'

Having found the buck firmly back in his own lap, Savage now needed to find someone else to pass it to.

'Martin Dutton,' he suggested with a satisfied smile. 'Now he could be just the man for the job.'

Ashworth laughed. 'Could be. Look, Ken, if that's all, I do need to check something with my team.'

Now it was Savage's turn to laugh, although the sound carried more malice than humour. 'Your team, as you call them, are getting a bit of flak.'

Ashworth was eager to be away from the smoke-filled room. He got to his feet, saying, 'How's that then?'

Savage, adding to the problem by lighting another cigarette, said, 'Seems they visited the local Employment office, and when they came out, that car of Bedford's wouldn't start. The engine had boiled over and the clutch was burnt out,' he let out a chesty chuckle, 'and they had to catch a bus back to the station.'

* * *

The station grapevine always went into overdrive when reporting the misfortunes of unlucky officers, and the truth could never be allowed to spoil a good story.

This time Holly and Josh were the unfortunate targets, and every distortion which would add to their embarrassment had been applied.

They knew they would simply have to brazen it out until it died a natural death, or until another officer was overtaken by disaster and the perverted humour of the grapevine could get to work on that.

Holly felt the blood rush to her face as they weaved between tables in the police canteen. The place was fairly crowded so they had no choice but to sit next to a table of rowdy uniformed officers.

It seemed that the six constables had elected Pete Marlow as their spokesman, and as Josh went to get the tea, Marlow turned to Holly. 'What did you say to the bus driver, then? Follow that taxi?'

This brought forth much mirth.

'Ha, ha,' Holly countered.

Pete Marlow, a man in his mid-twenties, with close-cropped black hair and coarse features, ran through his extensive repertoire of policeman/bus jokes. But then, sensing that his audience were losing interest, he began to get more personal.

'Tell me, Holly,' he said, 'is it true you've given up trying to get a fella, so you got Poof the Magic Policeman to move in with you?'

Holly had experienced more than her fair share of problems in the love stakes and was deeply wounded by their harsh laughter. Her eyes misted over as she searched for a reply.

'Leave it alone, Marlow.' Josh's quiet voice came from behind her. He placed the cups on the table.

Marlow sat back in his chair. 'Who's talking to you?'

'I'm talking to you, and I'm telling you to go and be stupid somewhere else.'

'And if I don't want to . . . poofter?'

The surrounding officers realized this had now gone far beyond a joke, but all were riveted nonetheless.

Josh remained relaxed, dignified. 'Then I suggest we continue this discussion somewhere a little more private, like the car park.'

Ashworth, standing by the swing doors, watched the situation develop, but did not intervene until Marlow averted his eyes.

With his bluff called, the constable had little choice but to back down. 'Come on,' he said, 'can't you take a joke?'

Ashworth marched in then, clapping his hands smartly. 'Right,' he barked, 'there's a crime committed every three seconds, and you lot won't solve any of them sitting in here on your backsides . . .'

Within ten seconds there was not a uniform left in the canteen.

Ashworth took the seat beside Holly. 'I won't do any jokes about buses or cars,' he smiled.

'No, don't sir . . . please,' she said wearily.

'It is funny though.' And, despite himself, Ashworth grinned.

'Not when you've heard it all about six hundred times, it isn't,' Holly complained. 'And it's all been distorted. When we got back to the car it wouldn't start so I called the AA. The man said the clutch had gone and he gave us a lift back to the house to get Josh's car.'

Ashworth, sitting with elbows resting on the table, started to laugh softly and quickly put a hand to his mouth.

Holly carried on, 'Then he went away for the mini. He was going to tow it back, you see, and leave it in the drive.' She sighed dejectedly. 'None of this would have come out if he hadn't rung the station to say he'd had to leave it in the road because another car was blocking the driveway.'

The vibrations from Ashworth's elbows as he vainly attempted to control his laughter caused tea to spill from their cups.

Holly gave him a puzzled look, then glimpsing the humour in his eyes, she allowed herself a smile. 'I suppose it is funny really. Josh asked the man how much it would cost for a report on the car, engine, gearbox, the lot, and the man said he could give us one now, for free . . . he said the bloody thing was totally knackered.'

Ken Savage, on his way out of the station, was aware of raucous laughter coming from the canteen, but with his mind firmly fixed on the first drink of the day, he simply decided to ignore it.

CHAPTER 7

Gladys Smart sat alone in the small front room of her terraced home.

Although it was hardly large enough to accommodate the three-piece suite and fourteen-inch television set on its own stand, the room had once been her pride and joy, used only at Christmas and other family occasions — 'best bib and tucker' territory.

How things had changed, she reflected unhappily.

Her mind travelled far into the past, back to the 'Bunny Run'. She wondered what the youngsters of today, with their cars, money and drugs, would have made of that. They would laugh and jeer, no doubt, at the thought of young people spending every Saturday and Sunday night just walking up and down the town's main street, stopping to chat every now and again. There was never any drunkenness or violence then, just good clean fun.

Gladys closed her eyes and saw herself, once more, as a pretty seventeen-year-old, proudly wearing the floral dress which was her Sunday best.

How she'd led the boys a dance in those days, letting them walk her home, even allowing a brief kiss and cuddle. But it never went any further . . . not until she met Cliff.

In the Guards, he was then, and he looked a right treat in his uniform. Swept Gladys off her feet, he did.

Yes, she thought sadly, swept me off my feet . . . into a marriage of drudgery.

A tapping began above her head. She glanced up at the ceiling; her husband's stick was striking the bedroom floor with such force that the light fitting swayed to and fro.

With an effort, Gladys pushed herself from the chair, waiting a few moments for the strength to flow into her legs. The tapping became louder, more insistent.

'Wait a minute,' she muttered impatiently.

Standing at the foot of the steep narrow staircase, Gladys called, 'All right, Cliff?'

'No, I'm in bloody agony,' was her husband's frail reply. 'Where's the doctor?'

'I've phoned him,' Gladys said defensively. 'He said he'd be here as soon as he could.'

He carried on moaning but Gladys, pretending not to hear, returned to her chair . . . and her memories.

* * *

Ashworth always maintained that a house was more than just bricks and mortar; a house had a soul. Now his house felt empty, mournful, as if missing its mistress, as he was.

Sarah had thought it best to take the dog — Samantha had a large garden in which Peanuts could roam around all day — and Ashworth found he even missed her frantic barking at every tiny sound from outside.

He checked his watch; it was nine thirty p.m. and he had telephoned Sarah three times already, each time being assured that all was well and the birth was not yet imminent.

He poured two fingers of malt whisky into a glass, topped it up with soda, and attempted to relax.

He was worried about his daughter, he was missing his wife, but something akin to relief had accompanied her departure. At least it had removed the threat of Nigel Anthony getting in touch with her.

Far too restless to settle, he wandered, glass in hand, from lounge, to kitchen, to dining room, finally coming to rest in the hall. He sat on the stairs, eyes glued to the telephone on which he would soon receive news that he was once again a grandfather . . . or that things had gone very wrong.

The murders bothered him in every conceivable way. Holly and Josh had informed him that David Chambers' alibi was confirmed. They had located the boyfriend, Russ Evans, whose only concern had been that the death would bring his misdemeanours to the attention of his wife, the mother of his three children.

This, to Ashworth's mind, left him with only one suspect: Ian Johnson, husband of the first victim; and if Ashworth finally cleared him, he would have to face up to the possibility that he could be dealing with a serial killer. And that was something he did not even want to contemplate.

* * *

Gwen Anthony was proud of her body; her breasts did not sag; her middle still bore the taut hardness of youth; her legs were long and shapely.

Normally, when the weather was warm, she would sleep naked, enjoying the feel of cool sheets on her skin. But of late she had developed caution.

Gwen watched as her husband took off his bathrobe, staggering slightly as he hung it behind the door. His nakedness revolted her.

When he climbed into bed she quite unconsciously moved as far away from him as the tight confines would allow.

Switching off the bedside lamp and plunging the room into darkness, Gwen lay still, listened to her husband's breathing, smelt the stale brandy fumes on that breath.

Watching the illuminated digits on the clock, she waited until ten minutes had passed before assuming he had fallen into a drunken sleep. Only then did she allow herself to relax, breathe more easily.

Suddenly Nigel's hand gripped her thigh with such force, she cried out in pain.

'Come on, Gwen.' His speech was slurred, the edge to his voice unpleasant.

'Stop it. You're hurting me.'

'Come on then.'

'No,' she insisted, 'I don't want to. I don't want to do it. Can't you understand that?'

'Why not?' he asked viciously. 'Why don't you want to?'

Gwen was now faced with either giving in to her husband's demands, which were becoming increasingly more violent by the day, or enduring another row about Ashworth.

In a token of surrender, she opened her legs.

She derived no pleasure at all from their lovemaking and suddenly a strong feeling of nausea swept over her, brought on by her husband's drunken pawing and the thought of what he had become.

With Nigel's dead weight on top of her, Gwen knew that soon she would have to take steps to bring this nightmare to an end.

* * *

Gerald Fox opened the door to the flat he shared with his mother.

He carefully hung his tweed jacket on the old-fashioned hall-stand, complete with umbrella compartment and shoe-rack, then studied his reflection in the hall mirror and tidily flattened his hair.

His mother called from the kitchen, 'Is that you, Gerald?'

'Yes, mother.'

'You come in here. Your bedtime drink will be cold.'

He entered the tiny kitchen and found his mother pouring hot milk into a mug.

'These people, they work you too hard. Eleven p.m. and you just come home.'

She was a large woman, solidly built, with grey hair tied back and secured in a bun. Her facial bone structure was delicate, but somewhat marred by the pinched set of her mouth.

'Have you eaten?' she asked.

'Yes, mother.'

'Well, have you not a kiss for your mother?'

Fox lightly brushed her cheek.

'What is that I smell on your breath?' she demanded.

Fox's face reddened. 'I stopped off for a beer on the way home . . . with some of the guys.'

Abruptly his mother stopped stirring the drink and stood with hands in the pockets of her flannelette dressing gown.

'And who are these guys? Who takes my boy out drinking? Eh?'

'Some people from work,' he lied.

She beamed. 'It is good you make friends in this new country. It is good to have friends.'

Fox sighed. 'I was born here, mother.'

'You have no sense of history. Now, go in and sit down. Tell me about your day.'

The living room was furnished with a three-piece suite arranged in a semi-circle around the television set, and a battered dresser on which dolls in Polish costumes were displayed.

Fox sat on the sofa while his mother fussed around him with the hot drink.

'The police came to see me today,' he told her after taking a sip.

'The police?' There was fear in her eyes.

'Yes. You know that woman who was murdered?'

'The one that was on the news?'

'Yes. Well, another woman was murdered last night, and I interviewed both of them at work. They were claimants.' He sounded almost proud.

'You be careful, Gerald. The police, they do strange things. They plant evidence—'

'Mother,' Fox laughed, 'this is Britain in the nineteen-nineties, not Poland when you were a little girl.'

'Police are police. If your father was alive he would tell you—'

'Father is alive, mother,' he said brutally. 'You know that.'

She shook her head rapidly. 'No, no, he is dead. You will not admit it. Anyway, I do not wish to talk of these things.'

Gerald Fox's eyes held a cold glint as he watched his mother flounce from the room.

* * *

'We shouldn't be doing this, Josh,' Holly whispered.

'Just a few more minutes,' he pleaded. 'We're not doing any harm.'

They were sitting in Josh's Nissan, opposite the block containing Gerald Fox's flat.

'He's not coming out again,' Holly said, 'and in any case, what's he done?'

'I've just got a feeling about him,' Josh replied, lightly drumming his fingers on the steering-wheel.

'You're beginning to remind me of someone,' Holly said pointedly.

'God forbid,' he said, realizing she meant Jim Ashworth.

'Look, Fox left work, spent the evening in a gay bar . . . end of story.'

Josh turned to face her. 'He went in and he came out. Who's to say he didn't leave by another entrance, do whatever he wanted to do, then slipped back, spent some time in the bar and left by the front door where he knew we'd be watching. What do you think?'

Holly gave him a look of disbelief. 'I think you've been watching too much television. God, even your ley lines idea was better than that.'

'Yes, I know it's crazy,' he admitted, 'but there's something funny about him.'

'That's all well and good, Josh, but we can't just barge into his life and start investigating him. We've got no reason to suspect him of anything.'

'No,' he agreed, 'we haven't.'

Holly saw an opportunity to broach the subject which had been on her mind all evening. 'If I hadn't been with you, you could have followed him into the club.'

'Yes.' Josh sighed and turned to look out at Fox's flat.

'Josh?' She sounded tentative. 'What do you do? You know?'

'I'm a policeman,' he replied blandly.

'I know that, you bloody idiot,' she laughed. 'I mean . . . sex.'

'I don't,' Josh said easily.

Holly was surprised. 'You don't?'

'No.' Suddenly he was serious. 'It's this Aids business, and everything else. I just don't think it's worth the risk.' He laughed. 'I'd go down a bomb at gay lobbies, wouldn't I?'

'I bet.' Holly felt slightly embarrassed now and stared out of the passenger window.

'I know what you're getting at though,' Josh said. 'If we're to go on sharing the house, we've got to get some ground rules. I mean, if you ever want to bring a man home, I'll just make myself scarce.'

'Oh, it's not that,' Holly said hurriedly. 'I just wondered, that's all.'

'I could murder a cup of tea,' Josh remarked, breaking the atmosphere.

'Let's give this up, Josh,' Holly said with enthusiasm. 'Let's get some chips on the way home . . . yes?'

'Okay. But something will turn up against Fox eventually, I'm sure of it.'

* * *

The gloriously warm weather was still holding out as the following day dawned. Although too early in the year for high pressure to produce the oppressive heat of summer, the warming sun was fast drying out and healing the ravages of a long hard winter, allowing the rejuvenation of all living things to begin.

Ashworth could not concentrate on anything until he had telephoned Sarah to check on their daughter. She assured him that Samantha had passed a comfortable night and the doctors were quite happy with her condition and that of the unborn baby.

Replacing the receiver, he glanced at his wristwatch and realized what a saint of a woman he had married; it was only seven a.m., and although he must have got Sarah out of bed she had not complained once.

It took him thirty minutes to shower, shave, and hastily consume two cups of tea; and he left the house at seven thirty sharp, for he had things to do today.

Feeling it was almost a sacrilege to pollute the wonderfully clean air with petrol fumes, he started the Sierra and headed for the station.

* * *

Ashworth had been sitting at his desk for an hour when, back at Holly's house, a bare-chested Josh emerged from the bathroom.

'Sorry, Holly,' he said. 'I'll get dressed as quickly as I can.'

Holly took her turn in the bathroom. The steaming water was hot to her touch as she put the plug in the washbasin.

'Shit,' she muttered as it burned her fingers.

The previous night, tea and chips had progressed on to lager and conversation and it was 2 a.m. before they finally got to bed.

But the fact that they had overslept was not the sole reason for her bad temper; she was strongly attracted to Josh and was finding it increasingly more frustrating to think that nothing of a physical nature could ever take place between them.

Slipping out of her bathrobe she caught sight of her misty image in the steam-covered wall mirror and poked out her tongue at the reflection.

Holly's personal life had been in a state of decline for some years now, but during these last few months, since meeting Josh, the realization had surfaced that she was a woman who actually needed sex, in one form or another, to function properly as a person.

This realization had caused conflict between two entirely different sides of her character; and the strict, very correct, middle-class young lady was beginning to wilt under attack from the highly sensuous girl who even now felt mildly aroused by her own soapy hands running over her body.

* * *

Ashworth made no direct remark about their lateness as they bundled into the office at 9.20 a.m., but he dispensed with the pleasantries of wishing them a good morning.

'Right,' he said briskly, 'I've made a list of things I want us to get done today.' He looked pointedly at the clock. 'Firstly, I want to interview Ian Johnson here at the station, and away from that mother-in-law of his. Secondly, I'm far from happy about the supermarket manager who was messing about with Jenny Chambers. Check into what time he arrived home that night.'

Holly sat at her desk, sorting through her bag for her notebook. 'As I said at the time, sir, it's a little delicate. The man's got a wife and three children.'

'Handle it with care then,' he told her gruffly. 'Tell the wife Jenny Chambers worked for her husband . . . that much is true. Just say you need to check out his movements on the day she was murdered. Say it's routine.'

'You still think it's the husband or boyfriend in both cases then, sir?'

'We have to check it out.'

'With respect, sir, that's not what I asked.'

Holly had found the best policy with Ashworth was to fight her own corner, for such was the strength of the man's personality it was quite common for him to sweep others aside, without even realizing he was doing so.

Ashworth glanced at the clock again; as far as he was concerned the morning briefing was almost over.

'I admit it's unlikely,' he said, 'but we haven't got anything else.'

He paused for a moment. 'Have you two got any ideas?'

Josh, aware that his mouth was hanging open, closed it quickly. 'You're asking for our ideas, sir?'

Ashworth raised his eyebrows questioningly. 'That's what I said.'

'Well . . .' Josh hesitated. '. . . there's this Gerald Fox from the Employment office. If you remember, he interviewed both women.'

'Is that all you've got?' Ashworth asked, showing distinct signs of irritation.

'Not really, sir.' He glanced apprehensively at Holly. 'You see, Fox had both women under surveillance. He was aware of their movements.'

'But what motive had he got?'

'None that most people would understand, sir.'

He went into detail about the Bradford killings, informing Ashworth that Fox had recently been transferred from there.

The explosion which they expected did not occur. Instead Ashworth seemed to be giving this information serious consideration.

Eventually he said, 'Has he now? Have you done any follow-up work on him?'

'Not as yet, sir, no, but we did watch him last night.'

'And?'

'He left work, spent the evening in a club, then went home.'

Ashworth seemed disappointed. 'There's not much we can do to him for that.'

'Yes, that's the problem, sir,' Josh agreed. 'As Holly pointed out, we can't just start investigating him without good reason.'

'Look into him . . . ask around,' Ashworth said eagerly. 'If he starts to look like a possible, we'll think of a reason to investigate him officially.' He paused. 'I take it last night's overtime was unpaid?'

'Of course it was, sir,' Josh replied.

'Good,' Ashworth said cheerfully, 'then perhaps you'd consider doing some more. Going by your computer calculations, when would the next murder take place?'

Josh counted it out on his fingers. 'Four days' time, sir.'

'Sir, are you saying you want us to watch Fox?' Holly asked.

'Yes, unofficially, that is,' Ashworth warned. 'And if you do that', he smiled, 'I might even let you off for being late this morning. Oh, and talking about you being late, I've been here since a quarter to eight so I'm off to the canteen for a bacon sandwich and a cup of tea.'

Heading for the door, he called back, 'Holly, you go and see the supermarket manager's wife. Josh, ring Johnson — tell him that I need to see him at the station. Send a car for him if necessary.'

With that he made an energetic exit.

'I don't believe it,' Josh said as soon as the door was closed.

'Don't believe what?' Holly queried.

'Well, usually at this stage in an investigation, Ashworth's got his suspects and starts homing in on them . . .' He picked up the receiver and dialled Johnson's number. 'But this time he's actually asking us what we think.'

'Can I use your car?' Holly asked.

'Yes, sure.'

'Actually, Josh, I think you're being unfair to him. Perhaps he's just learnt from his past mistakes and he's trying to involve us more.'

'Could be, either that or he's having a nervous breakdown.' He threw her the car keys. 'Oh, hello, Mr Johnson, this is DC Abraham, Bridgetown CID . . .'

CHAPTER 8

Holly took the scenic route to Chambling Drive on Bridgetown's Yorkmoor Estate.

The drive was pleasant and took her mind off the reason for her visit. In the fields she saw tiny lambs, eyes frightened and blinking rapidly, exploring their new world from the relative safety of their mothers' sides.

The warm breeze catching her hair through the open car window instilled in her a strange desire for freedom, to be released from the constraints of her job, of society, of life itself. She suddenly longed to return to the womb; begin again, armed with the knowledge she had acquired, on a charted course along which only happy events occurred.

But this ineffectual flight of fancy quickly evaporated before the advancing tide of bricks and mortar as the housing estate came into view.

She found Chambling Drive and parked outside number 23: a pretty three-bedroomed detached with frilly net curtains at its double-glazed leaded windows. The open-plan front garden was neat; roses, set in a bed at the centre of the lawn, had been severely pruned and were only now showing new green shoots.

As Holly rang the bell a child started to cry inside the house. The door was opened by a harassed young woman, cradling a baby in her arms.

'All right, all right,' she soothed, placing a pink dummy between the baby's petulant lips.

'Sorry,' said Holly. 'Am I the cause of this?'

'And I'd only just got her to sleep,' the woman stated angrily.

The baby pulled the dummy from its mouth and hurled it down the garden path.

'Sorry,' Holly repeated as she produced her warrant card. 'DS Bedford, Bridgetown CID. I need to ask you a few questions.'

'Oh?'

'Can I come in?'

'Yes, I suppose so.'

The woman continued to soothe the baby as Holly retrieved the dummy and followed her into the house.

'In there.' The woman indicated the lounge. 'I'll take this one upstairs and try to get her down again. Oh, I'd better wash that.'

She snatched the dummy from Holly's hand and clambered up the stairs, cooing in the screaming baby's ear.

Holly entered the lounge which was much as she expected: suite and carpet expensive and relatively new; up-to-date television, video recorder and stereo; the garden beyond double-glazed patio doors appeared well-tended and tidy.

She wandered over to the wall unit and studied an impressive array of framed photographs. Russ Evans, the handsome supermarket manager, was obviously fond of the camera; there were numerous shots of him with two children at various stages of their short lives, and one of him proudly holding the new baby.

The rigours of childbirth had undoubtedly aged Mrs Evans; in the wedding photograph she was a pretty, trim-waisted girl, but the woman who greeted Holly at the door had not yet regained her figure after the arrival of their latest addition, and although her hair was still thick, fluffy and well-styled, as it was in the photograph, her face looked tired and dark smudges spoilt the appearance of her brown eyes.

Holly glanced around at the collection of toys littering the carpet. Upstairs, the baby's crying was spasmodic, eventually giving way to contented gurgling sounds. When these ceased, Mrs Evans's stealthy steps could be heard on the stairs.

'I am sorry,' Holly whispered as she came into the room.

Mrs Evans put a finger to her lips for silence as she gingerly closed the door.

'No, I'm sorry,' she said heavily. 'I was just a tiny bit rude, wasn't I?' Her smile was apologetic. 'Our other two are at school and I'd just got her off to sleep.'

She automatically picked up toys from the floor, piling them neatly into a cardboard box in a corner of the room.

Finally she said, 'This must be about the murdered woman who worked at my husband's supermarket.'

'Yes, that's right.'

Holly watched as Mrs Evans deposited the last of the toys into the box. She had struggled into jeans a size too small and the discomfort was evident on her face. Holly wondered whether she ever suspected that her efforts to control her husband's amorous eyes might be in vain.

Mrs Evans's next statement proved otherwise. 'Is it true what the papers are saying? That both women were committing adultery?'

Holly nodded. 'Yes, we believe so.'

'What's it coming to?' Mrs Evans said, shaking her head sadly. 'I just thank God I've got Russ. At least I can be sure he wouldn't do anything like that.'

Dropping a stray building brick into the box, she said, 'I'm sorry, won't you sit down?'

Holly settled on the sofa. 'Nice house,' she remarked. 'It's making me green with envy.'

'That's what I mean about Russ. He's all home and family.'

You poor cow, Holly thought as she smiled sweetly at Mrs Evans. 'This is just routine, you understand. We just need to check out your husband's story.'

'Oh yes. Don't worry. I know Russ has nothing to hide.'

'Good.' Holly studied her notebook. 'So, what time did he arrive home the night before last?'

Mrs Evans's look was blank. 'Well, he didn't. Surely he told you?'

'Told me what?' Holly asked quietly.

'That he didn't come home that night. He spends half the week here, and the other half in Morton. He manages the two supermarkets.'

Holly looked again at her notes, at Russ Evans' version of events recorded there, then, tapping her forehead in a great show of frustration, she said, 'You know what I've done, don't you? I've gone and left my notes at the station.' Laughing, she added, 'Sometimes I think it's right what men say about us . . . perhaps we're not up to the job.'

Mrs Evans gave a weak laugh; with two small children and a baby to care for, sexual equality was not a subject which would dominate her thoughts.

'Help me out,' Holly smiled. 'Your husband spends half the week here, and half in Morton, you said?'

'That's right. He's got a flat there. It's inconvenient, but the money's good.'

'Oh, it's all right, it's coming back now. On the night Jenny Chambers was killed he was in Morton, wasn't he?'

'Well, not quite. He spent the day in the Bridgetown supermarket, then when that closed he drove to Morton to supervise the shelf-stacking.'

'Got you. Did he say I might be calling on you?'

'I don't think he mentioned it.'

'No reason why he should, I suppose.' Holly put away her notebook and stood up. 'Well, I apologize once again for disturbing you, Mrs Evans.'

'That's all right. If you could just be quiet on your way out . . .'

'I will.' She tiptoed across the hall, mouthing, 'Thanks again,' as she timidly opened the front door.

Climbing into the car, she muttered, 'Right, Mr Evans, you'd better have some answers ready, and they'd better be bloody good.'

Inside the house, the baby began to cry with renewed vigour.

* * *

As Holly drove towards a confrontation at the Save U Supermarket, Ashworth was experiencing one of his own in front reception at Bridgetown station.

Ian Johnson had arrived, accompanied by his domineering mother-in-law. Ashworth was beginning to wonder whether the man could function without her.

Johnson, smartly dressed in grey suit, white shirt and blue tie, looked slightly bemused as Mrs Thomas launched her attack.

'You've no right to do this,' she yelled at Ashworth. 'I'm perfectly entitled to be with Ian while he's being interviewed. I'm writing to my MP about this.'

Ashworth remained mild. 'You're quite correct, Mrs Thomas,' he said, 'I don't have the right, but then I didn't claim that I had . . .'

'I won't have my son-in-law hounded,' Mrs Thomas declared stridently.

Unperturbed, Ashworth continued, 'I have simply requested to see Mr Johnson without you being present. Now he's perfectly entitled to deny the request but I must add that if he does I shall draw my own conclusions from it.'

Martin Dutton watched with amusement; he knew Ashworth always predetermined a course of action, and anyone who impeded its flow was likely to feel the sharp edge of his tongue. He winced when Mrs Thomas, ignoring his words, accused him of exceeding his authority.

Ashworth, his voice now loaded with controlled anger, said, 'Mrs Thomas, will you please listen to what I'm saying. You will not be asked to sit in on any interview I conduct with Mr Johnson . . .'

Any retort the woman might have made was swallowed due to the look on Ashworth's face and his clipped tone which did not invite further debate.

'. . . nor have you any right to request to be present. If and when I interview Mr Johnson in an official manner, he can ask for a solicitor, but in the present legislation mothers-in-law are not mentioned. Now I'll arrange for a cup of tea for you.'

He strode over to the desk. 'Martin, could you . . . ?'

'Yes, I heard, Jim . . . your voice does carry sometimes,' Dutton smiled, 'I'll see to it. Oh, and thanks, Jim.'

'For what?' he asked, glancing at Mrs Thomas who sat glaring at him from the visitors' bench.

'For lumbering me with the vigilante business.'

'Not guilty,' Ashworth insisted. 'I just said no and passed it back to Ken Savage—'

'Knowing full well he wouldn't do anything that might infringe on his leisure time,' Dutton said amiably. 'I think he sees the working day as just an interval between getting drunk, so he would pass it down the line to muggins, wouldn't he?'

'The thought never entered my head,' Ashworth said with a smile.

'I'll bet. I was thinking of sending young Bobby—'

'Martin, if this buck gets passed around many more times, the tea lady will end up doing it.'

Dutton grinned. 'My old sergeant always used to say, steer well clear of a campaigner with a bee in his bonnet. It's good advice.'

'Well, as a good sergeant, that's what you should be telling Bobby.'

'It's him or me, Jim, him or me,' Dutton laughed. 'I'll go and see about that tea.'

Ashworth turned to Ian Johnson. 'Would you care to follow me up to the office?' he asked politely.

* * *

Holly parked in a small, deserted car park at the Save U Supermarket.

Inside, a rather tetchy female supervisor informed her that Mr Evans was in a meeting and would probably be tied up for several hours. But an insistent Holly asked for him to be brought out of the meeting, explaining that she was conducting a murder enquiry and felt Mr Evans might be able to help.

The fact that the woman capitulated immediately proved that Holly was, quite unconsciously, developing an abrasive streak not dissimilar to Ashworth's.

The line of checkout girls viewed her with some curiosity as she waited by the supervisor's desk behind the tills. Some moments later a rather flustered Russ Evans came striding through the store and out of the checkout closest to her.

'Yes?' he asked abruptly.

'Could we go somewhere more private please, Mr Evans?'

'I'm in the middle of a business meeting,' he snapped. 'What's this about?'

'Porkies,' Holly told him flatly.

'Porkies?'

'Yes, Mr Evans, the porkies you've been telling me.'

A disturbed look flushed Evans's face. 'But I've told you the truth,' he insisted.

'Mr Evans,' Holly said sweetly, 'yesterday I told you I'd accept that Jenny Chambers was simply working for you, and I wouldn't probe or try to uncover anything that might upset your family unless it was absolutely necessary . . . now I took that decision out of the goodness of my heart.'

'You're leaning on me,' Evans said uneasily.

'No, I'm just pointing out that if I get messed about I get bloody-minded, and that has a direct influence on how much goodness I have in my heart.' She gave him a brittle smile. 'Can we go somewhere private?'

His expression said 'bitch' as plainly as if he had spoken the word. Turning on his heel, Evans marched towards the front of the store and stopped at the tobacco kiosk.

'Is Joe in his office?' he asked the salesgirl.

'No, Mr Evans,' she replied sharply. His ill-mannered interruption while she was dispensing change to a customer had made her lose count, and with annoyance she started again.

He lifted the wooden flap to the kiosk and Holly followed him through to a door at the back which led into a tiny room. It had a sink with electric kettle and coffee on the draining board, and a single wooden chair.

'Security guard's office,' Evans informed her.

'Nice,' Holly commented drily.

He turned to face her. 'Look, what do you want? I've been as honest as I can.'

'No, you haven't,' Holly pressed. 'You told me that on the night of the murder you left here and went home.'

'That's right, I did,' Evans insisted.

'But when I went to see your wife earlier today—'

'My wife?' he said, horrified. 'Why bring her into it?'

'Because I had to check your story,' Holly told him firmly, 'and you didn't go home that night. You went to Morton.'

'Oh God.' Evans turned away in exasperation. 'I went to my home in Morton . . . that's what I meant.'

'Pull the other one and my ears twirl round,' Holly retorted. 'Look, you gave your address as 23 Chambling Drive. You never mentioned Morton.'

'Because home to me is where my wife and kids are,' Evans explained.

'I went home, that's what you said, so wouldn't it be safe to assume you went home to your family? You didn't say you went to your flat in Morton.'

'You're twisting what I said,' Evans accused. 'I thought you people were supposed to be polite to the public.'

Holly, sensing the man was frightened, mounted her attack. 'Listen, Mr Evans, for how I feel, this is polite. Thanks to you, I've now got to go all the way to Morton and find out if anyone saw you there.'

'Why in God's name have you got to do that?' he asked hotly. 'Can't you just take my word for it?'

'Huh, take your word for it?' Holly said with incredulity. 'Don't you realize the trouble you're in? I'm not involved in this investigation to pass the time . . . we're looking for a murderer. All I thought I'd have to do was ask your wife what time you arrived that night. From her answer I could have determined whether or not you went straight home.' She sighed impatiently. 'But now I've got to go to Morton, find out if anyone saw you there, and if so, what time.' She looked him straight in the eye. 'Don't you understand, Mr Evans? . . . I'm regarding you as a suspect.'

'Oh my God,' Evans muttered. He moved to the sink and stared into it. 'Nobody saw me in Morton,' he said quietly.

'If I were you, I'd start praying someone did.' She turned to a fresh page in her notebook. 'Give me your address in Morton.'

'42 Cresswell Rise,' he said despondently. 'I suppose this increases the chance of my wife finding out?'

'Depends where you were around ten fifteen — that's roughly the time Jenny Chambers was killed.'

'I was on my way to Morton.'

'That's about an hour's drive, so if you left here at ten, you should have arrived there at eleven,' Holly surmised.

'Yes.'

Evans turned to look at her, his eyes blank and distant.

'Mr Evans, I think you know far more about Jenny Chambers's death than you're telling me . . .'

Evans shook his head in denial.

'. . . and that changes a lot of things because I need to take the shortest route possible. I haven't got time to pussyfoot around your tangled love life.'

'You're going to tell my wife, aren't you?'

'If it saves time, yes, but you could save me the time and yourself a lot of trouble by telling me the truth.'

'I've told you everything,' Evans protested. 'I've been totally honest about my movements that night.'

'We'll leave it there then,' Holly said casually, 'but I'll be in touch.'

She headed for the door. 'By the way, where will I find you for the rest of this week?' With a cynical smile she turned to him. 'At home with your wife and family . . . or at home in Morton?'

'I'll be . . . oh God, you're going to find out anyway, so I might as well tell you.'

'I think it would be a good idea,' Holly counselled. 'And perhaps we could go somewhere a little more comfortable than the security guard's cupboard.'

* * *

Ashworth was facing a similar problem back at the office; he knew Ian Johnson was concealing information which could be vitally important, but he had no idea why.

He had seated Johnson in front of his desk, had dismissively sent Josh for three cups of tea and now, under the pretence of looking through a wad of papers, he was silent for a number of minutes.

Finally he cleared his throat and looked up. Johnson was staring straight ahead, the same bemused expression on his face.

'Right, Mr Johnson, let's get down to it. May I call you Ian?'

Johnson shrugged. 'Yes.'

'Good. Now, Ian, I'm going to be totally frank with you as there's no one else here; I think it's funny that Mrs Thomas seemed frightened to death to leave you alone with me.'

'She's just trying to protect me.'

'From what? Me?'

Johnson nervously ran his fingers through his hair. 'I've had a shock.'

'Yes, you have,' Ashworth agreed, 'and there's another thing that's puzzling me: neither of you has asked how the investigation's going, or whether we've found out who Margaret was having an affair with.'

'Can't you understand grief?' The man seemed forlorn, on the verge of tears.

Ashworth, keeping the compassionate side of his nature in check, went on, 'These are the questions I would expect you to ask, Ian. Shall I tell you why I think you haven't asked them? I think you knew your wife was having an affair, and I think you know who the man was.'

Josh entered then with a tray holding three mugs. Ashworth's expression told him this was an inappropriate moment so he hurriedly set down Johnson's tea and passed a mug to Ashworth. Then, selecting some papers from his desk he took them into the other office.

As the door closed, Johnson said, 'The neighbours have been talking, haven't they?'

'Yes, they have,' Ashworth said evasively.

'They told you about the row in the garden, didn't they?'

'Some of it,' Ashworth lied.

He was too short-staffed to carry out door-to-door, and as the murder had taken place some distance away from the family home, Ashworth had deemed it unimportant, but he would never have told Johnson that.

'Why don't you fill me in on the details?' he said quietly.

Johnson sat with head in hands and mumbled inaudibly.

'Sorry, Ian, I didn't catch that.'

He sat up straight but avoided Ashworth's eyes. 'I said I thought she might be having an affair.'

'And did you know with whom?'

'I knew she was doing some work for Terry Giles.'

'You confronted her with this, I take it?'

'Yes, that's what the row in the garden was about.'

'And was that on the day she was murdered?'

Johnson looked up sharply. 'You know it was.'

Ashworth took several sips of tea before he spoke again. 'Shall I tell you what I think, Ian? That final row — when you realized your wife was seeing Terry Giles — pushed you over the brink. There you were, working all the hours God sent, trying to hang on to your home, and your wife was being unfaithful.'

Ashworth crossed to the glass wall, stared out at the town, as he said softly, 'I think you followed your wife that evening, saw her with Giles. It just got too much for you—'

Johnson yelled, 'No, no.'

Very slowly Ashworth returned to the desk, leant forward in front of him. 'You killed her, son, didn't you?'

'No, honest to God, I didn't.'

'So where were you that evening?'

'I told you, I was just out walking.'

'Can't you see how that doesn't make sense to me? The very day you have a row with your wife about this, she goes off for another liaison with her lover, and you just go for a walk.'

Johnson made no answer, and Ashworth knew he would extract very little else from him at this time; far better to give the man something to think about, something to maintain the pressure, than push him to breaking point.

Sitting down again, Ashworth said, 'I haven't got enough to hold you on, Ian, not yet. But what I can do is search your home and take away certain items for forensic tests. So that's what I'm going to do, and while I'm waiting for a magistrate to grant me a search warrant, one of my officers will sit with you . . . just to make sure you don't dispose of anything.'

He studied Johnson's slouched form for a few seconds, tried to ascertain the effect his words were having on the man.

Then he went to the other office, told Josh to go with Johnson and wait with him until uniformed officers arrived to assist with the search.

CHAPTER 9

Holly was extremely pleased with the information she had gleaned from Russ Evans; and had greatly enjoyed flexing the muscles which came with her promotion.

Although not the type to go power-mad she was nevertheless determined to make a positive contribution to the investigation, rather than simply carry out Ashworth's instructions in a robotic fashion.

Starting the engine of Josh's Nissan, Holly decided to take a minor detour on her way back to the station; and while meandering along the twisting lanes she filed away in her mind the facts which Evans had told her.

There could be little doubt now that the man was a suspect; he had both motive and opportunity; and Holly knew it would be very easy to build a case against him.

After a while she stopped the car and gazed at the object of her desire. A man in a light suit glanced through the window and raised his hand in recognition. Holly felt a tremor pass through her; a delicious, sensuous wave of anticipated pleasure.

She locked the car and kept her movements unhurried as she crossed the road. 'Don't seem too eager,' she told herself, 'he'll only take advantage if he knows you're desperate for it.'

On the forecourt she stopped in front of the Nissan Micra. Its gleaming red bodywork so highly polished she could see her reflection in it, and its grey upholstery so clean it looked unused. She knew then she had to own the car.

'Hi,' a pleasant voice rang out behind her. 'Back for another look then?'

'Just passing,' Holly said, trying to sound offhand, 'so, yes, I thought I'd have another look. I can't quite make up my mind.' She circled the car, scrutinizing the bodywork.

'I never forget a face,' the man said, 'but names escape me.'

'Holly Bedford.'

She looked up at him. He was very attractive, tall, immaculately dressed; his boyish face handsome, his black hair thick and wavy. Automatically Holly stole a look at his left hand and was disappointed to see a wedding ring there.

'Gary Williams,' he reminded her smoothly. 'Now, if I remember rightly, you're the lady with the mini to trade in.' He glanced across the road at the Nissan Sunny.

'I got rid of it privately,' Holly announced grandly, making a mental note to collect the twenty-five pounds promised by the scrap dealer.

'That's good,' he said. 'I could do you a really marvellous deal on it now.'

'Like what? I'm looking for a ten per cent discount, at least.' She tried hard to sound businesslike. 'And I've got someone I want to give it the once-over.'

'Oh, is that a boyfriend?'

For some reason the question annoyed Holly. She was about to make an acid remark when she stopped. He was, after all, very good-looking, with an open disarming smile.

She said, 'It is a male friend, yes.'

'Pity.'

'We are just friends though,' she heard herself say.

'Ah, that sounds more promising,' he smiled, holding her gaze. 'I'll tell you what I'll do — ten per cent of four thousand is four hundred. I'll knock five hundred off and let you have it for three thousand, five hundred.'

Holly could hardly contain her excitement. 'What's the catch?'

'There isn't one. As it's a cash deal I've got a lot more leeway.'

'I'll have to think about it. I've got some others to look at,' she said, hardly daring to leave the car in case someone with three and a half thousand came along and spirited it away.

'Why don't you come back tonight and have a test drive?' the man asked casually. 'Then perhaps we could have a drink while we chat over the deal.'

'Wouldn't your wife object to that?'

'We don't get along.'

'She doesn't understand you . . . right?'

'She doesn't,' he said, his eyes flirting.

'Shame.' Holly turned away. 'About seven then.'

'I'll look forward to it,' he called.

Holly could feel his eyes on her all the way across the road. Gary Williams was a red light, and she hadn't yet made up her mind whether to stop or drive straight through into the danger zone.

* * *

Gladys Smart sat at the kitchen table with a copy of the *Sun* newspaper spread before her.

'Why is everything tits and bums nowadays?' she muttered to herself.

It had been so long since she'd had anyone to chat to, talking out loud was now an unconscious habit; she often asked herself questions, then provided the answers.

'Everything's sex, sex, sex. But then again, I suppose it always was for some.'

Her husband's groans drifted down through the ceiling and Gladys felt like crying. He was in constant pain now, too weak to move.

Even walking along the landing to reach the lavatory was beyond him and on occasions, when it was impossible to distinguish requests for the bed pan from cries of agony, his bodily functions were performed where he lay. Now, his only source of relief were the injections administered by the doctor.

Gladys tried to close her mind to his moans. If some sort of release was not forthcoming in the very near future she feared for her own sanity.

The doorbell rang.

'Thank God, the doctor,' she said, on her way along the passage. 'You might be able to get a bit of a nap this afternoon, Glad.'

She opened the door. 'Oh, I thought it was the doctor.'

'It is,' Gwen said cheerfully. 'My husband couldn't make it, so I came instead.'

'You'd better come in then,' Gladys said with clear disappointment. 'I like Dr Anthony. We always have a little chat. He's nice.'

'I'm nice too,' Gwen assured her. 'Now, where's your husband?'

'Upstairs, in the front bedroom.'

'Right, I'll find my own way up.'

Back in the kitchen, Gladys could hear the doctor's movements, could just make out her cheerful remarks which were wasted on someone in the latter stages of terminal illness. She put the kettle on as Gwen began to descend the stairs.

'In here, doctor,' Gladys called, her dry throat cracking with the effort. 'Would you like a cup of tea?'

'Thank you, that would be nice,' Gwen said, putting her bag down beside the table.

As Gladys threw a tea bag into the pot, she asked, 'How much longer, doctor?'

'Difficult to say, I'm afraid. He's in the latter stages . . . could be days or even a month.'

'A month?' Gladys said wearily.

'Look, let me make the tea,' Gwen suggested kindly. 'You sit yourself down.'

As Gwen watched Gladys lower herself into the chair, she asked, 'How are you coping with it?'

'The best way I can, I suppose.'

Gwen poured boiling water into the tea pot. 'It's very difficult at the moment but would you like me to try and get him into hospital?'

'No,' Gladys replied staunchly. 'He don't want to go into hospital. He's told me he wants to die at home.'

'You've got a son, haven't you?' Gwen asked, pouring the tea. 'Can't he help out?'

'A son?' Gladys snorted. 'I haven't got a son.'

'But I thought . . .'

'He's Cliff's son, not mine.'

Gwen put the teas on the table and sat down. 'Is this his second marriage then?'

'Oh no, my dear, we've only been married once.'

'Mrs Smart, I don't understand . . .'

Gwen was beginning to worry that the constant strain might be causing a kind of breakdown.

Gladys said, 'Your husband didn't when I told him about it. He's a nice man, your husband, really kind and gentle. You're a lucky woman.'

'Yes,' Gwen said, still aware of the discomfort from her bruised thighs.

'It would surprise most people your age,' Gladys chuckled. She enjoyed passing on a story beyond the comprehension of others.

'A wee slip of a girl I was then . . .' she began. '. . . been married just three years and thought the sun shone out of Cliff's backside. Then one day — it was a Tuesday — I was getting a breast of lamb ready for his dinner and there was this knock on the front door. Well, when I opened it, there was Daisy Cranform from the next street . . . her who brought disgrace on her family by getting pregnant outside wedlock. She was holding this baby in her arms; wrapped in a white shawl it was. "Here, Gladys Smart," she said all cocky like, "this belongs to your Cliff". What do you mean, I asked her . . . a bit sharp I was too. "I'll tell you what I mean," she said, "he was going to leave you for me until he found out he'd put me in the club, then he didn't want to know". So, she said, "if you're getting his wage packet, you can have his bastard as well". And with that she handed me the baby and just marched off.'

'Well, doctor, I didn't know what to do. I put it in a chair and it bawled its head off all day. Anyway, when Cliff come home, I told him and he said, well you'll just have to bring it up, that's all there is to it.'

'But why didn't you just leave?' Gwen asked, totally absorbed.

'You didn't then,' Gladys replied sadly. 'Don't forget, I'm going back over fifty years . . . the man was boss then. There weren't no social security to run to for your keep and a nice little flat. And your family didn't want you, 'cause they'd been glad to see the back of you in the first place.'

'That's awful,' Gwen sympathized, realizing she hadn't touched her tea.

'Oh, I was better off than a lot, I can tell you, doctor. There was them round here used to come home from the pub and give their wives a damned good hiding . . . and make them sleep in the coal hole if they felt like it. Oh, yes, I was lucky in some ways. As long as Cliff got his meals and everything else he wanted, he was all right. Every week I got my money, even when he was working short time, and he never once laid a finger on me.'

'You didn't have any children of your own?'

Gladys smiled wistfully. 'I used to read poetry when I was a girl . . . does that surprise you?'

The statement puzzled Gwen. 'No,' she said.

'I was carrying at that time — when Daisy come round, I mean — although I didn't know it. But I lost the baby . . . it was the upset of it all, I suppose. 'Course, they didn't tell you nothing in those days, explain like, but it seemed something went wrong and I couldn't have any more.

'But whatever they might have said, I knew what it was: all the love inside me just shrivelled up and died, see, so I couldn't make any more babies.'

She laughed miserably. 'Cliff didn't mind . . . his life was happier for it. In those days, babies were just an inconvenient risk men put up with when they had their bit of fun.'

All at once Gladys brightened. 'Look, we've hardly touched our tea and it's gone cold. I'll make another pot.'

'No, don't bother for me,' Gwen said hurriedly, 'but if you want another cup, I'll make it.'

'I won't bother either then,' Gladys said, rising awkwardly to her feet. 'All day long I'm making pots of tea and half the time I don't drink them.'

She picked up the cups and hobbled across to the old white enamelled sink, saying, 'My old bones get stiff if I sit too long.'

'Would you like me to have a word with your son . . . well, your husband's son?' Gwen asked. 'He does have a responsibility.'

'No, thanks . . . Ron's a bad lad. I always looked after him, mind, he weren't neglected, but I didn't have any love for him . . . nor did his dad.'

She turned and looked at Gwen with sad eyes. 'And in this life it's only the love you hand out that comes back to you. Isn't that right, doctor?'

Gwen wondered how Nigel had reacted to Gladys's tale of heartbreak; somehow she couldn't picture him sitting through it all, listening patiently.

'What are you going to do, Mrs Smart,' she asked gently, 'when this is all over?'

'When it's over,' she intoned, and her normally dull eyes sparkled, her tired face creased into a smile. 'When it's over I want to visit one of those romantic places, like Paris or Rome, and I want to sit at one of those cafés on the pavement. Just sit there, I will, with my drink . . . and think about what might have been.'

As Gwen drove away from the house she reflected on the fact that her own life was hardly perfect — but it could be far, far worse.

CHAPTER 10

Holly positively bounced into the station. The confidence which came with having a male — and a very good-looking male at that — proposition her had boosted her ego to such an extent, her reflection in the car window was transformed from that of an ugly duckling to a graceful swan. Added to which, she had almost bought a beautiful car and was well on the way to solving Jenny Chambers's murder single-handed.

No doubt Ashworth would shoot her theories down but, when he did, she would simply throw them back into the air.

She tripped into the office. Ashworth was at his desk, and Josh, back from baby-sitting Ian Johnson and his personal effects, was at the computer, drinking tea.

'Holly, I thought you'd deserted,' Ashworth remarked cheerfully. 'Just as we're close to solving Margaret Johnson's murder.'

'The husband?' Holly asked.

'Looks like it. He still can't account for where he was at the time of his wife's death, so I've had his shoes and clothes brought in for Forensic to have a look at. He can stew for a few days until we get the results. How did you get on with lover boy?'

Holly had been wondering what to wear for the test drive, but Ashworth's question brought her mind back to the job.

As she settled behind her desk, she said, 'When I was a little girl we had a new vicar in our parish . . .'

Ashworth gave her one of his hard stares.

Unperturbed, she continued, 'At his ordination, when they came to the bit about, does anyone know of any good reason why he shouldn't become a parish priest, this little guy stood up at the back of the church and shouted, yes, he was having it off with my missus in Brighton.'

'Holly . . .' Ashworth warned.

'Please, sir, let me finish,' she insisted. 'Anyway, he became the vicar and for two years there were countless scandals; he had affairs; was drunk more often than not; but he wasn't removed until after he'd been pulled over by the police for suspected drink-driving. He was so far gone, while the officer was getting the breathalyser, he started urinating in the gutter—'

'Holly,' Ashworth broke in, 'fascinating as your girlhood memories may be, I can't for the life of me see what they have to do with the case.'

She chose to ignore the cynicism in his voice, and concluded, 'Truth is stranger than fiction, sir.'

'Of course,' Ashworth said, spreading his hands expansively. 'It's when you come out with little gems like that I realize why I recommended you for promotion.'

'I'm just trying to prepare you, sir,' she laughed, 'because Russ Evans's life makes the vicar's seem humdrum. He's got a wife and three kids in Bridgetown and a common-law wife with a young baby in Morton.'

'And he was having Jenny Chambers on the side?' Josh gasped.

Holly nodded.

'Find out what he's on and get me some of it,' Ashworth quipped. Then, 'Does this put him in the frame for the murder?'

'Very much so, sir. He divides his week between Bridgetown and Morton. Now, on the night Jenny was murdered he claims that after he left her he drove to Morton, but the journey took half an hour longer than usual because of road works.'

'And in that lost half an hour he could have committed the murder,' Ashworth mused. 'But what would his motive have been?'

'I've worked that out, sir,' Holly said confidently. 'Evans is a very good-looking man, and I've an idea his personal life has got into a mess because he can't say no.'

Ashworth knew the feeling . . . but murder?

Holly caught his doubtful look. 'Please hear me out, sir. Most married men faced with a pregnant girlfriend would have tried to sort something out: leave the wife or get rid of the girlfriend. But not Evans . . . he sets up an elaborate plan to somehow divide his time between the two families.'

'Is either woman aware of the other's existence?' Ashworth asked.

'No, sir, from what I gather, both think of Evans as a devoted father and husband.'

'I see. So what you're putting forward is, Jenny Chambers could have fallen for Evans in a big way and wanted to be more than just a casual lover.'

Holly smiled; Ashworth's perception, his ability to read the thoughts of others amazed her, almost as much as his quaintness of phrase; 'casual lover' amused her — so much better than 'bit on the side'.

'So, he had neither the time, nor financial resources, to set up a third home,' Ashworth remarked, 'and he said no in a most positive way . . . he smashed Jenny's head in with a hammer.'

Holly's spirits sank. 'You don't like it, sir?'

'On the contrary, Holly, I like it a lot. Good work,' he beamed, drumming his fingers on the desk top. 'It's coming together. I don't know what the odds are against two adulterous women getting murdered by partners or lovers on consecutive days, but that's what it's beginning to look like.'

Josh asked, 'So you don't want me to follow up on Fox then, sir?'

'Yes, I do,' Ashworth encouraged, 'most definitely. I want all leads followed up on this one. We'll take nothing for granted.'

He stood up. 'And why don't you two call me Jim, or guv? Let's lighten this place up a bit.' He headed for the other office, announcing, 'I'm going to phone my wife.'

When the door had clicked shut behind him, Holly leant towards Josh, whispering, 'What's wrong with him? Why the good mood?'

Josh shrugged.

'And why does he keep ringing his wife?'

In hushed tones, Josh told her about Ashworth's daughter. 'But there is something wrong with him,' he added solemnly. 'Have you noticed how receptive he is? Usually at this stage his mind's closed, but this time I've got a definite feeling that if I told him I thought you'd committed the murders, he'd have you followed.'

They fell silent, and Holly wondered how she could broach the subject of the car without hurting his feelings.

She decided to come straight out with it. 'Josh, I think I've done a deal on the Micra. I'm getting it for three and a half thousand. What do you think?'

'Great,' he replied without enthusiasm.

'I did follow your advice,' she quickly added. 'I'm having a test drive tonight.'

'But, Holly, I wanted to watch Fox.'

'That's all right, I can catch the bus and drive the car home,' she said excitedly, simulating the turning of a steering-wheel.

'Okay,' Josh said moodily.

* * *

The rain began late afternoon. For well over an hour a strong south-westerly lashed it viciously against the station's glass walls which rattled with such ferocity, those in CID feared they would break.

But it was a productive afternoon. Holly established that there were no road works between Bridgetown and Morton on the night Jenny Chambers was killed. She passed this information over to Ashworth and was surprised by his reaction.

He simply said, 'What do you want to do?' And when she appeared slightly reticent with her reply, he added, 'Well, come on, it's your case.'

'I'd like to make him sweat, sir . . . leave him until late tomorrow. With his tangled love life, the thought of a night in custody should really panic him.'

Ashworth said, 'All right,' and left it at that.

* * *

Christmas 1975; that was the last time Holly had felt such intense excitement. 1975; the year of the Sindy doll, complete with her own wardrobe. And now the gleaming red motor car had taken on a similar degree of importance in her rather empty life.

The rain had stopped, but the wind still howled, carrying rubbish from the gutters along with it; the stronger gusts lifting soft drink cans and depositing them noisily several yards along the road.

After a lengthy search through her clothes, Holly opted for jeans, mostly because they were difficult for amorous car salesmen to penetrate. And when the wind whipped around her legs as she climbed from the bus, she was grateful for their protection, seeing in her mind's eye a flimsy skirt permanently lifted by it.

But her confusion over Gary Williams was clearly reflected in her choice of top: it was tight, short-sleeved, and the outline of her black bra was visible through its white fabric. In short, it was as brazen as the jeans were demure.

She crossed to the showrooms, relieved to see the Micra still in its place.

Gary came out to greet her. 'Hi, Holly, made up your mind yet?'

'No, but I'd like to test drive it.'

The smell of its interior was beautiful, the gears were smooth, and just as important, nothing rattled. And the small car did not seem to be in any way affected by the cross-winds as Holly guided it along the lanes around Bridgetown.

They had been out for an hour and her confidence was growing. Gary glibly pointed out the car's virtues: ease of parking; economy of running; and — after some excellent lines in suggestive patter — the intervals between services.

'What do you think?' he asked, as Holly passed the same farm for the third time.

She was non-committal.

'Tell you what,' he said, 'pull into that lay-by and let's talk about it.'

Holly steered onto a piece of tarmac, large enough for three cars, at the side of the road.

As she pulled up, Gary undid his seat-belt and turned towards her. 'Come on, Holly, you must have made your mind up by now.'

'I don't know,' she hedged. 'It's a lot of money. If you could knock another hundred off . . .'

'I'm getting the feeling I'm being stitched up here,' he complained genially. 'I've cut my profit margin to the bone as it is.'

'Just another hundred and I can afford it,' Holly urged.

A large car edged towards them along the narrow road. It drew level, slowed, and its horn blasted out into the still evening. Gary raised his hand in acknowledgement.

Holly glanced over her shoulder at the departing vehicle. 'Who was that?'

'Dr Anthony. He buys his cars from us. We're the main Jaguar dealers for the area,' he explained. 'Why?'

'It's nothing, I just know his wife. She's a pathologist. I deal with her a lot.'

'What do you do then?' Gary asked with interest.

'I'm a policewoman . . . or should that be police person. I'm never quite sure nowadays.'

'Plain clothes?'

'God, you're observant.'

Gary relaxed into his seat and said with a smile, 'I can see it's half true what they say about women in CID . . .'

'What's that then?'

'That underneath all those plain clothes, you all wear the same uniform: black knickers, black suspender belt . . . black bra.'

'Yes, quite true,' Holly agreed with annoyance. 'I'm also a fixture of the station because I've been screwed on the front reception desk. Let's get all the dirty jokes about policewomen out of the way in one go, shall we?'

'How about coming for a drink with me?' he asked, toying with her hair.

Holly slapped his hand away lightly. 'The car,' she reminded him.

'Is that a definite no . . . about having a drink with me?'

'I don't want to talk about it,' she laughed, 'until we've sorted out the car.'

'That means you might then?'

She hit the steering-wheel with mock anger. 'Will you talk about the car first?'

'Okay, I'll tell you what I'll do — it's only got one month's road tax left on it. I'll tax it for six months . . . how's that?'

'All right,' she smiled, 'you've got yourself a deal.'

'Now can we talk about the drink?'

Holly turned to stare out of the side window; twilight had slipped into darkness. 'When?' she asked quietly.

Gary's fingers returned to her hair. 'Tomorrow night?' he asked softly, caressing her cheek and gently pulling her head round.

'Oh God,' she whispered as his lips touched her own.

Her arms willingly encircled his neck as she escaped the confines of the seat-belt. Her fingers curled through his hair, pulling him towards her, and their mouths opened wide in a passionate embrace.

Engrossed as they were, neither noticed the car, using only sidelights, stop some twenty yards from the lay-by. As the driver watched, he listened to the voices inside his head.

When he could stand it no longer, he quietly backed into the entrance of a field and drove off in the opposite direction.

Holly felt Gary's hand slide up over her breast. 'No,' she breathed, while at the same time guiding that hand, encouraging it into a slow caressing rhythm.

It was not until his hands moved down to fumble with the fastener of her jeans, that Holly called a halt.

She pulled away, breathless. 'No, not here.'

'Does that mean, if we were somewhere else . . . ?'

Holly was fast becoming aware of her true self. She slowly turned to face him and smiled. 'That's how it sounded, yes . . . but you'll have to wait and see.'

* * *

If Holly was doomed to spend the remainder of the night longing for sex, then Gwen Anthony, in strict contrast, was hoping against hope for a respite.

Gwen heard her husband's car pull up outside the cottage. She glanced at the clock; it was just eight forty-five.

When he entered the lounge her heart sank. She could tell by his expression that he was hyped up. And she knew the large brandy he poured before crossing to the inglenook fireplace would do little to calm him. He knocked the drink back in two swallows.

'I was talking to Mrs Smart today,' she said, trying to sound at ease. 'She was telling me about the terrible life she's had.'

There was no response from Nigel.

Gwen pushed on. 'You know . . . the wife of the cancer patient.'

'I know who you mean,' he lashed. 'That woman's had her life ruined because her husband couldn't keep it in his trousers.'

Too late, Gwen realized she had chosen the wrong subject. They did not speak again.

As Gwen steadily sipped a couple of dry sherries, she watched her husband devour three-quarters of a bottle of brandy.

Eventually, she left the room and climbed the stairs to the bathroom. She had brushed her teeth and was rinsing her mouth when the door opened.

Straightening up, she carefully replaced the glass on the washbasin before turning to look at her husband.

This was going to be hard but she was determined to see it through.

'Gwen.' He slurred her name as he advanced towards her.

'No, Nigel,' she said firmly, trying desperately to remain calm.

He reached out, viciously grabbed the back of her hair, pulled her face close to him. 'Why, Gwen?'

She could smell the brandy on his breath, could see the demented gleam in his eyes. 'Because you're beginning to frighten me, that's why.'

He tightened his grip. 'You like it.'

Gwen knew she was walking a tightrope; at any moment this could explode into violence, but she persisted. 'I don't, Nigel. You hurt me. And I don't like the things you say while you're doing it . . . or the things you want me to say.'

He forced her head back, causing her to wince. 'I just call you a filthy little whore,' he said with quiet menace, 'because that's what you are.'

The pain was becoming hard to bear and Gwen cried out, 'Stop it, for God's sake, stop it.' Tears spilled from her eyes.

The outburst merely urged him on. 'You know what I want you to say, Gwen, but you won't. What you've said to Ashworth . . . but I want you to use my name instead of his.'

Nigel's face broke into a terrifying grin as he panted, 'Do it to me, Jim . . . really do it . . .' He sneered. 'You shouldn't talk in your sleep, my love.'

Without warning, Nigel hit her; a hard, glancing blow to the temple.

The pain, the shock, galvanized Gwen into action. She tore at the hand holding her hair, digging her long nails into the flesh until his grip slackened.

Cursing, Nigel pulled back his hand to hit her again, but before he could aim Gwen beat his face with her clenched fists, driving him back.

'You bastard,' she screamed, again and again as her fists landed.

He stumbled under her onslaught, collapsed on the floor in an uncoordinated heap.

As Gwen stepped over his prostrate form, Nigel grabbed her ankle and she lurched forward; only her outstretched hands saved her from collision with the bathroom door.

Her senses reeled and her lungs ached as she fought for air, but her will for survival provided the strength to kick out with her free leg.

She grunted with satisfaction as her foot sank into soft flesh and the tight grip on her ankle slackened. A primeval roar emerged from her throat as she kicked out again and his fingers finally lost their tenuous grip.

Escape loomed large in her mind. She scrambled from the bathroom, slamming the door behind her. Nigel's muffled cries followed her along the landing.

In the darkness she did not see the small wooden chair which stood in a square at the top of the stairs; it came at her as if from nowhere and she pitched over it, landing with bone-shaking force.

As Gwen slid along the polished floor-boards, the bathroom door was ripped open. Pursuing footfalls brought her quickly to her feet, babbled words of fear spewing from her lips.

Her moans increased as she skidded into the small bedroom at the rear of the cottage. At first she feared her fumbling fingers would be unable to turn the key, but at the third attempt it ground into place.

Gwen reached up to slide the bolt at the top of the door, and as her fingers touched the cold metal, Nigel smashed into it. Shock from the impact travelled down her arm and through the length of her body as she pushed the bolt into place.

The door shook and trembled as, once again, Nigel threw his full weight against it. Gwen took a chair and jammed it beneath the handle. Any moment now she expected the door to buckle and splinter under the assault.

Then suddenly there was silence, an eerie, ominous quiet, more frightening than the hostilities preceding it. Gwen's legs were shaking uncontrollably, her breathing was ragged.

Five minutes passed, then a whimpering cry sounded from outside. 'Let me in, Gwen. I'm sorry . . . I'm sorry.'

She held her breath as he pleaded, made no response. Then he moved back along the landing, but it was not until she heard steady rhythmic snores that she relaxed.

Pale moonlight illuminated the bedroom, picking out the furniture. Gwen sat on the single bed, and looking down, saw that her dress had been torn in the struggle. Her hands ached terribly from the blows she had landed.

There was only one course of action open to her now. She would have to leave. And for the first time she felt regret for that amorous interlude shared with Ashworth, for there was little doubt that their merging of bodies had caused some form of mental breakdown in her husband.

But for the present, flight was impossible; her clothes, her belongings, even the keys to the Land Rover, were all in the bedroom where her drunken, deranged spouse was sleeping.

She lay back on the bed and closed her eyes, knowing that sleep would evade her.

CHAPTER 11

Holly pulled aside the bedroom curtains, peered down with satisfaction at the wonderful red car in the driveway, and hugged herself.

Just then, Josh's Sunny pulled up at the kerb. He walked to the house without taking his eyes off the gleaming Micra.

Holly could hear him moving about, going first to the kitchen, and on to the lounge. Then, not finding her in either room, she heard him climb the stairs.

Hurriedly she grabbed her bathrobe and put it on to cover her short nightdress.

Josh knocked tentatively. 'Holly?'

'It's open,' she called.

'Sorry,' he said, entering the darkened room. 'I didn't know you were in bed.'

'I wasn't.' She switched on the bedside lamp. 'I was just admiring the car. Isn't it great?'

'Yes,' he admitted. 'How did you persuade them to let you have it tonight? Surely you didn't take that much money with you?'

'No, but they let me bring it away, and I'm taking a Building Society cheque in tomorrow.'

'They're very trusting,' he said lightly.

'Yes.' She resented his prying into her affairs. 'I got six months' road tax out of them as well. He's doing that tomorrow.'

'He?' Josh quizzed.

'Josh,' she said curtly, 'is anything bothering you?'

'It's none of my business, but unless I'm mistaken—'

'You're right, it's not any of your business, Josh,' she said firmly.

'Sorry,' he said, holding up his hands for peace.

An awkward silence set in and Holly sat on the bed.

'I followed Fox tonight,' Josh announced after a time, 'and I think I may be close to getting a result.'

Holly patted the bed. 'Come on, sit down and tell me about it.'

Josh settled beside her. 'Well, he was following a woman called Karen Waters. She lives in a block of flats on the council estate, and she's unemployed but she goes out a lot.'

'Is she single or married?' Holly asked.

'She's single,' Josh said, studying Holly's discarded underwear with little interest. 'I spoke to several people who think she might be on the game. So, I followed Fox while he followed her. She went to a couple of pubs, then took a guy back to her flat. I made a few discreet enquiries, posing as a council tax inspector, and apparently the woman's noisy, causes a lot of nuisance, so the neighbours were only too willing to drop her in it.'

'But why would Fox want to murder a prostitute? It doesn't fit.'

'I don't know,' Josh admitted, 'but I reckon she's the next victim.'

When Holly remained silent, Josh turned to face her. 'You don't seem very impressed.'

'I'm not really,' Holly shrugged. 'I think you're wrong about Fox. He's just a very diligent person who takes his job seriously.'

'You've changed your tune, haven't you?' Josh scoffed. 'At first you said he was worth looking at. Anyway, I'll be watching Karen Waters closely.' He pushed himself off the bed and looked down at her. 'I don't suppose you fancy a bit of unpaid overtime tomorrow night?'

'I can't tomorrow. I'm busy,' she replied, annoyed with herself for feeling embarrassed.

Josh was obviously put out. 'Right,' he said, 'I'll leave you in peace then. Goodnight.'

'Goodnight, Josh.'

* * *

The clock on the tower of Bridgetown's Norman church peeled out the 3 a.m. chimes for anyone who might be interested at such an early hour.

Gladys Smart shifted her weight in the chair. So shallow was her sleep of late, the tiniest disturbance tended to wake her. As the third chime sounded in the distance, her husband stirred in the bed.

'All right, Cliff?' she asked anxiously.

'It's agony, Gladys.' His voice was little more than an anguished croak at the back of his throat.

'Do you want your tablets?'

'Give me four.'

'No, Cliff, the doctor said no more than two at a time.'

'What difference does it make now?'

He tried to sit up, but the effort left him breathless. Gladys poured water into a glass and took the top off the painkillers.

'Four, Gladys . . . please,' he begged.

'All right, Cliff,' she soothed.

One at a time, she put the tablets to his mouth, placed the glass to his dry lips. The Adam's apple bounced in his scrawny neck; even swallowing had become a painful exercise.

With the last tablet taken, he lay back exhausted. 'It won't be long now . . .' His feeble voice faltered on the words. 'I can see God's angels around the walls.'

'Rest, Cliff,' Gladys said softly. 'Let the tablets work.'

‘They’re beckoning to me,’ he rambled, ‘but they won’t let me follow till I’ve made my peace.’

As if granted strength by some divine force, he sat up in bed. Gladys, thinking the moment of death had arrived, suddenly felt frightened and very alone.

‘I’ve wronged you, gal,’ he sighed, ‘done you a terrible wrong.’

‘Cliff, lay back,’ Gladys urged.

But he wanted to speak and she bent closer to hear his words.

‘We’ve never even talked about it, have we, gal? Not while the lad was growing up; not since he left home. Both of us spending our lives pretending it never happened.’

He swallowed hard, tried to catch his breath. ‘I remember all that sloppy poetry you used to read, gal, and one bit always stuck in my memory: It’s not until the fire has been extinguished, that a man can see the havoc caused . . .’

‘Lay back, Cliff,’ Gladys implored.

He began to cry and his face reminded her of a baby’s, almost a replica of his son’s fifty years before.

‘I want you to forgive me, Gladys . . . I just want you to forgive me.’

Gladys cried too, and cradled him in her arms, aware of the bones poking through his skin.

‘I forgive you, Cliff,’ she sobbed.

And as she spoke a feeling of peace swept over her.

* * *

At nine a.m. the next morning Holly indicated right and pulled into the station car park. Even the sound of the directional indicators had a crisp new ring to it. She parked, enjoying the satisfying click as she pulled the handbrake lever up.

Ashworth, standing by his Sierra, made an appreciative face as she climbed out of the car, and Holly felt herself swelling with pride as he walked over.

‘Very nice,’ he remarked. ‘Very nice indeed.’

'It takes a bit of getting used to after the mini.'

Ashworth's eyes twinkled. 'What, you mean having one that actually goes along the road?'

She laughed. 'Yes, fair comment. It's only done twenty thousand,' she informed him proudly.

Ashworth did a tour of inspection around the vehicle. 'These engines go on for ever, so they tell me.'

'How's your daughter?' Holly asked.

'She keeps going in and out of labour. The doctors are saying if she doesn't start for real soon, they'll have to do something.' He smiled. 'They also say there's nothing to worry about, but that's not stopping me.'

'I hope it all goes well, sir.'

'Thank you.' He wandered back around the car. 'If you don't mind me saying, you've got some chipped paintwork here.'

Holly joined him and looked to where he was pointing. 'I didn't notice that.' She inspected the four places where tiny flakes of paint were missing.

'It's nothing to worry about,' Ashworth told her, 'but I'd get it fixed, or you could have the start of body rust.'

They climbed the back steps to the station.

'I'm expecting at least one arrest today, Holly,' he announced optimistically.

* * *

Nigel Anthony came awake slowly. His head ached, his face and body hurt dreadfully. Hazy memories of the previous night came back to him. There had been a fight, he was sure of that.

He looked down at himself. Still fully clothed, his expensive suit was crumpled and flecked with blood.

Trembling fingers went to his face; his nose felt swollen and sore. Wincing with pain, Nigel swung his legs off the bed and forced himself to stand erect. The room swam around him.

When it had slowly and painfully settled into focus, he studied his reflection in the dressing table mirror. His nose was indeed swollen and distorted, but it was difficult to tell whether the bruises beneath his eyes had been caused by Gwen's punches or an over-indulgence of brandy.

He searched the cottage. Gwen was nowhere in it. In the bedroom once more he ripped open the wardrobe doors; her clothes and belongings were still inside.

Stumbling down the stairs as fast as he could, he found her doctor's bag still resting beside the hall table . . . but the Land Rover was gone.

She had left him. The thought seemed to come from a distance, gradually creeping forward to hit him in the face. But his disturbed mind could not link her disappearance to his own behaviour.

He angrily assumed she had gone to Ashworth.

* * *

Mrs Fox circled the small flat. She was worried about her son. Even the suffocating love she felt for the boy could not blind her to his sometimes strange behaviour.

And his recent behaviour certainly was strange, starting with the arrival of that silver car which was occasionally parked outside. Since then Gerald had become nervous, fidgety, was forever looking out of the window.

As a young girl, in Poland, she had seen this behaviour in many people: dissidents, and others likely to attract the attention of the police.

But what could her Gerald have done to interest them? He was a good boy. A homosexual, perhaps. She chuckled. He thought she did not know; as if a boy could hide that from his mother. But, surely, the police could not persecute him for that?

Police are police, she thought, whatever country you are in.

'But Gerald is a good boy,' she told herself, despite the strong doubts she had to the contrary.

* * *

The morning meeting in CID was conducted in a mood of great optimism. Ashworth sensed that today would see the murders solved, therefore alleviating his greatest worry.

Josh, meanwhile, felt certain he was about to stop a third murder, and at the same time apprehend the killer.

Holly's attention was somewhat divided in that illogical way which can occur when matters of personal morality are involved: half her mind was enjoying the prospect of Russ Evans behind bars, unable to deceive further women; the other half savouring the thought that in less than twelve hours she would be one step along the road to becoming the mistress of Gary Williams.

Ashworth listened attentively as Josh recounted his story about Fox, seemed pleased when told that the man could make his move tonight.

'Good,' he said, leaning back in his chair. 'What's on your mind, Holly? You look very thoughtful.'

Holly blushed while forming the answer, 'Well, sir, I want to bring Russ Evans in to explain that missing half hour.'

'The traffic jam at the road works, you mean?' Ashworth tapped his pen on his desk. 'Odd, isn't it? Why should the man make an excuse like that? It's so easy to check out.' He gave her a stern look. 'You have checked it thoroughly, I take it?'

'Very thoroughly, sir,' Holly replied stiffly. 'In fact, I've double-checked it.'

'Good,' Ashworth said with a smile.

Whenever a good mood was upon him, Ashworth could not resist allowing the teasing element of his personality to come to the fore.

'Now all I have to do is wait for Forensic to come up with the results of the Ian Johnson tests.'

He stood up and crossed to the glass wall overlooking the main road. 'We're in for some fun and games by the looks of it. They're erecting barriers across the road. Just when we don't need road works we've got them.' He chuckled. 'And where were they when Russ Evans needed them?'

The telephone rang and a pneumatic drill started up simultaneously.

Josh answered the call. 'Hello?' he said, raising his voice above the outside noise. 'It's Forensic, guv.'

'I'll take it in the other office,' Ashworth called.

In the annexed room, Ashworth skirted around the desk and grabbed the receiver. 'Ashworth.'

'Hold on, Jim . . .' It was Gerry Talbot, Head of Forensic. '. . . I'm just going through the report to make sure I've got the information right. I didn't do the tests myself.'

As Ashworth waited there came a temporary respite from the pneumatic drill but Holly and Josh, in the main office, made no adjustments to their voices. Consequently, Ashworth could hear every word.

'Why can't you call him, guv? It's obvious he loves it.' That was Josh.

'I don't know,' Holly replied. 'I can't think of him as guv, any more than I can Jim.'

'It's only a term.'

'Yes, Josh, but it's a term of endearment.'

Josh laughed. 'You're crazy, do you know that?'

'Look, to me it would suggest some form of affection which I just don't feel for him,' Holly said with impatience. 'I like him, but he's not human enough for me. I bet even when he knows he's wrong he won't admit it to himself.'

Still waiting on the end of the telephone, Ashworth thought drily, what is it they say about eavesdroppers?

The drill started up again, sparing him further insight into his shortcomings.

Talbot was back. 'Okay, Jim?'

'Right, Gerry, what have you got for me?'

'I'll just give you the bad news, because that's all there is. Ian Johnson's clothes and effects are in the clear. Nothing on them at all.'

'Damn.'

'Sorry, Jim, I can tell I haven't made your day.'

'Thanks anyway, Gerry.'

Replacing the receiver heavily, Ashworth repeated, 'Damn.'

But in all honesty, he was not greatly surprised; even as he was forcing the piece into the puzzle he knew it did not fit.

Ashworth's good mood was swiftly evaporating; the drone from the road works, the rise and fall of his detectives' voices — all were beginning to annoy him.

He marched back into the main office, pinching the bridge of his nose — a mannerism which those of long acquaintance associated with the gathering of a storm.

'Right,' he shouted abruptly, 'Forensic found nothing on Johnson's clothes . . .' His brow knitted. 'Close that blasted window, Josh. I can't hear myself think in here.'

Josh complied, and as the sounds became muffled, he said, 'Johnson could have burned . . .' But, catching sight of Ashworth's expression, his voice trailed off.

'I want you two to get Johnson, bring him back here, and then I want that supermarket manager, Evans, brought in—'

'But I wanted to let him stew till late afternoon, sir,' Holly cut in.

'No, have him in now.' Ashworth's tone made it plain he did not welcome the interruption. 'He can stew in the interview room while I'm dealing with Johnson.'

So much for it being my investigation, Holly thought, snatching her bag from the desk.

She was heading for the door when Ashworth snapped, 'And tell Johnson's mother-in-law she is not to set foot in this station.'

Holly stopped, looked him straight in the eye. 'Are those the exact words you want me to use, sir?'

Ashworth relented. 'Well, no, dress it up a bit . . . but keep her out.'

CHAPTER 12

By the time Johnson and Evans were installed in adjacent interview rooms, all who had come into contact with Ashworth had felt the sharp edge of his tongue.

Ian Johnson looked up quickly as Ashworth hurried in, closely followed by Holly.

Ashworth wandered across to the dirty window overlooking the car park while Holly grabbed a straight-backed chair to face Johnson across the yellow Formica tabletop.

Despite frequent use of air-fresheners, the room smelt strongly of cigarette smoke from earlier interrogations during which the interviewees must have smoked incessantly.

Ian Johnson was no exception; he put a cigarette to his lips with trembling fingers and watched Ashworth's broad back.

The Chief Inspector took a sweet from his pocket, unwrapping it slowly before popping it into his mouth. 'All right, Ian, what have you got to tell us?' He did not turn around, but continued staring out of the window.

'I want a brief.' The answer came without conscious thought.

Ashworth passed the sweet around his mouth. 'Is that what your mother-in-law told you to say?' He turned then.

'Wise up, son. Forensic found nothing on the articles we took away from your home.'

'I knew they wouldn't.' Johnson stubbed out the cigarette and, the moment his fingers were idle, started toying with his lighter.

Ashworth's attitude softened. 'We don't think you murdered your wife, but we do need to establish where you were at that time.'

Johnson looked from one to the other.

'Had you got someone else?' Holly prompted. 'If you had it would be quite understandable.'

Johnson's laugh was hollow. 'God, I wish I had. Perhaps then all this wouldn't have come as such a shock.'

'Tell us, Ian,' Ashworth coaxed, taking a chair and sitting beside Holly. 'What have you got to lose?'

Johnson lit another cigarette and shook his head. 'I'll get into trouble.'

'You're in trouble, son,' Ashworth informed him brusquely. 'Believe me, we'll keep digging until we find out where you were. Why don't you just tell me — save me all that time? I'll personally try to minimize any trouble you're in.'

Johnson seemed to consider this. 'I was doing some driving on the side,' he finally blurted out.

Ashworth, expecting a far more serious confession, wanted to laugh. 'You were doing some driving on the side?' he echoed.

Johnson caught his expression. 'Yes, it may not seem like a lot to you, but look at it from where I'm sitting. I was using the work's van, so I was having to book more miles than I was doing to cover the extra driving. I was working cash-in-hand, so the tax man will be after me . . .'

He shot Ashworth a pleading look. 'I was only doing it for Margaret . . . so we could keep our home. I just thought if it all came out, it'd look more and more like I'd killed her.'

'All right, Ian,' Ashworth said quietly.

'Do you believe me?'

'Yes, I do.' Ashworth stood up. 'Now, I want you to give me the name of the firm you were moonlighting for so we can make discreet enquiries as to your whereabouts at the time we're interested in. As for the Inland Revenue, you can still enter accounts for last year on a profit and loss basis. You'll have to pay tax, but you won't be in any trouble.'

'Thank you,' Johnson said gratefully.

'Thank you for helping, Ian.'

Ashworth left the room without further discussion. Holly took the relevant details and followed. She found him leaning against a wall, unwrapping another sweet.

'I didn't know you had such a sweet tooth, sir.'

'It's the cigarette smoke . . . it sometimes brings the craving back,' he explained dismally. 'How long did you want to keep Evans waiting?'

'I wanted it to be as long as possible, sir, but as he's here voluntarily it might be discourteous to keep him too long.'

'I feel discourteous today,' Ashworth said bluntly. 'He'll keep while we have lunch.'

* * *

Gerald Fox sat alone in a corner of the Department of Employment canteen, picking at his chicken salad.

The young policeman was beginning to worry him. Why was he always following? At first, thinking the officer might possibly be attracted to him, Fox had been flattered, excited. A good-looking policeman would make a welcome change from the runaway youngsters, working as rent-boys, who were the sole outlet for his insatiable sex drive.

But if he was attracted, why didn't he make an approach instead of just following him everywhere?

Laughter drifted across the canteen, and Fox automatically looked to see if it was aimed at him. Then, satisfied that those at the crowded table were simply enjoying a friendly debate, he looked away quickly, not wishing to draw attention to himself.

If the police were interested in him, it could only be because he was homosexual. Some of his boys must be under-aged.

And don't the police love pushing gays around? You only have to witness their attitudes when they visit the clubs.

Fox cursed the part of himself which could not be controlled: his sexuality.

Resting his cutlery on the plate, he thought of his mother; perhaps he had inherited her paranoia.

But one thing he was sure of: there was nobody in the police force, nobody, to match him intellectually.

As Fox left the canteen, no one afforded him a second glance.

* * *

Ashworth was grateful that Russ Evans did not smoke.

For two and a half hours he and Holly went over the man's story again and again. But Evans would not budge; every time he told it, all the details matched his previous statements.

Ashworth, for the umpteenth time, said, 'Mr Evans, we're not getting any nearer to how you spent that half hour you can't account for.'

'But I've told you.' Evans's nerves were fraying; he was considering the consequences of a night spent incarcerated in a police cell. They had promised him that, if he could not supply a satisfactory explanation.

'No, you haven't,' Ashworth insisted firmly. 'What you're giving us is a cock-and-bull story about road works.'

'It's true,' Evans shouted. 'There were two lanes of the expressway closed, half way between here and Morton. I'm telling you the truth.'

Ashworth decided on a below-the-belt approach. 'You're good at the truth, are you, Mr Evans? When your wife asks what you did while you were away, you tell her, I take it?'

Evans hung his head in despair.

'Yes, we're getting to it now, aren't we?' Ashworth pushed home his attack. 'No, you tell her about lonely nights

. . . how you've missed her and the kids. You tell her a cock-and-bull story, because that's what you're good at.'

'I've told you the truth,' Evans said, emphasizing every word.

'And I keep telling you the truth — there were no road works on the expressway between here and Morton on the night in question. How do you explain that?'

Ashworth was exasperated; he felt the interview was going nowhere. 'Right,' he said, 'would you like a cup of tea?'

Evans shook his head. 'No.'

'Well, I would,' Ashworth said, rising from his seat. 'We'll leave you alone to think things over, Mr Evans, and when we come back we'll ask you the same questions . . . and if you give the same answers we're going to hold you overnight.'

What little colour the man had drained from his face. 'You can't do that.'

'Oh, but I can,' Ashworth informed him, 'and if I can't get some answers, by God, I will.'

'I've got responsibilities,' Evans said hotly.

Ashworth gave an empty laugh. 'Oh yes, I know that. Would you like me to contact all those you're responsible for? Shall I get them to come and visit you? Maybe they should all come together, get to know each other . . . they could compare notes.'

Evans got to his feet; his face hostile. 'You're a bastard.'

'It's been said.' Ashworth leant across the table. 'But Jenny Chambers can't compare notes, can she? Jenny Chambers is dead; and someone killed her in the half an hour you can't account for. So think on, lad . . . and sit down.'

Ashworth pointed firmly to the chair and Evans sank resignedly into it.

* * *

Gladys Smart opened the front door. 'Oh, thank God, doctor, he's in real agony.'

Nigel Anthony brushed past and made his way up the stairs, glad of the low wattage bulb which lit the passage way, making his swollen nose and bruised eyes less noticeable.

Gladys waited at the bottom of the stairs until he reappeared. 'I've been trying the surgery all day but they said you weren't in.'

'No, both my wife and I are off sick,' he told her abruptly. 'They rang me at home.'

He stopped well outside the arc of light given out by the bulb. 'I've given him the highest dose I can. He should be more comfortable soon.'

'I hope so, doctor,' Gladys sighed. 'He keeps begging me to give him all his tablets . . .' She began to cry bitterly. '. . . and if you hadn't come when you did, I would have. I just can't stand to see him like this much longer.'

Showing little compassion, Anthony said, 'I'll call in tomorrow,' and walked to the front door without looking back.

* * *

Josh had been out to his car to collect some reports he had typed at home. Entering the station, he paused at the reception desk to straighten the bulky papers and listened with amusement to the discussion between sergeant Dutton and a group of uniformed constables.

One PC complained, 'Come on, sarge, have a heart, I've been out till past two a.m. three mornings this week . . .'

Dutton, a kindly, compassionate man, was well used to hearing gripes from his harassed officers but, although sympathetic, he knew he had to maintain control.

'We're undermanned at the moment — it's as simple as that,' he said stoutly.

The same PC grumbled, 'My missus says she'll leave me if I don't start getting home on time.'

'Well, if I were you, I'd thank the powers that be and help her pack before she changes her mind,' Dutton laughed, hoping humour would defuse the situation. 'Now, come on, lads, it's the job.'

Grinning, Josh headed for the stairs with the papers under his arm, sounds from the debate following him.

Suddenly he stopped and turned. 'Say that again,' he called.

The startled group looked towards him.

* * *

The rational part of Nigel Anthony's mind was functioning well that afternoon. He visited the bank and chatted with the manager about the joint accounts he held with Gwen.

If she had left him for Ashworth, and he was certain she had, he wanted to make quite sure that a great deal of money did not follow the same path.

On his way home, Anthony called into the garage.

'Hello, Dr Anthony,' Gary Williams called. 'What can I do for you?'

Anthony came into the office. 'How are you, Gary?'

'Fine. You?'

'Yes, thank you.'

Gary noticed the doctor's battered face but, like the bank manager before him, made no comment.

Anthony, conscious of his marked features, turned and studied the gleaming new cars through the office door, saying, 'This is a little delicate . . . has my wife been in?'

'No, Dr Anthony.'

'I want you to do me a favour if she does. Will you check with me first before letting her have anything on account?'

'Yes, of course,' Gary said, eager to safeguard commission from the new Jaguar Anthony ordered every two years. 'Is that just on buying a car, sir?'

'No, the lot, servicing, everything.'

'Right, I'll make a note of it.'

'And what were you doing in a lay-by with a certain young policewoman then?' Anthony asked lightly, still with his back towards Williams.

'I was selling her a car,' Gary replied innocently.

'Oh yes?' Anthony half turned, pulled a knowing face. 'Is it true what they say about the plain ones?'

Gary gave his man-to-man laugh. 'That they're grateful, you mean? I'll have to keep you guessing on that one.'

'Just don't let your wife find out,' Anthony said, smiling, as he headed for the door.

Gary watched him cross the showroom. At the door he turned and waved.

Gary waved back, a highly polished professional smile on his lips as he thought, I'll end up with a face like yours if she does.

* * *

As Josh strode along the corridor, he could hear Ashworth's raised voice. Not savouring the prospect of passing on the information given to him by the uniformed officers, his knock on the door to the interview room was timorous.

'Come in,' Ashworth barked.

Josh pushed open the door. 'A word, guv, please.'

Ashworth joined him in the corridor, slamming the door behind him. 'Don't give me any bad news, Josh,' he warned. 'I don't need it.'

'Sorry, guv, but Evans's story holds up.'

Ashworth glared at him. 'How? Holly checked out the road works.'

'They weren't road works as such, guv,' Josh informed him hesitantly. 'A lorry spilt its load on the expressway between here and Morton that night. Uniformed had to seal off two lanes until it was cleared up.'

'Damn.' Ashworth hit the wall with the flat of his hand.

Josh continued, 'In the darkness, with the traffic cones, the ordinary motorist—'

'All right, all right, there's no need to draw pictures,' Ashworth snapped. 'The times check out, I take it?'

'Yes, guv.'

Without speaking, Ashworth returned to the interview room, and Josh followed him in.

'Right, Mr Evans, additional information has come to light which does seem to confirm your story.'

Evans's face showed relief, while Holly frowned.

'There were no road works that night,' Ashworth informed them, 'but there was a crash which led to two lanes of the expressway being closed.' He pointed a warning finger. 'Mind you, we'll still have to make enquiries at Morton, but we'll use discretion.'

Evans let out a long breath. 'Does that mean I'm free to go?'

Ashworth pinched the bridge of his nose. 'Yes, go on, get out,' he spat unceremoniously.

When Russ Evans had gone, Ashworth paced the room, frustration evident in his every move. 'So, we end the day three steps back from where we started.'

'I don't agree, sir . . .' Josh began.

'We've lost our two main suspects,' Ashworth continued brusquely. 'Forensic haven't come up with anything, and we haven't yet found the hammer used to kill the Chambers woman.'

'There's still Fox, sir,' Josh reminded Ashworth as he sat down.

'Yes.' He reflected on this. 'He's my last hope. Right, give me those reports. I'll work in here. That office is like a mad house, what with the racket from outside; and the sun on all that glass reminds me of a rowdy Turkish bath. Whoever designed this building . . .'

Holly and Josh beat a hasty retreat.

CHAPTER 13

Gwen Anthony carefully negotiated the rutted track leading to her cottage. The ground was awash on account of the recent rain, making it impossible to decipher when the tyre marks of her husband's Jaguar had been made, or in which direction he had been travelling.

An intense feeling of trepidation came over her as she passed the lay-by, for the cottage lay around the next bend.

'Come on, Gwen,' she said aloud with false cheer, 'there's nothing more damaging to a girl's ego than wearing the same knickers for two days.'

Although one purpose of her visit was to collect some clothes, the real reason was far more practical: she needed her credit cards, cheque book, and any cash she could find.

Gwen eased into the last bend. Her plan was simple: if Nigel's car was there she would turn round and drive back to the main road. Her Land Rover would easily outrun the Jaguar on this uneven surface.

The parking area was empty.

Gwen's relief was tinged with sadness as she viewed their lovely cottage; its thatched roof with tiny windows set in it; the studded front door which for hundreds of years had provided a sturdy barrier against unwelcome visitors.

Her movements were hasty as she alighted from the vehicle; and she almost ran to the small garden gate.

Turning the key quickly in the lock, Gwen swung open the door, not bothering to close it behind her as she took the stairs two at a time.

In the bedroom she lifted her suitcase off the top of the wardrobe and flung open the mirrored door. She rapidly took out dresses and shoes, throwing them in a heap on the bed. The chest of drawers was next.

Satisfied that she had everything, Gwen bundled the clothes into her suitcase, closing it as she sprinted down the stairs.

Finding her handbag in the lounge she checked inside and found her credit cards and cheque book.

'Cash,' she muttered.

She placed her suitcase and handbag beside the open front door, stopping for a second to peer anxiously outside.

The only sounds were evening birdsong. The peace and tranquillity contrasted sharply with the tension which made her stomach cramp.

Her heels sounded as she ran to the room her husband used as a study. Rifling through the bureau which served as a desk, Gwen came across five ten-pound notes in a pigeon-hole, and hurriedly stuffed them into her pocket.

She made her way to the door, and glancing back, noted with some satisfaction that, due to her haste, the room appeared to have been burgled.

In the hall a forewarning shiver ran the length of her spine, alerting her to danger. Wildly she looked around for whatever could have caused it.

At first it was not apparent, but when it became so, the implications left her rooted to the spot.

The front door was closed.

* * *

Josh was following Gerald Fox at a discreet distance. The brake-lights of the man's Escort glowed red as it slowed then stopped at a halt sign.

Josh, thirty yards behind, pulled over to the kerb; he had no wish to alert Fox to his presence by stopping directly behind him.

The Escort turned left into the High Street and Josh fell in behind. He had followed Fox so often now, it no longer required conscious thought on his part, and Holly was occupying his mind as he kept the Escort's rear lights in view.

Josh knew she resented his attempted intrusion into her personal life, but he felt his intentions were honourable.

From her choice of literature, her preferences in television programmes, and subtle observations he had made, it was apparent to him that Holly was a young lady with a very robust libido. She was also extremely vulnerable, easily hurt, but she did her best to conceal this side of her nature by adopting a sometimes brisk, one-of-the-boys attitude.

Josh's main fear was that she could all too easily fall prey to the advances of a married man such as Gary Williams and could find herself involved in an affair which went nowhere, but would be powerless to stop it.

But for a quirk of fate, Josh thought with a smile, I'd have made somebody a good mother.

Well ahead, the indicators of Fox's car blinked as it turned right into the car park of the Princess Alexander, a club frequented by Bridgetown's homosexual population.

Josh stopped opposite just as Fox approached the main entrance. Before pushing open the swing doors, he turned and stared in Josh's direction.

'Balls,' Josh exclaimed, quickly turning his head away. He was certain Fox had seen him and the thought worried him.

After half an hour, Josh became restless. Something was wrong. That thought kept coming back into his mind: if Fox knew he was being watched, was Josh's idea that he might be the murderer so ridiculous?

It would be simple for the man to leave a busy pub by another exit, drive away, return after an hour, say, and re-enter without anyone noticing.

Josh was presented with a dilemma: if he went barging into the pub and Fox was still inside, then his cover would be blown. So, what should he do?

He looked at the large car park. Of course; he could look for Fox's car. But that would mean a fairly detailed inspection of over a hundred vehicles, for under the neon lighting they all took on the same colour. And if Fox came out and found him prowling around the car park . . .

Even if Fox wasn't in the pub, that in itself would prove very little; it was not unusual for gays to vanish for an hour for reasons other than to murder people.

Josh could not contain himself. He got out of the car and hurried towards the brightly-lit entrance. Sensuous music was playing in the background as he pushed open the door.

'You a member?' a voice greeted him as he stepped into the marble-floored entrance hall.

'No,' Josh told the bouncer, a large thickset man with broken nose and smart tuxedo.

'Well, unless there's somebody to sign you in, you don't get past the door,' the man responded flatly, his expression stating he was not a supporter of the gay cause.

Josh flashed his warrant card. 'Go and play Charles Bronson somewhere else, okay?'

The man sneered and grudgingly stood to one side. Relations between Bridgetown station and the hired muscle of the public houses had never been friendly, each accusing the other of trespassing on their territory.

Josh worked his way around the dimly lit bar, moved around bodies swaying to the thump of the music.

Fox was nowhere in sight.

The Lounge proved quieter but no more fruitful. Neither did the aptly-named 'Snug', where couples sat, holding hands, engaging in whispered conversations.

With eyes smarting from cigarette smoke, Josh carried on through a door at the rear of the room and found himself in the car park. A laborious inspection of all parked cars followed, and as he worked his way down the last row it was apparent that Fox and his car were missing.

Josh was torn between waiting for him to return and watching Karen Waters's flat to safeguard her welfare.

He chose the latter and sprinted to his car, realizing that Fox could quite easily have passed straight through the pub, and if that was so, he had already been gone for forty-five minutes.

* * *

Holly sighed with contented relief, all mundane thoughts chased away, along with the sexual frustration which was her constant companion.

For now, nothing else mattered but her rare feeling of satisfaction, the opulent smell inside the almost-new Jaguar, that delicious feel of soft leather on the backs of her naked thighs.

After Gary had climbed off, Holly savoured the feelings, the sensations, for a full five minutes before moving. Then, pushing herself up from the seat, she busily rearranged her skirt.

'Want a ciggy?' Gary asked.

'No, thanks, I gave up . . . oh, go on then, why not?'

He lit two cigarettes and passed one to her. It was now over three years since she had stopped smoking and the first few inhalations left her dizzy, produced a sensation similar to floating on a cushion of air. She giggled.

Gary pulled out the ashtray. 'Better be careful,' he warned. 'This is a client's car.'

'I wonder if he'll ever know what went on in the back of it?' Holly laughed.

'I hope to God not, he's a marriage-guidance counsellor.'

Holly laughed louder, then felt a slight falling-to-earth sensation when Gary, as if prompted by the mention of marriage, glanced at his watch.

'Somewhere you've got to be?' Holly ventured.

'No, no, it's all right.' His face was illuminated by the glow of his cigarette as he drew on it. 'I just wondered what the time was.'

'I hope you can lie a bit more convincingly when your wife asks where you've been,' Holly taunted, 'or we're both in trouble.'

'I don't get on with my wife,' Gary insisted, carefully stubbing out his cigarette in the tiny ashtray.

'But you still wouldn't want her to find out, would you?'

He remained silent.

'I'm not pushing you, Gary, it's just that I want us both to know what's happening here.' She laughed airily. 'Maybe you shouldn't have picked a detective for your bit on the side.'

'Holly—'

'No, listen . . . we're having an undercover affair, right? You take me to a pub that's in the middle of nowhere, and you still nearly jump out of your chair every time someone comes in.'

'It's my kid,' he protested.

'I don't care what it is, Gary, that's what I'm saying. I just don't want you feeling you have to lie to me. I'm not going to do the fall-for-the-married-guy bit, and by the same token, I'm not going to be just your bit on the side. I remain a free agent.'

'You're a very forthright lady.'

She stubbed out her cigarette. 'Why complicate something that's complicated enough?'

Gary picked up her frilly black pants. 'Can I keep these as a souvenir?'

'What if your wife finds them?'

'She won't. I'll leave them at work. Yes?'

'Why not,' she laughed. Then, sobering, 'We're going to have to find somewhere else to do it, you know.'

'Why?'

'Gary, my love,' she said, sinking back into the luxury of her seat, 'I'm a police officer. If a patrol comes along and catches me being bunked up in the back of a car, I'll lose my job.'

'What about your house?' he asked.

Holly shook her head. 'It's difficult.'

'The boyfriend?'

'He's not my boyfriend,' she countered. 'We work together, and at the moment he's staying with me.'

'And he doesn't try it on? What's wrong with him?'

'You wouldn't believe me if I told you. Come on, we'd better be getting back,' she prompted, catching him looking at his watch again.

'Yes, I suppose so,' Gary said, trying to sound reluctant but falling short of it.

The Jaguar purred along winding unlit country lanes until they were close to the gateway of a field where Holly had parked her Micra.

Gary dropped her a hundred yards away from the car, as married men were prone to do with their girlfriends; and even on such a deserted stretch of road he seemed agitated, eager to be away.

Holly strolled along the lane, enjoying the cool air wafting up her skirt and dancing on her naked skin.

Her little speech in the Jaguar had been an attempt to hold onto her independence, her self-respect; and also to reinforce the lie she kept telling herself: that there was no room in her life for love, domesticity, or any of the boring things that went with them.

As she neared the car, Holly noticed something strange about it: the angle of the roof was wrong. She quickly walked around to the front nearside, and found the tyre was flat. Stooping down, she touched the rubber, pushed her fingers into the spongy wall.

'Shit,' she swore aloud. 'Bloody shit.'

It was then she heard breathing behind her and was turning when a blow caught her on the side of the head.

'Bitch.'

The word seemed to come from a great distance as Holly fought to stay this side of consciousness.

* * *

Josh looked at his watch. It was 10.45 p.m. and Karen Waters had not left her flat for two hours. Every so often he could see her silhouetted against the curtains as she moved about.

He started the car and drove to Fox's flat. When he saw the man's Escort parked outside, doubts started creeping into his mind as to whether Fox was, after all, the serial killer.

Seeing no need for further unpaid surveillance, Josh drove home. He parked with a feeling of disappointment on seeing that Holly's car was not in the drive, for he had a strong craving for company.

And he began to wonder if perhaps it might not be a bad idea to move back into his old digs; all of a sudden the thought of his landlady constantly fussing over him was extremely attractive.

* * *

The ringing of the telephone disturbed Ashworth's dream; its urgent insistence chasing away the image of him proudly holding the small screaming bundle of glowing pink miracle which his daughter had produced with her husband.

Naked, he climbed from the bed, switching on the lamp as he picked up the receiver.

'Hello?' he said; the recent deep sleep still in his voice.

As he listened, Ashworth came fully awake with a jolt. 'When?' he asked.

He listened again, with impatience. 'And which ward is she in?'

Jotting down 'Ecton' on a pad beside the telephone, he said, 'I'll be right there,' and rushed to get dressed.

The grey of dawn was shading the sky as Ashworth pulled into the hospital car park. And the air was cool and still as he made his way to the main entrance; his rugged, unshaven face carrying a worried expression.

He walked to the ward, the hospital odours powerful in his nostrils, his footfalls heavy in the early morning quiet.

Pushing through the swing doors he found his passage blocked by a diminutive night nurse obviously disturbed by his appearance, for his slightly tousled hair, yesterday's crumpled clothes lent him an unfriendly air.

'Yes?' she asked briskly.

'Chief Inspector Ashworth,' he announced. 'I believe DS Holly Bedford is in this ward.'

The woman relaxed as she scrutinized the photograph on his warrant card. 'Would you like to step into the office?' she asked in hushed tones. 'Most of our patients are still asleep.'

As he was ushered into a tiny room, Ashworth glanced at the name badge pinned to the woman's uniform, and said, 'What is DS Bedford's condition, Sister?'

'She's comfortable at the moment, and not in any immediate danger.'

He let out a relieved sigh. 'That's good. Have you any idea what happened to her?'

Ashworth towered over her in the confined space, and she craned her neck to look up at him, saying, 'As to how she sustained her injuries, no. All I can tell you is that she admitted herself last night, at eleven p.m. She had a wound to her right temple and had lost a considerable amount of blood.'

The sister indicated a chair, but Ashworth shook his head and continued standing.

She went on, 'The young woman was very weak and the doctor ordered a blood transfusion immediately. When she regained consciousness, she requested we contact a Joshua Abraham, explaining that this was a police matter. Mr Abraham is with her now. He asked us to call you.'

'Can I see her?'

The sister considered this.

'It is important,' Ashworth urged.

'Very well,' she said, 'but only for a few minutes. She's still in a very weak condition.'

Ashworth followed the sister through the packed wards. Beds were placed along two sides, and a row stood in the centre. Some patients were snoring, and there was a distinct smell of vomit in the air.

Holly's face was drawn; her pale complexion almost matched the white of her pillow. A tube from the plasma drip was inserted into her arm, and her forehead was concealed by a bandage. A worried Josh sat at the bedside.

'Holly,' Ashworth said softly.

She opened her eyes.

'Are you all right?'

'Yes.' She smiled bravely. 'I haven't had this much fun since my ingrowing toe-nail.'

'A few minutes,' the sister quietly cautioned. Ashworth nodded his agreement as she walked away.

He turned back to the bed. 'Can you tell me what happened, Holly?'

'I've told Josh, sir. Can he pass it on? I feel so sleepy.'

'Surely.' Ashworth touched her arm. 'We'll leave you to get some rest.'

Her eyes were already closed, sounds of the ward already becoming distant.

Ashworth looked across at Josh and gestured towards the door. As they left the ward, Ashworth bluntly asked, 'Well?'

'It's a bit tangled, guv. She's been drifting in and out of consciousness.'

'Just give me what you've got.'

Josh, irritable through lack of sleep, felt angered by the abrupt edge to Ashworth's voice, but remained pleasant as he said, 'Holly was returning to her car parked in Hanslope Lane, guv . . .'

'What was she doing in the middle of nowhere?' Ashworth asked as they headed for the stairs.

'It's a bit confidential, guv.'

'Don't give me confidential, Josh, one of my officers is down and I need to establish why as quickly as possible.'

'All right,' he said reluctantly, 'I believe Holly has formed some sort of relationship with a married man, and he dropped her off in Hanslope Lane.'

Ashworth's eyebrows were raised as he glanced at his constable.

'When she got back to the car,' Josh went on, 'it had a flat tyre. She was bending down to inspect it when someone hit her with what she believes was a hammer.'

Reaching the stairs which led to the ground floor, Ashworth prompted Josh to continue.

'Well, from what I can surmise, I think the blow must have all but knocked her out, and sheer instinct made her fight back. She landed several kicks on her assailant and believes one hit him in the face.' Josh turned to Ashworth. 'You know, guv, the judo stuff.'

'Yes.' Ashworth hated the over-use of words. 'Did she get a look at her attacker?'

'I don't think so. As I said, I think she was almost out, and probably half-blinded by blood.'

Josh, although young and reasonably fit was having difficulty in keeping up with his striding superior.

'So how did she get to the hospital?'

'She rested for a time, attempted to stem the flow of blood, then walked here.'

'Walked?' Ashworth sounded incredulous. 'It's over a mile.'

'I know, and she collapsed just as she made it to the hospital grounds.' He smiled. 'She keeps rambling on about her car and getting it safely back to the house.'

Ashworth shook his head as they walked across main reception. 'She's a plucky kid. We'd better get Forensic out there to have a look at it. Then, when they're done, we'll change the wheel and get it back to her house.'

An ambulance siren was blaring somewhere in the distance as they crossed the deserted car park.

Ashworth said, 'Right, we'll go back to my place for breakfast. I'll phone Uniformed from there, get them to stand guard over the car until the Forensic team can get there.'

Josh felt highly honoured by the invitation. 'Okay, guv,' he smiled.

Back in the ward, Holly, drifting in and out of drug-induced slumber, was wondering what the hospital staff must have thought when she was admitted with one vital piece of underwear missing.

CHAPTER 14

Gladys came awake with a start. Her aged body ached from sleeping in the rigid armchair.

Her husband, his face a deathly white, was lying in the bed, his frail form shaking beneath the covers.

'No . . . please,' he said pitifully. 'No more pain . . . I can't stand any more pain.'

Gladys pushed herself from the chair. 'It's all right, Cliff.'

As she leant over the bed, Gladys fancied she could smell the touch of death upon him. She poured water into a glass.

After mopping his fevered brow with a cool towel, she reached for the bottle of painkillers. His agonizing cries, his sobbing, made her stiff fingers fumble with the childproof top, but it finally sprang off and fell to the floor.

She looked again at her husband and shook two tablets out into her palm.

His earnest eyes pleaded with her.

She shook the bottle and more tablets tumbled out.

* * *

What Josh had not realized, when accepting Ashworth's invitation to breakfast, was that he would be acting as cook.

He expertly divided his attention between bacon sizzling under the grill, and eggs and mushrooms cooking in the large frying pan.

Ashworth filled the percolator and very soon the smell of fresh coffee mingled with the aromas from the food.

Fat spat in the pan and Ashworth eyed the food hungrily. 'How did last night's observation of Fox go?'

'Oh, I lost him, guv.' The business with Holly had driven everything from Josh's mind, and he had temporarily forgotten about Fox. 'I watched Karen Waters but he didn't go anywhere near her.'

'He could have attacked Holly though,' Ashworth surmised as the coffee machine gurgled.

'Yes, that's what I thought,' Josh said, dishing out the food. 'And I blame myself for that.'

'I don't follow.'

'If I hadn't been living at Holly's house, she could have taken her boyfriend back there.'

Josh turned off the gas beneath the frying pan, and Ashworth coughed lightly, saying, 'I usually have a slice of fried bread with mine.' Adding, 'Fairly well done, please,' as Josh delved into the bread bin.

Neither spoke again until the bread had been fried.

Ashworth poured coffee. 'You're being too hard on yourself, Josh.' He took his plate and cutlery over to the breakfast bar. 'If Holly was next on our man's list, it would have happened in any case.'

Josh joined him. 'Maybe,' he said dismally, pushing his food around the plate.

'Without a doubt,' Ashworth assured him. 'Now, if Holly landed a kick on her assailant's face, our man could be marked.'

'Yes, but like I say, Holly wasn't making a great deal of sense.'

'This looks good,' Ashworth said, loading his fork with egg, bacon and mushrooms. 'So, if we take a look at Fox today . . .'

'Will do, guv.' Josh sipped his coffee as he looked around the kitchen. 'This is a nice house.'

Ashworth merely grunted as he hungrily chased the food with his knife and fork.

'I'm thinking of buying a property . . . putting down some roots,' Josh said thoughtfully. 'But I couldn't afford anything like this.'

Ashworth pointed his fork at Josh's plate. 'You've hardly touched your breakfast.'

'Sorry, guv, I'm not very hungry.'

'Well, I'll have the bacon if you don't want it,' Ashworth said, shovelling it onto his own plate. 'Waste not; want not — that was my mother's maxim.'

He tucked in. 'With your salary you could get a mortgage on a starter-home, surely?'

'Yes,' Josh agreed, watching Ashworth and marvelling at his appetite.

'Right,' Ashworth said with an air of finality when he had finished. 'I'm going to shower and shave. Do you want to take a shower here?'

'No, thanks, guv, I'd better go home and change.' He stood up. 'What do you want me to do then?'

'Get a look at Fox, see if he's marked, then report back.'

'Right, guv, I'll see myself out.'

As the front door closed, Ashworth stared with distaste at the greasy plates and cooking utensils. He was not a man well-versed in domestic chores; and suddenly he remembered he had not telephoned Sarah to check on their daughter.

* * *

Josh drew an intriguing blank at the Department of Employment offices.

Gerald Fox, it appeared, was not at work and had reported in sick.

Armed with this knowledge, he returned to the station to find Ashworth slouched over his desk.

‘Fox isn’t at work, guv,’ Josh announced, taking off his bomber jacket and draping it over the back of his chair. ‘He rang in sick.’

‘Did he now?’ Ashworth sat back and smiled. ‘How very interesting. Maybe we should visit him in his sick-bed.’

‘We’ve still no reason to interview him formally though, have we, guv?’

‘If his face is marked we have,’ Ashworth stated jovially. Then, ‘Have you any idea who this married man is that Holly’s mixed up with?’

‘Guv . . .’ Josh looked sheepish.

‘It’s got to be addressed, Josh, unpleasant though it may be. And we also need to establish who else knew about it.’

‘Ask Holly, guv, everything I say is pure speculation.’

‘Right,’ Ashworth said briskly, ‘get your coat back on. Let’s go Fox hunting.’

* * *

When Mrs Fox opened the door, she felt that her worst nightmare was happening in her waking hours. For, in common with all who felt they had cause to fear the police, Mrs Fox could identify them easily, without the aid of uniform or introduction.

The shock of seeing them on her own doorstep caused her to push the door until it was all but closed.

‘Yes?’ she faltered, ‘What is it you want?’

‘We’d like to have a word with Mr Gerald Fox.’ Ashworth’s resonant voice filled the corridor as he took out his warrant card.

With horror, she read the details. ‘What you want with my boy?’

‘There’s nothing to alarm yourself about,’ Ashworth assured her, lowering his tone to a softer key. ‘I’m Chief Inspector Ashworth of Bridgetown CID . . .’

All at once the frightened Mrs Fox flung open the door and stood squarely in the doorway as if to deny them entry. ‘My son is not at home,’ she said firmly.

'We have contacted his place of work,' Josh said, 'and they told us he's off sick.'

The woman's eyes flitted between the two men. 'He has gone out. To the doctor maybe . . . I do not know.'

'May we come in and wait then?' Ashworth asked pleasantly.

'No,' she shrieked. 'In this country you cannot simply walk into people's homes.'

'You're quite correct, madam. We'll call back later then,' Ashworth said, quite fascinated by the woman's excited behaviour. 'Good morning.'

As they made their way back along the corridor, Josh said, 'The woman's terrified, guv. What do you think caused that?'

'It must have been you,' Ashworth smiled, 'because it certainly wasn't me.'

'Do we look for Fox?'

'Not much point . . . he's in the flat.' Ashworth looked back. 'We'll pay another visit later.'

'You're in a good mood, guv,' Josh observed as they left the building.

'I've had some good news about my daughter,' he beamed, 'and I'm beginning to think you're right about Fox, so I've every reason to be.'

* * *

Despite two further visits to the flat that morning, they were no nearer establishing the whereabouts of Gerald Fox. And on both occasions the behaviour of his mother bordered on the hysterical.

In the afternoon, Ashworth visited Holly and was glad to find her in far better condition than during the early hours.

The first thirty minutes were like any ordinary hospital visit: their conversation was general, stilted; Ashworth frequently consulted his wristwatch; and Holly willed the bell to signal the end of visiting.

But Ashworth was also there on official business, and with the formal pleasantries out of the way, he rather awkwardly launched into the real reason for his visit.

'Holly,' he said quietly, 'there are some questions I need to ask you.'

Her face was downcast as she stared at the sheet. 'I know, sir.'

Putting on a brave face, she went on, 'I'd been out for a drink with a friend who happens to be a married man. He dropped me off in Hanslope Lane, where my car was parked. I'd left it there—'

'That's not what I'm interested in, Holly,' Ashworth quickly stated. 'Was this the first time you'd been out with your friend?'

'No, sir, I spent some time with him the evening before' — her formal tone would have seemed more fitting in the witness box — 'but on that occasion it was business rather than pleasure.'

'Holly . . .' Ashworth shifted his feet. 'I'm finding this as difficult as you are.'

Holly looked directly at him for the first time. 'Will he have to be interviewed, sir?'

Ashworth shook his head. 'At the moment, no. Did anyone else know about this association?'

'I hope not,' Holly said miserably, looking away.

'No one saw you at the pub, for instance?'

'Well, of course there were other people there.'

Ashworth sighed deeply; this wasn't getting them anywhere.

'There was Dr Anthony. The male one.'

'He was in the pub?' Ashworth asked quickly.

'No, this was the evening before. We were parked in a lay-by . . .' A vivid crimson crept into Holly's cheeks.

'And you're certain Anthony saw you?'

'Yes, because he sounded his horn and slowed down as he went past. Gary told me he's one of his customers.'

'Interesting,' Ashworth remarked. 'But to your knowledge Fox didn't see you at any time, in the pub or outside.'

'No, if he'd been in the pub, I'd have recognized him.'

'And you didn't recognize the man who attacked you?'

'Like I said, sir, I was out really.'

'But you did land some kicks on him?'

'Well, he left me alone, so I must have done.'

'If you were out on your feet, how can you remember?'

'It's the martial arts training, sir . . . set pieces, and all that. A kick for the stomach or an even more sensitive area, then when the head comes forward, a follow-up kick to that.'

'But how can you be sure that's what happened?'

'My foot hurts, sir.'

Ashworth laughed. 'Well detected.'

Holly turned to him; a wretched look on her face. 'Sir . . .' She hesitated. 'I take it this will be treated in strictest confidence . . . what I was doing, I mean.'

'Holly, your personal and private life is no concern of mine,' he said. Adding heavily, 'And I hope you'll view mine in the same light.'

Holly flushed again, recognizing this as a direct reference to the gossip she had entered into about her superior and Gwen Anthony. Ashworth truly was a man who missed little of what went on around him.

'Thank you, sir,' Holly said with a grateful smile.

'Now, how long are you in here for?'

Holly, welcoming the change in subject, said brightly, 'Only for today, I think, just to make sure I'm all right. So I could be back at the station tomorrow.'

'No, no,' Ashworth said, shaking his head wildly, 'that's far too early. Make a full recovery first.' But his tone held the lack of conviction of a short-staffed senior officer.

The bell rang to announce the end of visiting. Immediately, Ashworth stood up.

'Thank you for coming in to see me, sir.'

Ashworth surprised her by leaning over the bed and kissing her lightly on the cheek. 'One of these days you will call me Jim or guv,' he smiled.

Holly smiled back but said nothing, and Ashworth, joining the departing visitors, made his way out of the ward.

* * *

For a few seconds, Ashworth delayed knocking on the door then, making a face at Josh, his knuckles wrapped sharply on the wood. His need to speak to Gerald Fox was now urgent, but he still did not relish another scene with the mother.

As if expecting their return, Mrs Fox opened the door no more than a fraction. 'What is it you want?'

'Sorry to bother you again, Mrs Fox . . .' Ashworth began.

'My son is not at home. I keep telling you.'

'We need to speak to him. Could you please inform us of his whereabouts?' Ashworth insisted.

Mrs Fox fluttered behind the door. 'I do not know. You must go away before I call the police.'

'But we are the police,' Ashworth said with little patience. 'Mrs Fox, we need to find your son.'

The door was closed in their faces.

Ashworth raised his hand to knock again, but then thought better of it. Opening up the letter-box, he shouted, 'Mrs Fox,' but there was no response. He turned to Josh and shrugged.

Mrs Fox stood with her back to the wall, holding her breath, listening for sounds from the corridor. When she heard their departing footsteps, she exhaled, but was still unable to relax.

The silence in the flat was oppressive, broken only by the insistent buzzing of a bluebottle against the windows as it sought escape.

She opened a door to one of the bedrooms. 'Why do the police keep coming here?'

'I've told you, mother,' Fox said, 'they're saying I did something . . . telling lies.'

'And did they really do that to your face?'

'Yes, mother, I told you. They beat me up.'

'My God. Please, my God,' Mrs Fox chanted.

Her son's voice rose above the anguished sound. 'You've got to help me, mother. I need to get away for a few days.'

* * *

Ashworth was having difficulty in relaxing. His daughter's labour pains had once again subsided, and he was beginning to wonder how a process which had existed since time began, could sometimes be so fraught with complications.

Over the last few days, he had taken to spending most of the evening on the stairs, sitting in the dark, wanting to be as close to the telephone as possible.

The time was 9.40 p.m. and, as habit dictated, the first glass of malt whisky and soda was in his hand. Resting an elbow on the stair behind him, Ashworth leant back.

An all-station alert was out for Fox, and short of applying for a warrant to search the man's flat — which he would not get anyway — there was little else he could do.

He sipped his drink; it was one of the few pleasures in his life which had neither diminished nor dimmed.

Then he heard the sound of a vehicle turning into the drive, its headlights illuminating the hall through a glass panel set in the front door.

Intrigued, Ashworth put his glass down beside the telephone and opened the door. Gwen Anthony, her shoes crunching on the gravel, came hurrying towards him.

'Sorry to disturb you, Jim.'

'Gwen . . .'

He was indeed disturbed to see her at his home, and glanced around, making sure her arrival had not been witnessed.

'I needed to see you, Jim. It's very important.' Her voice was strange, the words clipped.

'You'd better come in then,' he said, with barely hidden reluctance.

When Ashworth flicked on the hall light, he saw immediately a marked change in her face. Tiny pain lines distorted her mouth, the flesh beneath her eyes was discoloured and swollen.

Struggling to keep her voice normal, Gwen asked, 'How have you been?'

She began to cry as soon as the door was closed.

'Gwen, whatever's wrong?' Ashworth's obvious concern was not reflected in his rather clumsy movements as he reached out to hold her.

Gwen clung to him, deep sobs racking her body. 'He raped me,' she whispered.

Ashworth held her at arm's length. 'Who did, Gwen? Your husband?'

She nodded, unable to speak.

'When?' The question was terse.

'Last night,' she sobbed. 'I've left him . . . I went back to the cottage for some things and he was waiting.'

She cast a desperate look at Ashworth. 'He hurt me, Jim . . . really hurt me.'

'Right, that's it,' Ashworth said, breaking away to grab his jacket from the rail.

'What are you going to do?' Gwen asked anxiously.

'What I should have done when this business started,' Ashworth said angrily. 'I'm going to settle this man-to-man.'

Gwen uttered a cry of distress. 'No, Jim, no,' she said, 'that can only make matters worse.'

Her tenuous grip on his arm did little to restrain him; and with all the grace of an enraged bull elephant, Ashworth struggled into his jacket.

'I think he killed those women,' Gwen said quietly.

Ashworth stopped in his tracks. 'My God, Gwen, I thought I was the only one to have suspicions in that direction.'

Wiping the tears away from her frightened eyes, Gwen said, 'I really think it's possible, Jim.'

'Right. Lounge,' Ashworth commanded, grabbing her arm and marching her out of the hall.

'Sit down and I'll get you a drink.'

'I'm driving,' she said as he placed her in an armchair.

Gwen looked around, realizing she was invading the home of a woman whose husband she had not only coveted, but had managed to steal for one brief, fleeting moment.

'It's whisky,' Ashworth said in the curt manner he always adopted in an emergency. 'And don't worry about the Land Rover, you can take a taxi.'

He passed her the drink. 'Here, you need this.'

Gratefully, Gwen gulped down half of it. 'I don't know what's gone wrong with my life, Jim.'

Ashworth settled on the sofa and gazed at her with a feeling of sadness. He let her finish the scotch, then asked, 'What makes you think he murdered those women?'

Gwen took a tissue from her pocket and blew her nose. 'Remember the night you went to see him in the Bull and Butcher? Remember he came home covered in mud, said he'd fallen over?'

Ashworth nodded grimly; this was just reinforcing the thought that had struck him at the time.

'That was the night the second woman was murdered.'

'Yes, but that doesn't prove anything, Gwen.'

Ashworth still did not want to accept that any of this could be possible.

Gwen disagreed. 'His mind's gone. Sometimes he's like a lunatic. Last night, when he . . .' She could not say the words a second time. 'His hands were round my throat, he was calling me a cheating cow, threatening to kill me . . . and I thought he would.'

She began to sob again, but swallowed hard and brought herself under control. 'Both women were committing adultery, weren't they? His mind's gone, Jim. He killed those women because in his sick mind he was getting back at us.'

Anthony's words from the past echoed in Ashworth's mind: At home . . . and in your job. He mentally pushed them away.

'There was another attack last night,' he said. 'Holly Bedford — but she fought the man off. It seems likely that she marked his face, so if your husband's face is bruised—'

'No good, Jim, the night before I left, we had a fight and, believe me, after that he was certainly marked.'

Ashworth suddenly felt very hot. He slipped out of his jacket, leaving it on the sofa behind him.

'If you're right, Gwen, even if we catch him, he'll have won, because when all this comes out at the trial, it'll destroy my marriage and my job.'

'And that, in his deranged state of mind, is what he wants,' Gwen said miserably.

Appearing much calmer now, she asked, 'Where does Holly Bedford fit into this? Is she having an affair?'

'I believe so.'

'Really?' Gwen said tartly, remembering Holly's holier-than-thou attitude towards her.

'We've still got a chance though,' Ashworth said, reassuring himself, rather than Gwen. 'There's someone else in the frame, and he's dropped out of sight.'

'What can you do about Nigel?'

'Nothing, officially,' he said lamely. 'I'll just have to keep my eye on him. Where are you staying?'

'The Mount View Hotel, at the moment, but Nigel's frozen all the bank accounts so I won't be for much longer. I've some money of my own but . . . oh, what the hell, let the solicitors sort it out.'

Gwen stood up with obvious difficulty. 'Sorry to dump all this in your lap, Jim.'

'You haven't.' He sighed heavily. 'I've been thinking along the same lines for some time now.' He rose to his feet. 'We've got ourselves into a fine old mess one way or another, haven't we?'

'Haven't we just? For the first time in my life I wish I'd had it stitched up before puberty.'

She smiled weakly, but Ashworth did not feel like laughing.

'Are you all right to drive?'

'Of course, I've only had the one drink.' She lingered by the lounge door. 'You'll be in touch?'

'I shall have to be, Gwen.'

He let her out, watched her walk towards the Land Rover, and for the first time the sight of her body, its sway, its movements, did not kindle any sexual desire within him.

As Ashworth closed the door, the telephone rang. He snatched up the receiver. 'Ashworth.'

It was Sarah; she was crying. 'Jim, Samantha's taken a turn for the worse.'

'Oh, God,' he moaned, feeling the pressure building inside his head.

* * *

The baby it seemed, with typical Ashworth stubbornness, was refusing to turn in the womb and engage itself; added to which, Samantha had developed a fever.

As the next day was Saturday, Ashworth confidently expected to be able to dash to his daughter's bedside. Even officers involved in double-murder cases could expect some free time. But it was not to be.

After a sleepless night, Ashworth received an early call from the station. Bobby Adams was the disrupting messenger; and even on the end of the telephone, his nervousness was apparent.

'Sorry to disturb you, Chief Inspector,' he stuttered, 'but there's been another attack on a woman. I wasn't sure if this was something that would need your attention—'

'Of course it needs my attention, man,' Ashworth barked, 'and stop going all round the houses . . . just get to the point.'

'Sorry, sir.'

The young officer's nervous stammer, which had fast disappeared as his confidence grew, now crept back into his voice.

He took a deep breath and said, 'The woman was attacked last night, sir, on the Barr Nature Reserve. She's in hospital at the moment, in a critical condition.'

'Thank you.' Ashworth's voice was ice. 'I'll come straight away.'

After breaking the news to Sarah, he started out for the station, managing to keep his temper in check on roads crowded with Saturday shoppers, but muttering more than a few oaths when the Sierra was caught in a traffic jam by the road works outside the station.

As he walked in, Ashworth relented slightly at the sight of Bobby Adams manning reception. His eager face beneath greased-down hair had a couple of razor nicks, suggesting he had not yet fully mastered the art of shaving.

The young constable, half expecting the earlier tirade to continue, stood rigid.

Ashworth leant on the desk and gave him a smile. 'Bobby, I'm sorry about earlier,' he said. 'I was worried about my daughter and I had no right to take it out on you.'

Bobby, relaxing a little, managed to ask, 'How is she, sir?'

'It's a bit complicated,' Ashworth replied, not wishing to go into details.

'I hope everything goes well, sir,' Bobby said with absolute sincerity.

Ashworth patted his shoulder. 'Good man,' he said, then walked off.

* * *

Gladys Smart digested the doctor's words as she studied his battered face.

'But he don't want to go into hospital,' she declared, with as much firmness as she could muster. 'He wants to die at home.'

Anthony merely shrugged. 'Well, it's up to you. He's in the latter stages and this chest infection is a bad one.'

He followed her down the creaking stairs. At the bottom, Gladys asked with dread, 'How long, doctor?'

'Three days at the most,' he replied, heading for the front door. 'I just want you to realize he's dying; and I want you to decide whether you can cope with that, or whether you want me to get him into hospital.'

'No, no,' Gladys insisted, 'I promised him.'

'All right, all right,' Anthony humoured, 'don't upset yourself.'

'The pain's terrible for him now, doctor. Every time he coughs, he screams with the agony of it,' she quaked. 'He keeps begging me to give him the bottle of painkillers so he can be out of it. I don't know what to do . . .' Her voice broke and she quickly brought a hand to her mouth, but her eyes spoke volumes.

Anthony looked down on her kindly. 'I know, and I shouldn't be telling you this but I'm not totally against that sort of thing.'

'It seems pointless prolonging his life like this.'

'I agree, but there's nothing I can do about it. I have to preserve life while it's there.'

'I know, doctor.'

Anthony opened the door, and paused. 'You'd be surprised how often it does happen though. A patient with so little time to live . . . well, no doctor I know would order a post-mortem in those circumstances. There'd be no point.'

He let himself out, and Gladys called after him, 'Thank you, doctor.'

CHAPTER 15

Josh glanced up from the computer as Ashworth strode in; and he could tell by his superior's expression that pleasantries were not on the agenda.

'I've got some good news, guv,' he ventured.

Ashworth did not sit down, but chose to stand in the centre of the office.

'Close that window,' he ordered abruptly. 'I can't hear myself think.'

As Josh complied, Ashworth said, 'What is it then?'

With the sounds from outside now less deafening, Josh picked up his notepad. 'The Bradford police have detained Fox, and the encouraging thing is, he's got a black eye.'

Ashworth visibly brightened at the news. 'Has he now? Are they sending him down?'

'Yes, guv, he should be here early afternoon.' Josh studied his notes. 'The attack on the Barr Nature Reserve,' he continued, 'was carried out late last night. The victim's a young girl, but we don't know her identity yet. She's badly injured . . . in a coma. They've got her on a life-support machine.' He looked up. 'Her assailant was disturbed by a man named Brian Frederick; that's the Neighbourhood Watch bloke everybody's calling Vigilante Man.'

'What do you mean, everybody?'

'Everybody at the nick, guv,' Josh answered evenly. 'I've been to see Frederick, but he wasn't much help. At eleven last night he heard screaming on the nature reserve so he grabbed a walking stick and went to investigate. He was about a hundred yards in when he saw a man kicking the girl as she lay on the ground. Frederick made a lot of noise, shouting and yelling, and the man ran off. No description of him, I'm afraid.'

Ashworth brooded for a moment. 'Like you said, it's not much help.'

'Holly's still in hospital, guv, but she should be out later today.'

'Good,' he replied vaguely.

* * *

Ashworth was in interview room number 1, waiting for Fox to be brought in. As he sat, the building pressure was causing his upper back and neck to ache with tension; and a dull throb behind his eyes promised to escalate into a thumping headache in due course.

The door finally opened and Josh showed Gerald Fox into the room.

The Chief Inspector's first impressions were vitally important to him; and as Fox sauntered in Ashworth saw that he could well be the man they were looking for. Small, slight, with an effeminate air about him, Fox appeared timid, harmless, but for a second, Ashworth caught the flash of cunning in his brown eyes.

'Gerald Fox, guv,' Josh announced.

'Mr Fox, I'm Chief Inspector Ashworth. Would you like to sit down, please?'

'What the hell am I doing here?' Fox demanded, his normally quiet voice now shrill, lending a young girl's pitch to his words.

'Helping us with our enquiries,' Ashworth told him flatly. 'Now, sit down, please.' He pointed to the chair.

For a few moments it looked as if Fox would not yield but then, under Ashworth's baleful glare, he walked around the table.

'You've been harassing my mother,' he said as he sat down.

'We've done no such thing,' Ashworth countered. 'We visited your mother only to establish your whereabouts.'

'She's frightened of the police. You terrified her.'

'Make a complaint then,' Ashworth said, tiring of the way in which the discussion was proceeding. 'Now, Mr Fox, we're looking into the murders of two women, and vicious attacks on two more.'

'What's that got to do with me?' Fox asked sullenly.

'We think you may be able to help with a number of matters.'

'You've been harassing my mother, and now you're trying to frighten me.'

Ashworth, barely managing to keep a hold of his temper, said, 'Mr Fox, I have neither the time nor the inclination to be polite about this. You, through your work, had a very thorough knowledge of the movements of the two murder victims, and in the third attack the woman fought back, marking her attacker . . .' Ashworth stabbed out his finger. 'And your face is marked, Mr Fox.'

'I've a perfectly reasonable explanation for that,' Fox stated coolly.

Ashworth leant across the table. 'Then give it to me.'

'I got into a fight in a pub . . . well, outside it, actually.'

'Which pub?' Ashworth snapped.

'The Princess Alexander.'

'We can check that.'

'Check away.' Fox showed his uneven yellow teeth as he smiled.

'Right, when?'

'Thursday evening.'

Ashworth looked across at Josh standing by the door. 'At what time was this?'

'I don't remember, but the police were called,' Fox answered glibly.

'You were seen by the police?'

'No, I wasn't. By the time they arrived, I'd gone.'

'So, you were assaulted and yet you left before the police got there?' Ashworth sounded sceptical.

'Yes, it's called queer-bashing and your lot aren't very sympathetic about it. You always seem to believe we tried to touch somebody up and they took exception to it.' Fox's eyes were laughing at Ashworth.

'I'm far from happy with your answers,' Ashworth said bluntly.

'Tough shit,' Fox said, very slowly and very clearly. 'How long are you planning to hold me here?'

'Some time yet,' Ashworth said firmly. 'When did you go to Bradford?'

'I've been through all this.'

'Go through it again,' Ashworth insisted with some vigour.

Fox sighed, took on a bored expression. 'I went Friday morning to stay over the weekend with a friend . . . a male friend I haven't seen since I came here. Get the picture? It's all been verified.'

Ashworth glanced at Josh who nodded to affirm this was so.

Ashworth left his seat, began pacing the room. 'Right, Mr Fox,' he said gruffly, 'I'll tell you what I'm going to do. Firstly, I shall check out your story about the fight outside the pub. If I can't establish beyond doubt that you were there, I shall apply for a warrant to search your flat.'

He noted that Fox's expression had changed from insolence to one of concern.

'I don't want you frightening my mother,' he flared.

Ashworth, sensing he had touched a raw nerve, could not hide a slight grin. 'Your mother has nothing to be frightened about. You're entitled to have a solicitor present, if you choose.'

'She doesn't enjoy the best of health . . .'

Ashworth stopped pacing. 'I'd say you don't want us to see your mother because you're frightened of what she might tell us about you.'

'Look, you can do what you want to me,' Fox said, clearly disturbed, 'but just leave my mother out of it.'

Ashworth, feeling the tide had turned in his favour, strolled back to the table and leant forward menacingly. 'That's just what I'm not going to do, Mr Fox. I'm going to dig up everything I possibly can about you, from any source.' He straightened up. 'Now you're perfectly free to leave. So go home and think things over.'

Fox got to his feet and sullenly walked to the door, ignoring Josh's offer to escort him to front reception.

'Temper, temper,' Ashworth chuckled as the door slammed behind him.

'You were a bit hard on him, guv,' Josh remarked.

'He's our man,' Ashworth said, as if that explained his behaviour. 'We'll look into the pub story and take it from there.'

'The pub will need careful handling,' Josh pointed out.

'Then that's what we'll apply to it.' Ashworth glared at him. 'Have you got a problem, Josh?'

'It's a gay pub, sir. Neither the staff nor the patrons are known for their willingness to cooperate with the police. A lot of our lads on the beat aren't exactly paragons of understanding when they go in there.' He paused, then added diplomatically, 'It'll need a lot of tact.'

Ashworth took this as a personal affront. 'Are you suggesting I don't possess tact?'

'Yes, guv, in some circumstances you can be a bit blunt.'

Ashworth's reaction surprised Josh: he laughed.

'I see, so you want me to let you do the talking?'

'Yes, guv.'

'All right, you speak their language, so it might be for the best.'

Josh smiled inwardly, feeling his remark about lack of tact had just been strenuously endorsed.

* * *

Gladys Smart's feet seemed to weigh a ton, and her legs ached as she climbed the stairs. Breathing heavily by the time she reached the top, Gladys clung to the bannisters until her chest pain subsided and her breathing returned to normal.

For quite a few days now she had dreaded opening the bedroom door, fearful that she would find her husband in his death throes.

She could hear his feeble cries of suffering as she felt for the door handle. Its metal was cold to the touch and she caught her breath as the dry ill-fitting hinges screamed in protest when the door swung open.

Cliff was lying on his back, his gaunt face contorted with pain; and his eyes, all but vanished in their sockets, glowed with the fire of delirium.

'The doctor's on his way, Cliff,' Gladys said.

'Please, Gladys, the tablets . . . give me the lot,' he implored. 'Please put me out of this misery.'

He urinated, and as Gladys watched the dark stain spread across the bedclothes, he murmured, 'Please, Gladys, please.'

With her vision impaired by tears, Gladys reached for the bottle and shook it.

It was half full.

* * *

For the first time in her life Holly felt totally alone. Watching the visitors at other beds, catching their animated conversation, she felt pangs of isolation. To have had a relative there who annoyed her, who brought forth strong feelings of hatred, would have been far better than the loneliness which engulfed her.

Holly was to be discharged later that afternoon and, as the hospital buzzed with news that another woman had been attacked, she was eager to return to the station. The 'Adultery Murders' as the press were dubbing them, had taken on an acutely personal flavour for Holly, and she regarded the task of getting the perpetrator behind bars as an urgent priority.

It was then she spotted Gary Williams's handsome face as he entered the ward. Looking rather furtive, he paid careful attention to both visitors and patients as he strolled to Holly's bed.

Hurriedly running fingers through her hair, hoping it would fall into some sort of style, Holly wished she had put on her make-up.

Gary, satisfied that no one in the ward would recognize him, approached the bed with confidence.

'Hi,' he said, smiling.

Holly, extremely conscious of the dressing above her eye, her general appearance, felt ill at ease. 'What are you doing here?' she asked awkwardly.

'I came to see you,' he grinned. 'It's all over the papers . . . and I had just dropped you off, remember.'

'Oh, that's it is it?' she quietly retorted. 'Well, don't worry, your wife won't find out about us. Mind you, she would have done if I'd been murdered.'

'Holly . . . oh, this is all going wrong.' He pulled up a chair and sat by the bed. 'I told you the truth about my wife — we don't get on. But my kid's another matter.'

Holly studied his hurt expression and softened a little. 'I'm sorry, Gary, lying here doesn't do a girl's confidence any good.'

He reached for her hand. 'I'll see you when you get out, won't I?'

'Are you sure you want to? God knows, I wasn't a pretty sight before I got my face smashed in, but now . . .'

'Don't say things like that—'

'I'm not going to kid myself, Gary, I know you're only after one thing.'

'Oh, is that right? Okay, I know you won't believe I'm attracted—'

'Attracted to my what though?'

'Now come on, Holly,' he protested. 'At the time you weren't exactly reticent. I'll be polite and say I didn't have to talk you into it.'

As their whispered argument became louder, heads turned as patients and visitors alike regarded them with varying degrees of curiosity.

'All right, point taken,' Holly said, keeping her voice down. 'But I just don't want you thinking you're stringing me along.'

'I never thought I was,' Gary said, offended.

Holly turned away, was quiet for a moment, then said, 'Have you thought of anywhere we can go when I get out?'

'No, I haven't. How about your place?'

'There's Josh.'

'Josh? That's your boyfriend's name, is it?'

'He's not my boyfriend,' she insisted hotly. 'He happens to be gay, if you must know. He's just staying with me till he gets somewhere to live.'

'Can't you just ask him to move out?' Gary pushed.

'Oh, yes, great,' Holly flared, 'I'll be on my own most of the time then, won't I?' She glared at him. 'Don't forget, I was nearly topped because I was having it off with you.'

'Sorry,' he said. Then, after a while, 'This was a mistake, wasn't it?'

Holly sighed, and hit out at the sheets with frustration. 'No, it wasn't, it's just . . . Look, I'll ask Josh to go out a couple of evenings so we can be alone. Okay?'

'Okay.' He smiled. 'I'd better be going. I'll ring you when you get home.'

He leant across and planted a self-conscious kiss on her cheek.

'All right. Thanks for coming.'

As she watched until he was out of sight, Holly congratulated herself for not asking when she would be seeing him again — at least she had held onto her self-respect. But why had she reacted so violently?

You'll have to alter you attitude, she silently admonished, or this affair will be over before it's started.

CHAPTER 16

Ashworth did not feel comfortable around homosexuals. Although a broad-minded man, his moral values remained rooted in the 1950s and '60s. Even what they called their 'normal practices', he viewed with a certain degree of disdain; and the more perverse acts in their repertoire were completely beyond his comprehension.

Once, while watching a television programme on the subject, Ashworth had stared in disbelief as a man described how sexual gratification could be dramatically enhanced when dangling from the ceiling by a piece of flex around the neck.

He had turned in all innocence to Sarah, and asked, 'What's your neck got to do with it?'

So he was most definitely not at ease in the Princess Alexander where he mingled uncomfortably with the early afternoon drinkers.

'Would you like a drink, guv, while we're here?' Josh asked, trying to catch the barman's eye.

'No, let's just make our enquiries and get back to the station,' Ashworth replied gruffly as he glanced around the room.

He had not known what to expect, and found it reassuring that most of the men in the bar appeared outwardly normal.

The barman, however, proved to be an exception. His long hair was streaked with blond highlights and his pink jacket and floral trousers did little to disguise his campness.

'Yes, dearie?' he said to Josh.

'Bridgetown nick,' Josh stated briskly.

The barman gave a falsetto laugh. 'Never mind, dear, someone's got to do the job.'

'Very droll,' Josh smiled. 'Listen, we don't want any bother, we're just making a few discreet enquiries. Did you have a fracas in here on Thursday evening?'

'I'd have one any evening, anywhere, if it was on offer.' The high-pitched laugh came again. He touched Josh's arm. 'You'll have to forgive me . . . it's the mood I'm in.'

Ashworth glowered at the man. 'Sir . . .' he began. But Josh gave him a pleading look and he turned away, stood with his back to the bar.

'Isn't your friend butch?' the barman remarked.

'Thursday,' Josh prompted.

'Thursday, Thursday, Thursday . . . let me see.' He ran his fingers through his hair. 'I think there was a disturbance in the car park. Yes, that's right, but it wasn't much . . . as the MP said to his boyfriend.'

The man's laugh was beginning to grate on Ashworth's nerves, but he managed to stay silent.

'Did anyone witness it?' Josh asked.

'No, and if they had, none of our lot would mention it. The police came. The residents over the road called them.' He made a face. 'Right meanies, they are. But nobody was interviewed.'

'Thanks,' Josh said, 'you've been a great help.'

'When I'm on duty I'm helpful . . . when I'm not, I really start cooperating.' He winked. 'Keep that in mind, cheeky face.'

'I will,' Josh grinned, 'and thanks again.'

'Come on, Josh, let's get out,' Ashworth ordered.

Outside, in warm sunshine, on a pavement crowded with shoppers, Ashworth said, 'We've nearly got him, Josh.

The fight in the car park must have been a Godsend to him, gave him a perfect excuse for that black eye.'

They reached the Sierra and climbed in. 'How do we get anything on Fox though?' Josh asked, feeling for his seat-belt.

'His mother,' Ashworth declared confidently. 'If I can build up some kind of rapport with her, I think we might just find out a lot about that evil little son of hers.'

Josh snorted. 'If you can start up a rapport with her, you might just get the Nobel Peace Prize. She's running scared of us.'

'Wait till the old Ashworth charm starts to work on her,' he said. 'She'll be butter in my hands.'

'You're certain it's him then, guv?'

'Stake my pension on it.'

As they drove back to the station Ashworth whistled constantly, and Josh could only speculate as to what had caused his chief inspector's sudden buoyant mood.

* * *

For better or for worse . . . those were the words that kept running through Gladys Smart's mind as she viewed her husband for the last time.

As Nigel Anthony pulled the sheet up over his face, she felt a sense of loss which struck her very soul; but at the same time the blessed numbness of shock spread through her.

'Thank God he slipped away peacefully,' she said to herself rather than to Anthony. 'I suppose I'd better ring the undertaker.'

'Don't do that yet,' Anthony said quickly. 'I'll arrange for him to be taken to the mortuary. It'll be less distressing for you. Make the arrangements tomorrow.'

Gladys smiled gratefully. 'Thank you, doctor.'

'Now, I'm going to give you something to help you sleep.'

'No, I'll be all right,' she said adamantly. 'I just want to sit and think. There are a lot of memories . . .'

'I don't think that would be wise, do you?' Anthony said gently. 'Come downstairs with me and I'll arrange everything by telephone. Then I'll give you some tablets to make sure you get some rest.'

They left the room which smelt of death and excreta, and Anthony escorted Gladys down to the front room where he switched on the gas fire, even though the evening was warm.

He used the telephone in the hall to ring the hospital. And as they waited for the body to be taken away, Gladys became distressed, imagined she could hear her husband calling from the bedroom.

Applying his best bedside manner, Anthony calmed her and, once again, settled her in front of the fire.

He telephoned the son, broke the news of his father's death, and practically ordered the man in a very forthright manner to come to the house at once and look after the woman who had raised him.

Half an hour later, all matters had been attended to, and Anthony left the house.

He had acted out of concern for Gladys Smart; he wanted her to remain very much alive, very much in good health.

For her role was vital in the final humiliation of Chief Inspector Jim Ashworth.

* * *

When they arrived back at the station, they found Holly sitting at her desk.

'What are you doing here?' Ashworth exclaimed.

Holly grinned. 'Welcome back. Nice to see you, Holly. Have you made a full recovery?' she said sarcastically.

'You know what I mean,' Ashworth said with a guilty look. 'You're just out of hospital, you shouldn't be back at work yet.'

'I'd rather be here than at home by myself, sir.'

'All right,' Ashworth said, 'but it's desk duties for you. Is that understood?'

'Yes, sir.'

Ashworth eased into his chair. 'Now, before we update you on what's been happening, I want you to go back to when you were attacked. Can you remember anything, however insignificant?'

Holly fingered the dressing above her eye. 'I've been racking my brains about it. There's something, but I just can't get it. I think it's something to do with smell.'

'I'm not following you,' Ashworth said, interested but confused.

'Well, after the blow on the head, it was as if I wasn't really there; but the more I think about it, the more something tries to come into focus. I remember just after I bent down to look at the tyre, there was this breathing sound.'

'Asthmatic?' Ashworth prompted. 'Bronchial?'

'No, it was more like sexual excitement.'

Ashworth turned to Josh, and asked with typical insensitivity, 'Is that possible . . . I mean, with Fox in mind? Could men of your persuasion get severely aroused by an act of violence?'

Josh was perched on the corner of his desk beside the VDU. He smiled and pleasantly replied, 'Oh yes, guv. They're no different from heterosexuals in that respect. Whoever's committing these crimes could well go home to his partner with a strong sexual charge.'

'I see,' Ashworth mused. 'We live and learn.'

He focused on Holly once more. 'Can you remember anything else?'

'No, sir, as I said, something's there but I can't quite touch it. The smell reminded me of something I'd done recently, or somewhere I'd been, but total recall's not there.'

'Keep working on it,' Ashworth grunted.

'Do you think it's Fox, sir?' Holly asked.

'It's Fox,' Ashworth declared in a way that did not invite debate.

'I agree with you,' Josh said, 'but we've still got a lot of loose ends to tie up. And the man's clever; he's carried out four attacks and hasn't left one thing behind to connect him with them.'

Ashworth's brow wrinkled. 'Clever or lucky,' he said. 'Now, he told us he went to Bradford on Friday morning, and there was another attack here Friday night, so that's something we need to address. Does his story stand up, Josh?'

'Not really, guv. He told the Bradford police he travelled up on a single ticket—'

Ashworth caught on quickly and said, 'But if he knew he'd be coming back on Monday, why didn't he get a return?'

'Exactly. And the friend he was staying with substantiates his story, but what's that worth?'

'Nothing,' Ashworth said.

He noted Holly's puzzled expression and quickly brought her up to date with Fox's movements.

She said, 'If the two of you are right, I think you're going to have a job proving it.'

'I am going—'

'No, let me finish, sir,' she interrupted. 'I know you want me confined to desk duties, but let me see Fox. If he did this' — she touched the dressing — 'I'll know.'

'Holly . . .' Ashworth sounded doubtful. 'Are you sure this isn't becoming personal?'

'That bastard made me need stitches, sir . . . you can bet it's personal.'

Ashworth was not keen on the use of bad language but, such was the passion in Holly's voice, he made no comment.

'And if he's not stopped,' Holly went on, 'he's going to do it again. There's a woman out there—'

'All right,' Ashworth said, holding up his hand, 'there's no need to oversell your case. When we go to see him, you can come along.'

They were interrupted by the bustling entrance of Ken Savage.

'We've got a nasty one, Jim,' he said sharply. 'Euthanasia. A seventy-six-year-old woman whose husband was terminally ill. The poor devil only had hours to live, was in agony, and it seems she may just have given him enough painkillers to put him out of his misery.'

'How the hell did this come in?' Ashworth snapped.

'I know what you're thinking,' Savage said, raising his voice. 'We all feel the same about it, I'm sure, but Dr Anthony reported it to us, so we've got to investigate it.'

His gaze took in the two young detectives. 'I'm sure I don't have to remind you that euthanasia contravenes the law, so however we feel about this case we play it by the book . . . to the letter. Is that understood?'

'I think you've made yourself plain, Ken,' Ashworth said evenly. 'I take it this is the male doctor?'

Savage nodded.

'And what's he saying?'

'Just that the woman told him she was going to do it. He thought he'd talked her out of it, but when the man died he felt he couldn't sign the death certificate until a post-mortem had been performed. There were enough drugs inside him to kill a team of dray horses.'

'Couldn't the man have taken them himself?' Holly asked.

'I don't know,' Savage replied briskly. 'All I do know is Dr Anthony's downstairs waiting to make a statement.'

Ashworth was adamant. 'We'll take the statement, Ken, but this goes on the back burner.'

'We have a duty, Jim,' Savage warned.

'To protect the public.' Ashworth maintained an even tone; he had no intention of rowing with the Chief Constable in front of his team. 'We've got a maniac out there, and whatever this woman may have done, she's hardly likely to make a career out of it.'

'Yes, all right,' Savage said, 'but look into it as soon as possible.'

As the Chief Constable strode from the room, Ashworth cast a concerned look at his officers. 'Will you two take Anthony's statement?'

'Yes, guv.'

Josh signalled to Holly and she followed him out.

* * *

Nigel Anthony sat slumped over the table in the interview room.

His face still bore signs of his fight with Gwen, but although his nose was less swollen, the marks around his eyes had turned a more pronounced ugly blue. And somehow his hair seemed thinner, the widow's peak more pronounced. He smelt strongly of cigarette smoke.

The look of triumph on his face faded when the door opened on Holly and Josh.

'Where's Ashworth?' he demanded.

'The Chief Inspector's busy,' Holly replied as they took seats before him.

'I want Ashworth here,' the doctor insisted.

'I've told you, he's very busy,' Holly stated resolutely. 'He's asked us to take your statement.'

'He won't dodge me for ever . . . you tell him that.'

'I can't think of any reason why he should dodge you,' Holly responded, 'but if you feel he's not handling your claims properly, you can make a complaint.'

Anthony's protests subsided. He reached for the Benson and Hedges in front of him and pulled out a cigarette, fumbling in his pocket for a lighter.

'Unusual to see a doctor smoking nowadays,' Josh remarked in a conversational way, hoping to take some of the unpleasantness out of the situation.

'I'm not here to discuss my vices,' Anthony snapped.

'Right,' Holly said, 'what is it you want to report?'

'Murder,' Anthony replied flatly. 'One of my patients — Clifford Smart — had been suffering with cancer for over four years. I believe his wife administered a large overdose of painkillers.'

'You're claiming she carried out a mercy killing?' Holly asked.

As she watched the doctor toying with his cigarette, something clicked in Holly's brain, and adrenalin pumped through her system as her memory cleared. But for now, containing her excitement, she concentrated on Dr Anthony.

He was saying, 'No, that's not what I'm claiming. The woman killed her husband out of sheer hatred. Not to save him suffering, but because she wanted to see him dead.'

As Holly took this down in shorthand, she asked, 'And why should she want to do that, doctor?'

'Because she hated him, that's why. Throughout his life he'd had countless affairs. He'd even had a child by another woman and forced his wife to bring it up.'

'Have you any evidence to substantiate your allegations?' Josh cut in.

Anthony's eyes raked over him. 'The woman was always asking me how many tablets it would take to kill him. I, of course, warned her against any such action.'

'Doesn't make any sense,' Josh ventured. 'How long did you say the man had been ill?'

'Four years,' Anthony said, stubbing out his cigarette.

'And bedridden for how long?'

'Twelve months. Look, what does this have to do with anything?' Anthony protested.

'A lot,' Josh told him. 'So, the man had been bedridden for a year and he had, what . . . a matter of days to live, at the most.'

'Yes.' Anthony lit another cigarette.

'So why should she kill him then?'

Josh regarded these cases in the same compassionate way as many others would; this was obviously a mercy killing, and the less official probing carried out the better.

Anthony said, 'Because if she had done it any earlier, it would have been too obvious. As it was, if I hadn't remembered the questions she'd asked before, I would have signed the death certificate without a second thought.'

'No, it still doesn't make sense,' Josh argued. 'If this woman hated her husband so much, why would she put him out of his misery? Far better, surely, to sit and gloat over his agony.'

'You don't understand, do you?'

Anthony viciously ground out his half-smoked cigarette, and burning tobacco spilled over onto the table.

Suddenly he rounded on Josh. 'Has your partner ever committed adultery?'

'No, sir, I don't think I've ever been in that position . . . but then, some things are better not looked at too closely.'

'If you had, you'd understand that it does strange things to the mind.'

Holly had had enough. She said sharply, 'Right, can I have the woman's name and address, please?'

Anthony supplied the details then pocketed his cigarettes. As he made to leave, he said, 'Ashworth will be dealing with this, won't he?'

'We'll see to it,' Holly said, deliberately offhand.

'That's not what I asked,' Anthony spat with virulence.

Keeping her rising temper under control, Holly said, 'In a serious matter such as this, the Chief Inspector will be involved, yes.'

'Good, that's all I wanted to know. I can find my own way out.' He paused. 'Perhaps you would give the Chief Inspector my regards.'

As the door closed on his retreating figure, Josh turned to Holly. 'What was all that about?'

'God knows.' She was staring vacantly at the ashtray. 'Josh,' she said, 'I remember what the smell was.'

'Sorry?'

Holly ignored him, kept her eyes on the ashtray. 'I had a cigarette that night, the first in years . . . and the creep who tried to crack my skull open reeked of cigarette smoke.'

CHAPTER 17

Ashworth had decided to visit Mrs Fox alone. He wanted a good look at the flat; and he reasoned that a solo visit might bring forth a less hostile attitude from the woman.

He drove through the light afternoon traffic with outward ease, but inside his emotions were in turmoil. He was deeply troubled by Nigel Anthony's involvement in the death of Clifford Smart.

Ashworth had only spoken briefly with his detectives, and although he tried to appear nonchalant, the adultery theme disturbed him. So too did Holly's memory recall about the tobacco smoke, since Anthony's mental strain seemed to have led to a chain-smoking habit.

He stopped at a red traffic-light.

Had Anthony administered the fatal dose to Mr Smart? Could he be mocking Ashworth; committing murders under his very nose with a catch-me-if-you-can air?

The cars behind honked their aggressive message, alerting Ashworth to the fact that the lights had turned to green. Unperturbed he let out the clutch and pulled smoothly away.

In order to prove Anthony had not killed the man, he needed to establish that the seventy-six-year-old wife had. And that prospect was one he could not approach with relish.

He stopped the Sierra outside the flats. Gazing up at the ugly square building made up of grey stone and metal window frames, Ashworth wondered how the drabness of the place would affect the lives of those who lived there.

He knocked on the door of the flat. It was opened by Gerald Fox.

'What do you want now?' he demanded.

'A word, Mr Fox,' Ashworth said pleasantly. 'May I come in?'

'Who is it, Gerald?' his mother called from the kitchen.

'It's the police, mother.'

A worried Mrs Fox appeared behind her son. 'Why do you come here all the time? Why do you hound my boy?'

'May I come in?' Ashworth said again.

'No,' Mrs Fox replied, adamantly stepping forward to bar his way.

'Let him in, mother,' Fox said. 'I've got nothing to hide.'

The woman stood aside and Ashworth crossed the threshold. He had hardly entered the lounge before Fox turned on him.

'Right, what do you want?'

'I just called to say we've looked into your story, and it checks out.'

'Huh, so you're admitting you dragged me away from my weekend in Bradford and persecuted me for nothing.'

The man's confidence was growing by the second . . . just as Ashworth had intended.

'That would be one way of putting it,' Ashworth smiled, 'but I'd have said: We've eliminated you from our enquiries.'

Mrs Fox, who had appeared terrified when Ashworth first entered the flat, relaxed a little but still regarded him with suspicion and apprehension.

'Now you've told me, you can go,' Fox said sullenly. 'And stop bothering me.'

'Oh, Polish national costumes,' Ashworth said excitedly, pointing to the dolls on the dresser. 'These are fantastic,' he marvelled, studying them closely. 'Are they originals?'

'You know of such things?' There was excitement behind the timorous note in the woman's voice.

'Not so much Poland, but I've made a study of the Second World War and anything connected with it fascinates me.'

'The Nazis, they were evil people,' Mrs Fox stated heatedly.

'I agree,' Ashworth said, 'but it's still an interesting period of history.'

Mrs Fox stood stolidly, hands on hips, as she asserted, 'Not when you lose many of your family and friends in the concentration camps.'

Ashworth looked suitably chastened. 'I'm sorry, Mrs Fox,' he said, 'I didn't mean to cause offence.'

She brushed aside his apology with a wave of her hand. 'You haven't,' she said amiably, 'but sometimes the memories are painful.'

Gerald Fox had been watching with mounting concern. He took his mother's arm, saying, 'I don't want this man here, mother. He's from the police. He means to harm you.'

Mrs Fox shrugged off his grip. 'Shoo, you are just a boy. You do not want to understand about the war.'

Fox withdrew and glared at Ashworth until he was out of the room. A door within the flat could be heard closing quietly.

'I'm sorry,' Ashworth said, 'I've upset your son.'

'He is a strange boy. Sometimes I wonder where I went wrong.' She nodded towards the dolls. 'All I have left of my native land. That is sad . . . yes?'

'Very,' Ashworth agreed.

'You must think me a silly old woman to be so frightened of the police . . .'

Ashworth shook his head.

'. . . but I have seen people dragged from their beds in the middle of the night and they vanish . . . puff!'

'The police in this country are not like that,' Ashworth assured her.

'This you tell me. But the miscarriages of justice; the people who spend years in prison and then it is found that they have not done the things you say . . .'

'Mistakes are sometimes made,' Ashworth admitted, 'but I don't believe they are deliberate.'

Mrs Fox threw back her head defiantly, 'Huh, tell that to the people who rot in prison cells.'

'I can see you're a very spirited lady,' Ashworth flattered. 'I'm sorry I frightened you earlier.'

'Oh, I am a silly old woman.'

'I'd love to discuss the war with you, but I fear I'm in the way.'

'Maybe you call when my son is at work,' she whispered hopefully.

'Well, if I wouldn't be disturbing you, and you don't feel threatened by me, I'd very much like to.'

As Mrs Fox eyed Ashworth, her features softened. 'You, I think, are all right, but the others . . .'

Yes, Ashworth silently mused, I've always thought I'm all right, it must be the others.

He crossed to the door, asking, 'When will I find you in?'

'Always,' she said. 'Where is there for me to go? The people here, they call me the mad Polish woman.'

'I'm sure that's not true,' Ashworth said politely as he opened the front door. 'Until the next time then.'

So far, so good, he thought, hurrying along the corridor.

* * *

Back at the station Ashworth collected three cups of tea from the canteen and, hoping to pour them over troubled waters, he made his way to CID.

His assumption that he was sailing into troubled waters proved correct as soon as he got to the office.

'I wanted to come with you to see Fox,' Holly complained.

Ashworth did not feel like a confrontation so, placing a cup of tea in front of her, he said, 'And there's a very good reason why I didn't let you.'

'What is it then?' she asked morosely.

Ashworth passed Josh his tea and settled at his desk. 'Because you're getting too involved with this.'

'If it's Fox, I'm going to know,' she flared.

'I'll grant you that,' he said, remaining calm, 'but knowing and proving don't amount to the same thing.' He sipped his tea. 'No, if we go charging in now we're going to frighten him off.'

Holly pushed her cup to one side, as if to refuse it would repay Ashworth for his rebuff. 'So what do we do, just sit back and hope he makes a mistake?'

'Oh, don't worry, he's already done that.'

They looked at him questioningly.

'Yes, Mr Gerald Fox thinks he's more intelligent than I am,' he said without the least trace of humour.

Ashworth was pleased; the more he thought about it all, the more ridiculous it seemed that Anthony could be in any way connected with the attacks. It was Gerald Fox, and he was well on the way to proving it.

Gladys Smart still bothered him though, but he would put off dealing with her for as long as possible. If he could just get to the point where Fox's arrest appeared imminent, her case would take on less importance in the greater scheme of things.

As these thoughts filtered through his mind, Ashworth said, 'This mercy killing case, I want to delay it as long as possible.'

'Dr Anthony seemed very keen to push it, sir,' Holly said, relenting and sipping her tea. 'If I didn't know better, I'd say it was almost like a personal matter between the two of you.'

'You do know better, young lady,' Ashworth said brusquely. 'Dr Anthony and I have had a minor dispute, but it's well on the way to being sorted out.'

Holly was becoming more outspoken by the day, and Ashworth could well imagine it turning into a major problem. He knew he would have to stamp her down before too long, but for now he let it pass.

Josh, sensing the slight change in atmosphere, diplomatically changed the subject. He said, 'The general consensus of opinion in the nick is — what's the woman done? Her husband only had so many hours to live and it's hardly likely they'd have come up with a miracle cure in that time.'

Ashworth agreed, but said, 'The general consensus of opinion doesn't have to take the flak . . . I do. So, as the man upstairs said, we play it by the book.' He sat back with a sigh. 'And that's what I find so distasteful.'

He looked at his wristwatch. 'Right. Home. And barring any disasters tonight, we can have a day off tomorrow.'

* * *

But the arrangement of planets in the galaxy decreed that a day of rest was not in the offing for Jim Ashworth.

No sooner had he arrived home with guilty feelings for hardly giving a thought to his daughter's plight, than the telephone rang.

Praying it was not the station, he lifted the receiver. 'Ashworth.'

'Hello . . . Grandad,' Sarah greeted him.

'Oh, thank you, God,' Ashworth exclaimed.

His feelings of joy and relief were so potent, tears stung his eyes as he asked, 'Is Sam all right?'

'She's fine, and it's a boy. Six pounds, three ounces,' Sarah informed him happily. 'And Samantha says he looks just like you.'

'Really?' Ashworth said, swelling with pride.

'But apart from that, he's quite normal,' she laughed.

They talked for some time, happily sharing the moment, discussing the things that grandparents do on such occasions, and enjoying each other, even from a distance.

* * *

Rural Norfolk suited Ashworth's temperament. As the East Midlands gave way to wall-to-wall greenery, contentment swept over him; and the Sierra, in his expert hands, ate away the miles.

This was not a familiar route — Ashworth, because of his job, was not able to see as much of his children as he should — and he had to stop several times to consult the road atlas. But soon, the spire of the sixteenth-century church which dominated the tiny hamlet of Stoneharding, came into view.

The community there was small, and unfamiliar cars always attracted much attention, so quite a few curious stares followed Ashworth's progress. But as he pulled up outside a large, detached house at the end of the lane, village life returned to normal. The mystery had been solved. He was there to see the Barlows about their recent happy event, no doubt.

As Ashworth climbed out of the car, his son-in-law, Richard, came striding down the wide path of his huge front garden. Although only thirty-five, Richard already possessed a portly middle and thinning black hair.

His jovial face broke into a wide smile. 'Dad, did you have a good journey?'

Ashworth, ignoring the question and the proffered hand, hugged his son-in-law warmly. 'Congratulations, Richard,' he said. 'Well done.'

'I won't do the old one about it being my pleasure,' he grinned.

Ashworth chuckled heartily. He looked towards the house and spotted Sarah at the large lounge window. Somewhere in the house, the dog was barking wildly, and suddenly his need to see them became urgent.

Absence does indeed make the heart grow fonder. In the hall, he hugged Sarah with the same warmth, the same lack of self-consciousness, as he had done years before; and in Ashworth's eyes, she was still that attractive young girl who had so easily stolen his heart.

Peanuts, in her excitement, dashed all over the house, uttering a sound somewhere between a bark and a yelp until, finally, she lost control of her bladder. But no one seemed to mind.

Ashworth gulped down the much-needed cup of tea with such haste it burned his throat.

His grandchildren — Sally Anne, ten, and six-year-old Justin — viewed him with nervousness, as they always did for the first half hour of his infrequent visits. Afterwards, they would spend the rest of the day wondering why they had been so afraid of such a big softy.

* * *

The atmosphere in maternity wings always differs greatly from that of general wards, with joy and happiness frequent visitors.

Ashworth stared down in wonderment at the tiny pink form; this latest addition to the family. The sleeping baby seemed amazingly passive for someone of Ashworth origins.

The miracle of birth fascinated Ashworth; and it was his firmly held belief that all souls eventually returned from whence they came, to be born again. And he wondered how many lives this little chap had experienced, wondered what destiny had in store for him on this journey.

They spent a full two hours with Samantha, a bubbly, vivacious girl whose spirits had not been dulled by the arduous nature of the birth. But all too soon it was over and Ashworth was kissing his daughter goodbye.

'Sam, I'm sorry I wasn't here,' he said, 'and I'm sorry too that I have to go back.'

'It's all right, dad, but promise you and mum will come and stay with us soon.'

'I promise,' he said, smiling.

'Good.' She giggled. 'In that case, I'll tell you what we've decided to call him . . . James.'

'James Barlow. Now that has a ring to it,' Ashworth said proudly.

Back at the house, Sarah prepared a late lunch of roast lamb. Ashworth tucked in eagerly, welcoming her culinary skills after a week of police canteen food.

Later, Ashworth sat in an armchair with Justin on his knee, discussing things that are of vital importance to a six-year-old boy. When would the frog spawn turn into tadpoles? How many weeks now to the big school holidays?

His sister looked on with the lofty haughtiness that befits a ten-year-old girl with a younger brother who seemed only capable of discussing trivia.

'Grandpop?'

'Yes, Justin?'

The boy studied his toy tank as he asked, 'Where do babies come from?'

Ashworth, not used to explaining the reproductive cycle to children, phrased his answer carefully.

'Well, mummies have babies inside them all the time,' he began hesitantly, 'and when they think the time is right, they sit down and discuss it with daddy.'

'That's wrong.' Sally Anne spoke with authority as she twanged her knickers elastic through her dress. 'Julie Clayton, at school, says a man does something rude to a woman and—'

'Sally Anne, that's enough,' her father warned.

Ashworth shot Richard a thankful look and breathed easily once more, while Sarah chuckled softly into her wine.

A little while later, Peanuts reversed her earlier decision to mourn his departure when a large dish of roast lamb was put before her.

As Sarah escorted Ashworth to the car, they shared a companionable silence, and breathed in the perfumed air.

'How are things, dear?' she asked after a time.

'Rough,' he answered truthfully.

'Poor Jim,' she sympathized. 'I shall have to stay here for a few weeks, until Samantha's on her feet.'

'I know you will. I understand that.'

'I've missed you, Jim.'

Ashworth suddenly gripped her arms, gazed into her eyes, saying, 'Sarah, I've decided that without you my life wouldn't be worth a lot.'

'What's brought this on?' she said, slightly shocked, for he was not a man to convey his deeper feelings easily.

'It's just how I feel,' he said fervently.

And in the gathering dusk their lips met in a lovers' kiss.

As he drove back towards the church, Ashworth felt he was beginning a journey from paradise to hell. This was the first time he had ever viewed Bridgetown in that light, and he knew then his private life would have to be sorted out.

'Please, God,' he requested as his car sped past the church.

CHAPTER 18

A nightmare came to Holly that night.

She could smell stale tobacco smoke, and just as she turned, a blow caught her head, sent her sprawling across the shiny bonnet of her red car. Her first thought was for the vehicle and her arms went out to protect it.

'You filthy dirty cow,' the voice rasped. 'You've been with a married man.'

In the dream, Holly was naked; her flesh pale against the red bodywork. 'No, I haven't,' she shouted.

'You have,' the voice insisted. 'That's why you're naked. Jim Ashworth had you, just like he's had my wife.'

'No, he hasn't.'

She was running along the lane, but every way she turned the man was before her. The cigarette smoke choked her, blocked her throat, and she fell to her knees, heaving for breath.

'And now you must pay the price for being a cheating bitch.'

The man pushed his face close to hers. It was Nigel Anthony.

A hammer was smashed repeatedly into her skull, and Holly watched as the brains poured from her head.

'Jesus Christ,' Holly exclaimed, coming awake in an instant. She sat bolt upright, stifling the urge to scream.

'Jesus Christ.'

Climbing from the bed, her legs threatened to buckle, and her goose-pimpled flesh was perspiring.

Holly slipped on her dressing gown and padded through the darkened house to the kitchen. Flicking on the light, she was blinded by its brilliance for a few moments, but comforted too.

She crossed to a cabinet, took out a half bottle of vodka. After pouring a good measure into a mug, she lit a cigarette from a packet of ten bought from an off-licence the morning before.

Exhaling smoke, Holly tossed back the drink and poured another.

The stairs creaked and she gave a small involuntary cry of fear. Josh, clad only in striped boxer shorts, appeared in the doorway. He stared at the bottle, at the mug in Holly's hand.

'That won't help,' he told her gently.

'Leave it,' Holly ordered. 'Don't try to run my life, Josh, I don't need it.'

'All right.'

He turned and started back up the stairs.

'Josh, I'm sorry,' she cried after him. 'Can we talk?'

He reappeared in the doorway. 'Of course. But first . . .' He came towards her and took the cigarette. '. . . put this out, eh? It's just not you.'

Holly nodded and he stubbed it out in a huge ashtray which looked as if it might have been stolen from a pub.

Holly took another drink and laughed bitterly. 'I thought I was such a together lady, you know that?'

'You've had a shock, Holly. You could have been killed.'

He took a bottle of orange juice from the fridge, saying, 'If you must drink that stuff, at least have some of this in it.'

'It's not just that . . .' she said, allowing him to pour juice into the mug. '. . . but it has frightened me, Josh. I thought I could take care of myself.'

'You can,' he assured her. 'You fought him off, remember.'

'It was only luck.'

'No it wasn't, it was training and a cool head.'

'Maybe.'

Holly drained the vodka and, ignoring his meaningful look, poured another. 'But I don't know what'll happen the next time I'm in a tight situation. I'm scared, Josh.'

'Of course you are, you wouldn't be human if you weren't.'

Sensing this could be a lengthy discussion, Josh took a can of lager from the fridge.

'If it happens again, you'll react in exactly the same way,' he said, opening the can and taking a deep drink. 'That's not all that's bothering you though, is it?'

'Ever felt you're coming face to face with yourself?' she asked miserably.

'Frequently, yes.'

'Do you know what I've been telling myself these last few days?' she said, swaying slightly as the alcohol began to take effect. 'You know how all those police series on TV have the men knocking women off every which way? Well, I thought, how about having a real-life policewoman who doesn't give a stuff . . . just taking whatever she wants.'

She stared at Josh through hazy eyes. 'Do you think women are like that?'

'I don't know,' he shrugged. 'I don't think you are.'

She tossed back the drink. 'No,' she said flatly, 'but I need it, Josh. I need sex.'

Josh watched her pour another drink and, although it was unwise, he let her do it.

'Holly,' he said, 'you've got to decide what'll make you happy and go for it. That's what we all have to do.'

'Yes.' She let out a wretched sigh. 'Trouble is, what makes one part of me happy, makes the rest of me miserable.'

'Then you need to strike a balance.'

'I dreamt Dr Anthony attacked me,' she said, changing the subject with the rapidity of one who'd had too much to drink.

'Yes?'

'Do you think it's possible? I'm sure Ashworth's been giving his wife one. That would explain the adultery thing.'

'Shall we talk about it in the morning?' he suggested. 'With clear heads?'

'My head is quite clear,' she said, weaving an erratic path towards him. Then, 'You know what you said about deciding what'll make me happy and going for it?'

Her dressing gown came open, affording Josh a view of her body. He looked away quickly.

'Yes?' he said.

'Well, I want to go to bed with you.'

'Holly, that's impossible,' he said firmly.

'No, no, no, no . . . not for sex,' she slurred, clinging to his hand. 'Just want someone there with me . . . someone who cares.'

'Come on . . . upstairs,' he ordered patiently. 'I'll sort your head out, girl, if it's the last thing I do.'

* * *

While Nigel Anthony drifted through veils of brandy-induced sleep, Holly's was not the only nightmare in which he appeared.

His apparition floated before Ashworth for fleeting seconds that seemed like endless hours. The figure was misty, drifting; forming into a solid shape, only to disintegrate again in his troubled mind.

Ashworth witnessed the trial, the guilty verdict, and Anthony's devastation as he was handed five life sentences.

But that was not all. His own ruin featured larger than life. Everything he held dear: his wife, family, home, career; all assumed gigantic proportions, came hurtling towards him, and shattered into tiny pieces.

Ashworth came up through layers of sleep quickly, breaking into full consciousness with a start. The thoughts that haunted his waking hours could not now be curtailed by sleep.

As he lay still, listening to the night sounds, he realized that, for the first time in his career, he was functioning inefficiently. Every lead, every clue, every instinct propelled him towards Nigel Anthony, but he resisted arriving at that destination because of the consequences awaiting him there.

Instead, he continued to flounder about, seeking evidence against persons not remotely connected with the case.

But now the decision was being forced upon him. From tomorrow onwards he would try to establish what had really happened to Clifford Smart.

If Anthony had administered the fatal overdose to mock him — and in the solitary small hours of the morning, it seemed increasingly likely — far better to have it over and done with, than to endure the slow creeping inevitability of it all closing in on him.

CHAPTER 19

Ashworth's resolute frame of mind did not fade with the hard cold reality of morning.

In a few weeks' time Sarah would be home. And if that homecoming was to be marred by the revelation of his infidelity and its horrific aftermath, then so be it.

Ashworth was tired of lying.

He marched into the office spot on nine a.m. 'Right,' he said, 'I want Gladys Smart in today.'

All in CID were suffering, in varying degrees, from lack of sleep. Holly also had to cope with a hangover which made her head thump as her stomach churned.

A day of short tempers was in the offing.

'I thought we were leaving that for as long as possible, guv,' Josh said, the ever-present cup of tea in his hand.

'That was yesterday,' Ashworth stated flatly, sitting at his desk. 'I've now reason to believe Dr Nigel Anthony is tied up in all this.'

Holly glanced keenly at Josh, the sudden movement painful given her general condition and the stitches above her eye.

'What makes you think that, sir?' she asked.

Ashworth's glare said more than a thousand words could. 'I'm sure you're well aware of my reasons,' he retorted, 'and if your behaviour continues in this vein, you and I shall have a serious confrontation, sooner rather than later.'

Holly was genuinely taken aback by the outburst and her hackles rose as she asked, 'What behaviour? I was asking a question.'

Josh speedily assumed the position of peace-maker; a role he was having to adopt more and more of late. He said, 'What about Fox then, guv?'

'We'll have to keep an eye on him until he's out of the frame, but I'm not holding out any hopes.'

'And when do you want Mrs Smart brought in, sir?' Holly asked sharply. 'If that's not an impertinent question.'

Ashworth cast her another hard glare, was about to issue a reprimand, but thought better of it.

'Two p.m.,' he said resignedly.

* * *

'He's a right bastard,' Holly declared.

She was waiting to turn out of the station car park.

'You antagonize him,' Josh said calmly.

He watched the traffic-lights at the road works turn to red as a long line of traffic slowed to a halt.

'You can go now,' he said.

'I know that. I can drive a bloody car, you know.'

'Sorry.' He stared out of the side window, muttering, 'Keep your mouth shut, Josh.'

There were several reasons for Holly's anger. Firstly, she felt like death warmed up then allowed to cool again; secondly, Ashworth's tantrum had upset her; but mainly, the root cause was her own behaviour.

Josh had indeed spent the night with her; and the parts she could remember troubled her greatly.

Dimly she recollected having her arms around him after taking off her dressing gown. He had looked down at her body with what her drunken mind had taken as interest. Poor Josh, she thought, he must have been terrified.

Squirming with embarrassment in the car seat, Holly recalled whispering in his ear, 'Let me convert you, Josh,' while making playful attempts to pull down his boxer shorts.

Thankfully, what followed was a total blank. She knew only too well what had not happened; and she prayed that she had simply blacked out. That seemed the most likely explanation for he was still there in the bed when she awoke that morning.

Never again, she thought dismally, never again.

* * *

Why were the police coming to see her?

That was just one of the things worrying Gladys. She mooched about the house, every room now evoking both happy and painful memories.

Why wouldn't they release Cliff's body for burial?

Gladys came from a generation which never had two halfpennies to rub together, but always insisted that their nearest and dearest were dispatched to the hereafter with due ceremonies and respect. The fact that she could not do as much for her husband was causing Gladys acute anxiety.

And now the police wanted to see her.

It was ten thirty. Pacing the house made her tired, and the feeling of sickness brought on by too many cups of tea only added to her weariness.

The sound of the doorbell made her flinch. She was aware of her heartbeat as she scurried along the passage, favouring the right side because Cliff had parked his pedal cycle on the left for so many years.

Opening the front door Gladys viewed her two visitors: a tall, nice-looking young man, and a woman with a heavy dressing over one eye.

'Yes?' she asked timidly.

Holly's smile lit up her face, and Gladys thought how much prettier she looked.

'Hello, Mrs Smart, I'm DS Bedford, from Bridgetown CID. This is DC Abraham.'

They showed her their warrant cards.

'Can we come in for a few moments?'

'Well . . . yes,' Gladys said, a slight tremor in her voice. 'You'll have to excuse the place being a mess, but my husband's just died.'

'We won't look. I promise,' Holly said, smiling kindly.

They followed her through to the kitchen, and for the first time in her life, Gladys was ashamed of her old-fashioned sink, the chipped white wall tiles, her ancient gas cooker.

'Would you like to sit down?' She indicated the four chairs around a wooden table.

'No, we won't, thank you,' Josh said. 'Have you any idea why we're here?'

'Only what you told me on the phone . . . something about Cliff.'

Holly said, 'Your husband's death was due to a large overdose of painkillers . . .'

Gladys, her lower lip trembling, insisted, 'It was cancer. He'd had it for years.'

'No, Mrs Smart,' Holly said gently, 'the actual cause was an overdose. Somehow your husband took more tablets than he should have done.' She was speaking very slowly, very deliberately. 'This has been reported to us, so we have to investigate it. Do you understand that?'

'I think so,' she stammered.

'Now, neither DC Abraham nor I think you gave your husband those tablets—'

'I always gave Cliff his tablets,' Gladys interrupted.

'No, you're not understanding me, Mrs Smart,' Holly persevered. 'We don't think you gave him too many tablets, because if you did, you'd be in trouble. We think he decided to take them himself to end his suffering, and anyone who says differently has to prove it.'

'Prove it . . .' Gladys repeated softly.

'So all you have to say is that you didn't do it,' Holly said. 'Is that clear?'

Gladys nodded blankly. 'Yes . . . no . . . oh, I don't understand any of it.' Her eyes grew wide. 'Will I have to go to prison?'

'No,' Holly smiled, 'just keep telling the truth, Mrs Smart. You didn't give your husband too many tablets . . . yes?'

'All right.'

Gladys was very confused but reasoned that these youngsters were police and if they were saying that's what she should do, then it must be right.

'Okay then, I'll come and collect you just before two p.m. this afternoon and you can talk to Chief Inspector Ashworth at the station. Now, just remember you haven't done anything.'

Gladys started to tremble. 'The police station? Will I have to go there?'

'Yes,' Holly said, 'but there's nothing to worry about.'

'I'd better have a bath,' Gladys said suddenly, 'and change into my best things.'

As they climbed into the car, Holly muttered, 'Ashworth, you'd just better take it easy with that old love, or we're going to have a parting of the ways.'

'We've got to stick to the book,' Josh reminded her.

'No, Josh, in this case we stick the book,' was Holly's spirited reply.

* * *

Ashworth's morale was not high as he parked opposite Fox's flat.

What secrets hid behind its exterior? he wondered. Had the murderer of four people in Bradford and two in Bridgetown walked through the door he was now entering? Somehow, he doubted it.

The drabness of the seemingly endless corridor further depressed his spirits as he made his way to the flat.

'Who is it?' Mrs Fox asked in answer to his knock.

‘It’s Jim Ashworth . . .’ He deliberately did not announce his rank. ‘I was here yesterday.’

He heard a key turning and the door opened.

‘Good morning, Mrs Fox.’

‘I did not think you would call so soon,’ she smiled, patting her hair into place. ‘Would you like to come in?’

In a rather fussy manner she settled him on the settee, then vanished behind a curtain which separated the living room from the kitchen.

Ashworth listened to her industrious sounds as she made coffee. Presently, she appeared with two cups, and he gallantly moved the coffee table closer to the settee.

‘Thank you.’ Mrs Fox gave him a smile. ‘I am sorry, I have put two sugars in it. I never thought to ask. I entertain so little.’

‘Two’s fine,’ Ashworth assured her. ‘It smells good.’

‘Come with me. I will show you something.’

She signalled for him to follow her into the kitchen. With barely room for Mrs Fox in the confined space, Ashworth stood outside, holding back the curtain.

‘A coffee percolator,’ she announced proudly, as if Ashworth had not seen one before. ‘There are few luxuries in my life, but real coffee is one of them.’

‘Very nice,’ Ashworth said with strained enthusiasm.

‘Now, come and sit down.’ She guided him back to the settee.

Ashworth sipped the coffee. ‘Mmm, it tastes as good as it smells,’ he said honestly.

Subtlety had never been one of Ashworth’s virtues, and therefore he found it difficult to extract information without asking direct questions. As he finished the coffee he wondered how he could lead the conversation in the required direction.

‘You want to talk about the war,’ Mrs Fox said, settling beside him.

Ashworth glanced around the room, saw there were no ashtrays visible, so he took a chance. ‘You don’t smoke, I suppose?' he asked, patting his pockets as if searching for his cigarettes.

'No, I do not. I suffered a mild heart attack a few years ago, and the doctor, he said no more tobacco.'

'I won't then. Your son doesn't smoke either?' he asked, trying to sound casual.

'No.' Then Mrs Fox laughed. 'Well, he does, but he thinks I do not know. Boys, eh? His age and he is afraid to tell his mother he smokes.'

'Your husband doesn't live with you?' Ashworth asked, probing deeper.

'No, he is dead,' she said sadly. 'The Germans killed him in their hell camp, Auschwitz.'

'I see.'

'The first day of September, 1939: that was when the Nazis came into my country. And within nine months there were a dozen such concentration camps, but Auschwitz was the worst.' She huffed. 'The history books do not tell it all. Rape . . . huh, you might believe that a German soldier would not touch a Jewish woman, but it was not so.'

'Look, if we're to be friends, we can't keep being so formal, can we? My Christian name's Jim.'

'I am Sophie,' she smiled.

'And how old are you, Sophie? If you don't mind my asking.'

'I am sixty years old.'

'Had you known your husband long when the Germans took him?'

'We were childhood sweethearts.' She finished her coffee. 'Yes.'

They talked for over an hour, and Ashworth appeared to be listening intently as Mrs Fox related the numbers of people killed in the various camps, the execution methods used, and countless other memories of war-torn Poland, but his mind was sharply focused on the things he had discovered.

Mrs Fox paused and Ashworth seized his chance to bring the discussion to a halt. 'You're not really afraid of the police, are you.'

'In this country, no, but with the Nazis and the Secret Police in my old country . . . well, habits die hard. And my son, he has inherited paranoia. Before he left this morning he said, do not trust the police, mother, they will trap you.'

Ashworth looked at his wristwatch. 'I must be going,' he said, rising to his feet. 'We're not that bad, you know.'

'You are nice,' she declared. 'Not many people take the time to listen to an old woman.'

'How long have you been in this country, Sophie?' he asked as they walked to the door.

'Just after the war. Two years after, maybe.'

'Thank you for the coffee. May I call again?'

'Of course, whenever you like,' she said, waving him goodbye.

'Tomorrow,' he said to himself as he strode along the corridor.

To his knowledge, all the facts Mrs Fox had given him regarding wartime Poland were correct. The inaccuracies had all been to do with her personal life.

If his arithmetic was right, Mrs Fox would have been six years old when the Germans invaded her country, and her husband was of the same age. Yet somehow they had produced a child who was still only twenty-nine in the 1990s.

Ashworth surmised that due to her traumatic childhood, Mrs Fox's mind dwelt somewhere between reality and fantasy. No wonder her son wanted to keep her away from the police.

Ashworth needed to find out as much as he could before Gerald Fox took some action to stop his visits.

But in the meantime he had the distressing case of Gladys Smart to deal with.

* * *

A heavy atmosphere enveloped the interview room as Ashworth waited with Josh for Holly to arrive with Mrs Smart.

Josh, ill at ease, felt there was something terribly wrong with his superior: the man seemed to be jumping from suspect to suspect as if unable to sustain a train of thought for any length of time.

This morning it had been Dr Anthony, now it was Fox, but Ashworth seemed to be doing very little to prove anything against either. Surely if he had evidence against Dr Anthony he should have the man in, question him.

Indecision was not a fault many would lay at Ashworth's door, but it was showing its face in this case.

'Holly feels strongly about this one, guv,' Josh said, breaking the oppressive silence.

Ashworth, standing by the window, turned aggressively. 'And what's that supposed to mean?'

'Just that she . . . we feel sorry for the old girl.'

'And I don't?'

'That's not what I'm saying, guv. I just get the feeling that you and Holly are going to collide soon.'

'Yes, that's the impression I've got,' Ashworth intoned, 'and when we do that young lady had better run for cover.'

'But I think we can avoid that,' Josh ventured.

'How?'

'When we were interviewing Dr Anthony, he really did make this seem like a personal matter between you two—'

'Josh, this is getting out of hand,' Ashworth stated hotly. 'What we have here is quite simple: a terminally ill man has died of a massive overdose. We have to establish whether his wife administered that overdose, and if she didn't, who did.' He gave an empty laugh and added pointedly, 'Anyone seeing anything personal in that has been reading too much romantic fiction.'

The discussion ended abruptly as the door opened, and a hesitant Gladys Smart was ushered into the room.

Her 'best things' consisted of a floral cotton dress covered by an ill-fitting white cardigan. She was clutching a large black plastic handbag.

'This is Gladys Smart, sir,' Holly announced, giving the old lady a reassuring smile.

'Mrs Smart,' Ashworth said curtly, 'please sit down. I'm Chief Inspector Ashworth.'

She sat at the table, placing her large handbag between them as if to form a barrier.

'Do you know why you're here?'

'It's something to do with my Cliff.'

'That's right.'

Ashworth avoided looking directly at the woman, and his eyes rested on the handbag as he said, 'A post-mortem examination on your husband's body revealed he had taken a large overdose of drugs . . .'

He could feel Holly's eyes boring into his back; her hostility surrounded him. As a result, he attempted to soften his voice.

'Now, it's my job to find out how that overdose occurred.'

'Yes, sir, but I don't know nothing about it,' Gladys said, looking up at Holly.

'What was your husband's physical condition?'

Gladys appeared flustered, said nothing.

'Could he feed himself? Sit up in bed? That sort of thing,' Ashworth explained.

'Oh no, sir, he was much too weak for that. He hardly knew where he was for the last few days of his life.'

'And the painkilling tablets . . . where were they kept?'

'I always kept them downstairs, sir, like the doctor told me. I took them up when they were needed.'

'So, your husband didn't have access to the tablets at the time in question, even if he'd been capable of taking them by himself?'

Gladys stayed silent as her face reddened.

'Who else saw your husband, apart from yourself?'

'Dr Anthony. He used to call every day to give Cliff his injection . . . morphine, I think it was.'

'You have a son, I believe.'

'Cliff did.'

'Did he see his father that day?'

'No, he hardly ever came to see his dad.'

'So . . .' Ashworth pushed the handbag to one side. '. . . only you and Dr Anthony saw your husband on the day he died.'

'Yes,' Gladys stammered. 'Oh . . . you're getting me all mixed up.'

The sight of the quivering woman tore at Ashworth's heart but he pushed on brutally. 'Are you suggesting that Dr Anthony gave your husband those tablets?'

Gladys lowered her head, stared at the table top. 'I don't know, sir,' she replied timidly. 'I just know I didn't.'

'But if you didn't, then Dr Anthony must have done.'

Gladys made no response, simply sat with eyes cast down. Ashworth leant back, let out an impatient breath, and considered her for a while.

Eventually, he said, 'I want you to go home now and think about it, Mrs Smart, then come back tomorrow and tell me if there's anything you might have forgotten.'

Gladys looked up at him. 'Yes, sir,' she said, 'but I didn't do nothing, honest.'

'Holly, take Mrs Smart home, will you?'

Holly glared at Ashworth as she helped Gladys to her feet.

'The same time tomorrow,' he said briskly.

Holly's muttered 'bastard' reached Ashworth's ears as she led Gladys out of the door.

'I had no choice, Josh,' Ashworth said in his own defence. 'This has to be done by the book.'

'Of course, sir,' Josh said stiffly. 'Excuse me, I've got some computer work to see to.'

Then Ashworth was alone, wishing he could get away from himself as easily.

CHAPTER 20

After taking Gladys Smart home, Holly had failed to make an appearance; and Josh had remained monosyllabic.

It was now early evening, and as Ashworth prepared to leave the station, he sensed — or perhaps imagined — hostility in everyone he met.

Even Martin Dutton was not his usual chirpy self and seemed almost relieved when a member of the public came in to report his car had been broken into.

'Jim . . . a moment.'

Ashworth was about to push open the swing doors when Ken Savage's request stopped him.

'Glad I caught you, Jim,' Savage said, slightly out of breath. 'I've had a complaint.'

Whatever this was, Ashworth could well have done without it. He sighed heavily and said, 'My day has been full of them, Ken.'

'This one's from a Gerald Fox. He claims you're harassing his mother.'

'That's ridiculous,' Ashworth spluttered with exasperation.

'Why are you interested in her?' Savage questioned.

'This Gerald Fox who's doing all the complaining, is well in the frame for the murders and assaults. His mother invited me there, Ken.'

Savage relaxed. 'Ah, you're trying to extract information from her to incriminate her son, I take it?'

'Well, of course I am,' Ashworth flared. 'I'm not just dropping in for a cup of coffee.'

Savage raised his eyebrows in annoyance. 'Just tread carefully, Jim. The man's made a verbal complaint by telephone and he's backing that up with a solicitor's letter.'

'He'll have to prove I was harassing her, surely?' Ashworth reasoned. 'I can't do my job without talking to people, Ken.'

'As I said, just tread carefully, and try to get all your information before the letter gets here. We've got public relations to think about.'

Front reception was filling up fast. A queue had formed behind the man with the damaged car, who was now locked in argument with Sergeant Dutton.

And as two uniformed constables came through the swing doors, Savage took Ashworth's arm and guided him to a private corner.

'There is another matter . . .' Savage began hesitantly. 'The euthanasia case. Rumour has it you were a bit hard on the woman.'

Ashworth pinched the bridge of his nose, trying to hold onto his temper. 'Any officers putting their names to this rumour?'

Savage's look was apprehensive. 'I was hoping not to personalize this.'

'If someone's complaining about me, it is personal,' Ashworth bristled. 'It's Holly Bedford, isn't it?'

'Don't take it like that, Jim,' Savage said, his smile conciliatory. 'God knows what's wrong with the bloody woman. Bad time of the month probably.'

'No, she needs her backside kicked, that's what's wrong with her.'

'I'd rather not have a bust-up in CID,' Savage warned.

'Tell Bedford to stop exceeding her authority then.'

'Calm down—'

'I don't feel calm,' Ashworth insisted. 'To me it's quite simple — Bedford just wants to sweep this mercy killing under the carpet. Now, you square it with Dr Anthony, get him to withdraw his statement and I'll do that.'

'I know it's difficult—'

'That it is, and it's being made far more difficult by my own people.'

He squared up to Savage. 'Take charge of it, Ken. Stop trying to smooth everybody over. Now, I've still got work to do. You'll have to excuse me.'

Savage watched his angry exit. 'Still your same old reasonable self, Jim,' he muttered.

* * *

'You're not to see that Ashworth again, mother. I forbid it.'

Mrs Fox stood with hands on hips, eyes wide with indignation. 'You forbid your mother?'

'Yes, I forbid it.'

Those who had only witnessed the shy, retiring side of Gerald Fox would not have recognized the man circling his mother in the living room, lashing her with his strident voice; a snarl on his lips; an angry light in his eyes.

'When you are like this, I cannot deal with you, Gerald. You are like a crazy man.'

'Is that what you told the police?' he hissed.

'I tell the police nothing,' she said quickly. 'He was here to talk about the war.'

'You were talking about me,' Fox yelled.

'I was not. I swear—'

Fox pushed her viciously, sent her sprawling onto the settee.

She held up her arms for protection. 'No, Gerald, you must not do this to your mother,' she babbled. 'The demons are loose in your head. If you do not leave me alone, I shall tell the police all I know.'

The ceiling vibrated as someone from the flat above banged hard on the floor; and muffled shouts of complaint could be heard.

Fox looked up and dropped his voice to a whisper. 'Would they believe you though? Old mad Sophie, who gets it all wrong.' He bent over his mother menacingly. 'Remember the home I had you put in with the other loonies?'

Mrs Fox covered her ears, tried to block out his voice. 'No, Gerald,' she cried.

'If you talk to the police again, I'll send you back there . . . lock you up with all the other loonies.'

She began to sob, hands still over her ears, rocking from side to side. 'Please do not send me back there. It would kill me.'

Suddenly Fox was calm, his voice kind. 'Then don't talk to the police, mother, and I'll keep you here with me. I'll look after you.'

'Yes, Gerald.'

* * *

Ashworth dialled the number slowly, hesitantly, but all too soon the ringing tone was in his ear.

He felt his mouth go dry as a voice said, 'Doctor's surgery. Can I help you?'

'Dr Anthony,' he said. 'Gwen Anthony, that is.'

'And who shall I say is calling?'

'Jim Ashworth.'

'Hold the line, please.'

Ashworth waited, listened to the sounds of patients chatting; the rustle of papers as receptionists sorted through files and prescriptions.

'You're through,' the voice informed him.

'Hello?' Gwen said.

'I didn't know if you'd be there.'

'I've someone with me at the moment,' she told him, obviously unable to speak freely.

'I need to see you, Gwen. It's important.'

'Of course,' she answered quickly.

'Just tell me if this is all right . . . I'll meet you at eight p.m., after you've finished surgery.'

'The car park of the Mount View Hotel. That's fine. Thanks for calling. Bye.'

The line went dead. Ashworth replaced the receiver, and as he sat on the stairs he wondered fleetingly whether he would ever relax in a chair again within these four walls of his home.

* * *

The Mount View Hotel was an upmarket establishment of some one hundred rooms, and although its exterior resembled a tower block, its interior was luxurious. Ashworth had parked the Sierra in the car park and now sat waiting.

Gwen lightly tapped her fingers along the length of the roof before bending down to peer inside.

In spite of himself, Ashworth smiled at the sight of her. As the weather was warm she had discarded her top coat and looked stunning in a plain black dress and high-heeled shoes.

Ashworth climbed out of the car.

'When the receptionist said you were on the phone, I thought my luck had changed,' she said, very much like her usual bubbly self. 'Sorry I couldn't talk, but I had a sixteen-year-old girl with me, just going on the pill. The poor kid was terrified as it was.'

'I didn't know whether you'd be at the surgery,' Ashworth said as he locked the car.

'Not much choice really,' she shrugged, 'it's my living.' She nodded towards the hotel. 'You coming up?'

'Yes.' Then as he walked with her, 'Isn't it a bit awkward, with your husband there?'

'Not really. I keep out of his way, and make sure I'm never left alone with him.'

As Gwen collected her key from the reception desk, Ashworth recounted the story of Gladys Smart and told her of Anthony's accusations.

'And you think Nigel might have murdered him?' she asked with horror.

'Along with the women, yes.'

They entered the lift. 'Heads he wins; tails you lose,' Gwen remarked, pressing the button for the sixth floor.

'How do you mean?'

'Think about it. Who else but you would suspect him of the murders? And if you couldn't solve them, for whatever reason . . .'

'I'd lose my job, sooner or later.'

They reached their floor and pushed through people entering the lift.

'But that hardly fits in with hurting me at home,' Ashworth said as they headed for Gwen's room.

'Jim . . .' She hesitated. 'He's talking about filing for divorce . . . and naming you.'

Ashworth stopped. 'Game, set and match,' he said quietly. 'That certainly would destroy my marriage. And nobody suspects him of murder, so any attempt to investigate him on my part would look like a petty reprisal.'

'Quite. Come on, Jim, let's go to my room.'

Although the room was comfortable, it had an impersonal feel to it. Gwen flung her bag on the bed and invited Ashworth to sit in one of the deep armchairs.

'A drink, Jim?'

He looked decidedly preoccupied. 'What? No, I won't, thanks.'

'I will.'

She poured a large gin from a bottle on the bedside table, and topped it up with tonic.

'What are you going to do?' she asked.

'Press on and prove he committed the murders. That way I spike half of his plan.'

Gwen gazed at him over the rim of her glass. 'You're a hard man to beat.'

'Yes, but this time it looks as though I'll have to settle for a draw.'

Her eyes teased him. 'You'll always have someone to turn to if you need comfort.'

'You're back to your old self, I see,' he smiled.

'Life goes on,' she said with a shrug.

'What do you know about Gladys Smart?' Ashworth asked, deliberately steering to safer waters.

She told him Gladys's sad story, and Ashworth's face bore a grim look as he listened.

'Did your husband know about it?'

'Yes.'

'Gwen, do you think it's possible she did give him the overdose, to put him out of his misery?'

Settling on the bed, Gwen kicked off her shoes and drew up her legs, saying, 'When I saw Mrs Smart she was close to the end of her tether, but I very much doubt that she did. Remember, you're not dealing with a criminal mind here, simply a woman of seventy-six who comes from a generation frightened to death of authority. She'd be incapable of reasoning out post-mortems and all the procedure.'

'That's more or less what I thought,' Ashworth said dismally.

Gwen finished her drink. 'What do you do now?'

'Find out who didn't do it, and in the process find out who did,' he replied, getting to his feet. 'Thanks for your time, Gwen.'

She pushed herself from the bed and walked to him, a disgruntled look on her face. 'That's a bit formal, Jim. Don't you think?'

Despite his determination to remain resolute should this moment arise, Ashworth found himself disturbed by her body, her fresh smell.

She said, 'Like I say, life goes on. We're about to be hanged — does it make any difference how many other offences they take into consideration?'

Gwen's lips drew his and a tiny moan broke in her throat as they met. Their bodies touched, pushed against each other.

Ashworth wavered on the point of no return, but then he forced her away. Her face was flushed, her breathing heavy.

'Why not, Jim?' she urged.

Ashworth stared down at her. 'If you don't know now, Gwen, you never will.'

He left the room without another word.

Nigel Anthony, his eyes afire with loathing, watched as Ashworth returned to his Sierra. And although he had parked where he could not be seen, instinct made him duck down in the car seat.

'Tomorrow I'm going to put the final nail in your coffin, Ashworth,' he murmured with contempt.

CHAPTER 21

Next morning the warm weather broke, replaced by fine drizzle which fell incessantly from a leaden sky to dampen the spirits of all. But none more so than Ashworth's.

If he wished anyone a good morning en route to CID it was by courtesy of reflex action. Holly Bedford had crossed the line he drew for all of his staff, and now he must call her to account.

When he entered the office, both detectives knew from his expression that a storm had arrived.

'Josh, I'd like a word with Holly . . . alone,' he said abruptly.

Josh reached for his bomber jacket, mouthed 'good luck' to Holly, then made himself scarce.

Ashworth fixed her with one of his forceful glares but, from behind her desk, Holly returned it.

'Well, young lady, what have you got to say for yourself?'

'The first thing is, I'm a detective sergeant and I find being addressed as 'young lady' offensive.'

'Don't try to be clever with me,' Ashworth stormed. 'I'm referring to you going behind my back to Ken Savage.'

'And why shouldn't I, if I consider your behaviour necessitates it?'

Ashworth was momentarily speechless; he was not used to officers arguing back.

'I've also disobeyed an order,' Holly said. 'I told Gladys Smart we'd not be seeing her today.'

'You've done what?' Ashworth yelled.

'I don't know where your mind is, sir, but it's not on the job. You're going to kill that old dear. She was crying all the way home yesterday.'

'Holly, you're getting very close to the wire on this. In future you will carry out my orders to the letter. I am your superior officer and if you have any complaints, we'll see the Chief Constable together. Is that understood?'

'I'd heard you didn't pull rank,' Holly said saucily. 'I thought you liked to sort things out with your people.'

Holly's remarks, the cool manner in which they were delivered, goaded Ashworth.

'Well, young lady, if you were a man I would,' he retorted angrily, 'and I'd probably end up thumping you in the process.'

Holly's control finally snapped. Jumping up, she leant across the desk. 'Don't do me any favours,' she said. 'The last man who thumped me didn't walk away scot free, and you wouldn't either.'

Ashworth said no more but slammed out of the office, angered by the knowledge that he had by no means scored a resounding victory.

* * *

And from there his day deteriorated.

Sophie Fox did not answer his knock. She sat cowering in a corner of the tiny kitchen — the furthest point from the front door — whispering gibberish prayers to nameless gods as sights too terrible to comprehend flashed before her eyes.

She saw many poor souls, emaciated, dressed in rags, running towards a barbed wire fence. Their death cries, as bullets pumped into their bodies, held a triumphant ring, for dying before the relentless gunfire from the guards meant escape from the hell camps.

'No,' Mrs Fox moaned softly as Ashworth's second knock rearranged the pictures in her tortured mind.

She saw herself, not yet in her teens, pushed back on the floor and held there while a German soldier violated her. Others, fuelled by alcohol and fear crowded around, intent on causing as much brutalization, as much emotional pain as they could before fleeing from the liberating Soviet army.

Then all was quiet. No further knocks. The policeman must have gone away.

'My son, he is a good boy,' she cooed to herself. 'He is trying to protect me, as a good son should.'

As she crouched uncomfortably in the corner, Mrs Fox thought of her son and tried to rationalize those thoughts.

He was not frightened for himself, she reasoned, only for her. Those awful things she suspected he had done were all in her mind; figments of her imagination; not real. If she told the police, they would soon find out she was wrong . . . was mad.

That was why Gerald worried. He did not want her carried away, screaming, to the place where crazy people go; to where she had been taken three times already. That was what Gerald was afraid of; nothing else.

She got up with hope renewed, and wandered around the flat, humming softly to herself.

* * *

After his confrontation with Holly, Ashworth kept a low profile for the remainder of the day. Not that his troublesome detective sergeant bothered him overmuch; there were simply too many other things on his mind, more important things to be dealt with.

His abortive call on Sophie Fox left him dispirited; he spent the rest of his time doing precisely nothing.

Calling into the station at four thirty, he was almost relieved when Martin Dutton pointed to the ceiling with a look of foreboding.

Ken Savage, seated behind a full ashtray, smiled widely when Ashworth entered the office.

'Jim, pull up a seat, old son.'

Ashworth winced. Whenever Savage did his hale-and-hearty act, it meant he was about to broach a subject which would not be to Ashworth's liking.

He sat down and waited while Savage coughed loudly and repeatedly in an effort to shift the phlegm in his throat.

Finally, he began, 'I'm getting more complaints from this Fox character . . .'

'Ken, I was there this morning, and if the woman was in the flat, she didn't answer the door,' Ashworth said with fierce irritation. 'What's he complaining about?'

Savage did not answer immediately. He lit a cigarette, sat fingering the lighter.

Then, 'Just that, Jim. He said you called there this morning, and his mother was too terrified to open the door.'

Ashworth took in a long breath, exhaled sharply, then said, 'I knocked on the door twice. There was no answer, so I left. I shouldn't have to be explaining this.'

'Sit in my seat, Jim. This Fox is claiming he went home at lunchtime, found his mother so distraught he had to call the doctor.' Savage fixed Ashworth with a piercing stare, drew on his cigarette. 'The woman's got a heart condition, and a history of mental illness.'

'But I need to talk to her,' Ashworth insisted.

'If the media get hold of this . . .' Savage countered. 'Can't you bring the woman into the station so the whole thing's supervised?'

Ashworth shook his head. 'They're not that sort of questions.'

Savage considered him. 'How important is this, Jim?'

'Extremely important.'

'All right, but take another officer with you,' Savage said. 'I'm not going to allow the civil liberties wallahs to run the force, but I want you to tread carefully just the same.'

As Savage stubbed out his cigarette in the full ashtray, old filters and ash tumbled onto the desk. Tidying up with a few deft movements, he said, 'The mercy killing case — what have you got on that?'

'I didn't see the woman today. I decided to leave it till tomorrow,' Ashworth pronounced. 'She is elderly.'

'That's not the way I heard it, Jim,' Savage said tactfully. 'Word has it that Bedford overturned one of your orders.'

Ashworth sighed. 'Then you heard correctly. I'm having some bother with her.'

'Do you want me to step in?'

'No need,' Ashworth assured him. 'I'm firmly in control.'

Savage studied him for a while, then said, 'That's not how it looks, Jim. Bedford's an uppity lass and I'm looking to you to keep her in check.'

It did not escape Savage's notice that Ashworth could not meet his eyes as he said, 'I'm biding my time on that, but it will be sorted.'

'See to it. You're in charge of CID,' Savage said tartly.

But as he watched the dispirited Ashworth leave the office, he wondered whether the man was in charge of anything anymore.

CHAPTER 22

Gladys Smart was brought in the next morning. She looked pale and worn as Holly settled her into a chair opposite Ashworth in the interview room.

Josh was seated next to him. Holly moved back to stand beside the door.

Ashworth smiled kindly. 'Have you thought about what I said to you the other day, Mrs Smart?'

'Yes.'

'And have you anything else to tell me?'

'No, sir,' Gladys said softly. 'I haven't done nothing wrong, sir.'

'Only two people saw your husband that day: you and the doctor. So, one of you must have given him the tablets.'

'I haven't done nothing wrong, sir,' Gladys repeated, although her resolve appeared to be weakening.

'Mrs Smart, you can't just keep saying that,' Ashworth said sharply. 'I have to find out the truth. That's my job.'

Gladys took one look at his impatient expression and blurted out, 'Holly said if I just keep saying I haven't done nothing, I'll be all right.'

Ashworth's head pivoted round sharply and he looked at his sergeant. 'Will you excuse me?' he said to Gladys.

'Outside,' he ordered Holly, in a tone which made the old woman tremble.

He closed the door quietly and confronted the girl. 'What the hell are you doing?' he demanded.

'Trying to help an old lady who's somehow got tangled up in a dispute you're having with Dr Anthony,' she said defiantly.

'But you're not helping her.'

'Let her walk, sir, for Chrissake. Surely you can square that.'

'You deal with it then,' Ashworth said roughly. 'You let her walk, as you call it.'

Holly hesitated.

'Yes, I thought that would put a different complexion on it.'

'If we work together . . .'

'We're going to work together,' Ashworth assured her, 'because I'm insisting that we do. But it's going to be by the book, and if that doesn't appeal, I'll go to the Chief Constable and tell him I don't want you at this nick. Is that understood?'

Holly's expression was sullen as she muttered, 'Yes.'

'Good. Now take Mrs Smart home, and on the way explain to her that she won't be all right if she just keeps saying she hasn't done anything.'

Holly moved towards the door.

'And you can also tell her I'll see her tomorrow at three p.m. And you'd better make sure that's adhered to.'

The door to the interview room shook as Holly slammed it behind her.

* * *

Ashworth felt totally isolated as he sat alone in the CID office. How could the department function properly if he and his team could not bear to be in the same room?

Once again his thoughts returned to Mrs Fox. How could he get to her? Her son's threatened actions did not concern him, but if the woman refused to open the door, what could he do?

Fox was his last hope. If the man was merely trying to protect his mother, then Ashworth had an awful lot of music to face.

The telephone rang, and for a few moments Ashworth stared at it, nonplussed. Then he picked up the receiver. 'Ashworth,' he barked.

There was silence.

'Hello?' Still no response. 'Hello?'

He was about to replace the receiver when he heard, 'It is Sophie.'

'Sophie,' he said gratefully.

'I am sorry I did not answer the door yesterday.' She appeared to be whispering.

'Are you frightened of me, Sophie?'

'Some days are good for me, some are bad. Yesterday was bad . . . very bad.'

'Can I come and see you today?' he asked.

Her laugh was hardly joyous, as she said, 'You want to ask about my son, and yet you talk about the war.'

'You're a clever woman, Sophie.' Then, barely daring to breathe, 'Do you want to tell me about your son?'

There was a silence. Ashworth feared he had lost her. Then she said, 'I do not know. So many nights I go without sleep, thinking of these things.'

'Can I come and see you today?'

'Yes.' Her reply was quick, her tone conspiratorial. 'But we must be careful. My son, he suspects that I tell you things.'

'Is it safe to come now?'

'Yes, the guards, they have gone.'

Her words made Ashworth anxious. He said, 'I'll come straight away.'

* * *

The story of Gladys Smart's persecution at the hands of Chief Inspector Ashworth did the rounds, and in the telling became exaggerated out of all proportion.

Now most of Uniformed were waiting for the man to commit some sort of misdemeanour: speeding, or better still, a borderline case for the breathalyser which would allow them to pull him up.

Feelings were running high.

Even the staunchly loyal Martin Dutton had developed reservations. He, of course, maintained that the case must be looked at, the facts established; but an old lady questioned to breaking point, with no quarter given . . . no, that did not settle well.

The situation hardly seemed destined to improve either, for was not Ashworth now being accused of harassing a Polish woman?

And the rumoured fling with Gwen Anthony was not helping matters. Usually affairs were greeted with admiration rather than frowned upon by the male contingent, but this time they chose to make an exception.

Jim Ashworth had his enemies, nothing new about that, but now it seemed all flags were turning against him.

* * *

Ashworth was not a man given to elaborate emotional displays. He was prone to anger, yes, but always strove to control it. Most of the time he appeared calm, steady, but as he approached Fox's flat, he could hardly contain his excitement.

Mrs Fox wanted to see him on a matter regarding her son; and the said son was vigorously opposed to Ashworth's visits. So he surmised that some startling revelation must be in the offing.

The door was opened immediately in response to his knock.

'Come in . . . quickly,' Mrs Fox whispered. 'Before you are seen . . . yes?'

He entered the flat and Mrs Fox checked the corridor before closing the door.

'Sophie . . .'

'He has people watching me,' she said, clearly afraid. 'We must be very careful.'

'Are you frightened of your son?'

'Yes,' she admitted, 'but for me there is no escape. All my life it seems I have been in a prison.'

'Is he threatening you?' Ashworth questioned earnestly.

'Come, sit down, we do not have long.' She took Ashworth's arm, guided him towards the settee. 'The guards, they may be watching me.'

'Who are these guards?' he asked hesitantly.

'They are people who look after the liberties of others . . . and they imprison an old woman in her flat.'

'I see,' he said, settling into his seat. 'But, Sophie, this is a free country. You can see anyone you want.'

Mrs Fox sat rigid in an armchair. 'I cannot,' she said dully. 'This you must understand. I have been released into my son's care. They do not even trust me with my heart tablets or sleeping pills. Gerald, he gives them to me as if I were a child.'

Ashworth leant forward keenly. 'What is it you have to tell me about your son?'

'First I tell you about Poland, about my life. Then maybe you understand about my Gerald.'

She stared down at her hands as she began, 'I was only a child when I went to the Nazi death camp. I survived, but my sanity, it was gone. Sometimes I think it would have been better to perish with the rest of my family. Far better, yes, not to be in this world.'

She shrugged woefully. 'After the war, I come to this country. The people, they were so kind. They seemed not to have much, but they shared whatever they had with others . . .'

In the hope of speeding things up, Ashworth asked, 'Did you meet Gerald's father in this country?'

'Yes.' She nodded sadly. 'I worked on the land. There was this man . . . he owned the farm. We lived together but never married.'

'What happened, Sophie, between you and this man?'

'After Gerald was born, maybe three years after, I find this man is not good, not faithful to me.' She hid her face behind tremulous hands. 'The sickness inside my head, it came back.'

'And this had an effect on Gerald?'

'He hated his father and . . .' She stopped.

Ashworth crouched beside her chair. 'And what, Sophie?' he prompted.

She stared past him, her eyes unseeing. 'He overheard the rows I had with his father. Night after night they went on. We would fight, hurt each other. Gerald was only a small boy. All of this, it frighten him.

'Then my man he says he is sorry . . . all a mistake he makes . . . never will this thing happen again. He promise me. But it does, year after year, while my Gerald is growing up. I realize there is nowhere for me to go. I have a son to care for . . . no money of my own. All this, it turn his mind, make him sick like his mother . . .'

'Sophie, tell me about your son,' Ashworth implored. 'Tell me about Gerald.'

'He grew up not liking women, not trusting anybody.'

'Are you telling me your son is homosexual?' Ashworth asked, his heart sinking. 'But we know that, Sophie. He's above the age of consent; there's nothing illegal in what he does.'

'No, it is more than that,' she said miserably. 'He cannot stand people who break promises.'

'People who commit adultery,' Ashworth said flatly.

Mrs Fox slowly nodded. 'That is right. It does something to his mind, brings back all the unhappy memories of his childhood.'

'Tell me everything,' he pressed.

She looked at Ashworth then and he saw terror in her eyes. 'This is a hard decision for me to make,' she said. 'Without Gerald they will put me back in the hospital. I have given this matter much thought.'

'Did he murder the women, here in Bridgetown?'

Mrs Fox stared ahead, the terror replaced by a lifetime of torment. She opened her mouth to speak, and Ashworth felt an expectant tingle travel along his spine.

Then the door of the flat burst open.

Gerald Fox spilled in. 'What are you bloody doing here?' he demanded.

Ashworth got to his feet. 'I'm talking to your mother,' he replied calmly.

Two men stood in the doorway.

'Get out,' Fox screamed, lurching towards him. 'Get out.'

He swept the dolls from the dresser in one rapid movement.

His mother cringed in terror. 'No, Gerald,' she whimpered, 'not my dolls. Please . . . not my dolls.'

'Shut up,' Fox cried. He turned to Ashworth. 'You . . . get out.'

Ashworth ignored him. 'Are you all right, Sophie?'

Her tear-filled eyes met his. 'Yes, I am all right. I have taken my decision. You will go now, please.'

The two men advanced towards him. They wore donkey jackets and jeans, looked no more than twenty years old.

One said, 'Right, as you've been asked to leave, it might be advisable to do so.' He sounded surprisingly well-educated.

The men took hold of his arms and led Ashworth towards the front door.

'Who are you?' he asked roughly.

'We're a new movement,' the man informed him. 'We protect the people from the police.'

'If you don't take your hands off me, son, *you'll* need protection from the police.'

They passed into the corridor.

'Is that a threat?' the man asked, his tone self-assured.

Ashworth's annoyance was rising rapidly. He said, 'No, son, it's a promise. If you don't take your hands off me immediately, I'm going to knock the two of you through that wall.'

They let go.

'Thank you,' Ashworth said with dignity.

* * *

When news of the impending confrontation between Ken Savage and his Chief Inspector spread around the station, the general feeling was that Ashworth had once again overstepped the mark and should be brought to book.

Savage was very near the end of his patience as he faced Ashworth across the desk. 'You deliberately disobeyed an order,' he snapped. 'I told you to take another officer with you when you went to see Mrs Fox.'

As always Ashworth could not admit he was wrong, and he said heatedly, '*She* rang *me*, Ken.'

'That doesn't make any difference,' Savage insisted.

'She was about to tell me something regarding her son which I believe would have tied him in with the murders. But then he burst in with those two thugs.'

'Those two thugs, as you call them, happen to be university graduates and founder members of a civil liberties group.'

'Civil liberties, my backside,' Ashworth said with venom.

'Yes, and believe me, you further their case when you start threatening to beat them up.'

'They were assaulting me,' Ashworth said in his own defence.

'They claim they were escorting you from the flat because you'd been asked to leave. You had no right to be there, Jim, and that hardly entitles you to threaten to knock them through the wall.'

'What do you expect of me?' Ashworth demanded.

'I expect you to behave like a police officer . . . a senior police officer,' Savage said, picking up his cigarettes.

'I nearly had the information I need,' Ashworth stated hotly.

Savage threw down the packet. 'You've got to leave this, Jim. The woman's three jacks short of a full deck.'

'Are you denying me the right to gather information?'

'No, I'm not, and don't try to put words in my mouth,' Savage warned. 'If you've got anything on Fox, bring him in. I'll back you to the hilt — search warrants, anything. But what I'm not willing to do is let you blunder about in the hope of turning something up. And on this case, Jim, that's what you seem to be doing.'

Ashworth was about to speak, but Savage cut him short. 'Leave the woman alone. That's an order, and I expect it to be obeyed.'

Ashworth gave a dejected nod. 'Right,' he said.

Savage lit a cigarette, sat back and watched smoke drift up to the stained ceiling. 'I'm sorry, Jim, but these pressure groups are becoming a fact of life. We're walking on thin ice,' he said wearily. 'If it was left to me you could bluster your way around this, but as it is . . .' He left it there.

'Bluster? That's how you see me, is it?'

'Probably a bad choice of word,' Savage admitted, 'but you're forthright, Jim — even you can't deny that — and nowadays we have to be careful.'

He took in Ashworth's fixed expression. 'Where's your team?'

'I don't know, Ken,' Ashworth answered truthfully. 'They've fallen out with me as well. It would appear that trying to establish the truth is becoming a no-go area.'

Savage's mood softened. 'Don't get downhearted, Jim.'

But the fight had drained out of Ashworth.

'No,' he said, rising from the chair. 'If that's all . . .'

'For the moment, yes.'

As Savage watched him leave the office, he reflected that he had never before seen Ashworth at such a low ebb.

CHAPTER 23

Ashworth arrived at the station the next day still wondering whether he had kept the worry and apprehension from his voice while speaking to Sarah the evening before. But as she had made no comment and had talked solidly for thirty minutes about the baby, he supposed he had succeeded.

He pushed through the swing doors just in time to witness Martin Dutton vanishing into the office behind reception, leaving the area completely deserted.

Climbing the stairs to CID, Ashworth imagined the whole station had a strange ghost-town feel to it, as if everyone had disappeared before his anticipated arrival.

This peculiar feeling stayed with him until he opened the door of CID and saw the back of Josh's head outlined against the flashing VDU screen.

'Where is everybody?' he asked, attempting to sound cheerful.

Josh swivelled round in the chair. 'Mrs Fox has been found dead, guv,' he said.

Ashworth felt he had received a heavy blow to the abdomen. 'When? How?' he asked with bewilderment.

'Her son found her in bed this morning,' Josh said, decidedly offhand. 'Dr Anthony's there. And the Chief Constable said that due to the delicate circumstances, we'd better keep a low profile.'

'Yes,' Ashworth said, his brain already working. 'Ring Dr Anthony, Josh, and ask her to let me have the results of the post-mortem.'

'On Mrs Fox, guv?'

'Of course,' Ashworth said sharply.

'But there may not be one, guv. The woman had a heart condition.'

'Tell Gwen I want one. Go on, see to it,' he ordered.

Now he knew the reason for the deserted police station; everyone assumed he had hounded Sophie Fox into an early grave.

With some dread he made his way to Ken Savage's office. The Chief Constable was pacing the corridor outside, smoking furiously, and for once he surprised Ashworth.

'You've heard the news?' he asked without ceremony.

Ashworth gave a grim nod.

'I'm backing you all the way on this, Jim.'

'You are?' Ashworth said with surprise. 'Why?'

'Because I checked it out. It's on record that this Fox woman did ring you yesterday. Now that's hardly the action of someone who's terrified of you.'

'Thank you, Ken,' Ashworth said with a grateful smile.

'You keep a very low profile,' Savage advised, 'and I'll brazen it out with those civil liberties people.'

Ashworth returned to his office with feelings of relief. If he should go under for this, then Savage would probably go with him, so Ashworth could count on the man fighting tooth and nail to prevent that happening.

* * *

He did not see Holly until three p.m. that afternoon, when she brought in Gladys Smart for further questioning.

And in order to divert his mind from the task before him, Ashworth ruminated for a while on the fact that he would have to find out where his sergeant kept disappearing to in order to avoid him, for he badly needed to re-establish his authority in CID.

Gladys appeared frail, uneasy, as Holly once more helped her to the chair facing Ashworth and Josh.

'Mrs Smart,' Ashworth began after clearing his throat, 'have you thought any more about what I've been saying to you?'

'No, sir,' she whispered.

Ashworth knew he had to end this stalemate, had to know the truth, if only to quieten his own conscience. He already had enough to refer this case to the Crown Prosecution Service, but if he did that, the woman would undoubtedly be prosecuted.

He decided to change tack. 'Dr Anthony told us you hated your husband . . . wanted him dead.'

His words lashed into Gladys. 'No, I didn't, sir,' she said vehemently.

'He had a baby by another woman and forced you to bring it up. Is that true?'

Gladys began to cry.

'Is it true?' Ashworth persisted.

'Yes,' Gladys sobbed, her face a mask of worry, 'but I didn't hate Cliff. A few days before he died, he asked me to forgive him and I did.'

Ashworth bent forward, his steady gaze resting on her face. 'That's not how it looks to me,' he said. 'I think you gave your husband those tablets because you hated him for what he'd done to you.'

As Gladys looked up, tears coursed down her wrinkled cheeks, mucus hung above her lip.

'I done it, sir,' she said, her voice quiet, pathetic. 'I done it, but not because of what you said. I don't want all that coming out in court . . . not about the baby, I mean. I done it 'cause Cliff was in agony and he begged me to.'

Ashworth saw a ray of hope. He asked quickly, 'What made you think we wouldn't find out?'

'It was that Dr Anthony. He said he wouldn't order one of them things to find out why Cliff died . . . but then he did.'

Ashworth closed his eyes as the ray of hope vanished. Anthony might not have administered the fatal dose himself, but he had encouraged Gladys Smart to do so.

He looked back to the woman, and said gently, 'Thank you, Mrs Smart, I won't be taking a formal statement today.'

As Gladys sat there, still highly distressed, she made a pitiful sight. Ashworth dug into his pockets, took out a handkerchief and passed it to her.

'Thank you, sir,' she said.

He needed to get away and as he crossed to the door, Ashworth hoped that neither of his officers would follow. But his heart dived as Holly left the room before him and Josh could be heard leaving his seat.

Holly spun round as soon as the door to the interview room was shut. 'You bastard,' she said with loathing.

'Leave it, Holly,' Ashworth ordered harshly.

But Holly would not leave it. Pushing her face close to his, she said, 'You think you're God Almighty, don't you? Well, I'll tell you what I think you are—'

'Stop it, Holly,' Josh said, taking her arm, attempting to intervene.

'Stay out of this, Josh,' she warned, never once taking her eyes from Ashworth's face. 'I think you're a fucking bastard,' she hissed.

The words were delivered with such force, such rancour that saliva sprayed his jacket.

'I could have your warrant card for that,' Ashworth said, but there was no fire in the words.

'My warrant card? Right . . .'

Holly delved into her shoulder bag, and such was her haste, several letters and a tube of lipstick tumbled onto the floor. But then she found the card.

Holding it under Ashworth's nose, she said, 'Here it is.'

Then, as Josh looked on horrified, she threw it along the corridor. 'Go and get it,' she said, 'then you can stick it up your arse.'

A numbness crept over Ashworth as he watched it slide along the floor, becoming lodged under a door at the end of the passage.

'Get her away from me, Josh.' There was almost a pleading note in his voice.

Josh took her arm. 'Come on, Holly.' But she would not budge, so he pulled her roughly. 'Come on,' he insisted.

Holly allowed herself to be led away as Ashworth went back into the room.

'I'll take you home now, Mrs Smart,' he said softly.

A dejected Gladys Smart struggled to her feet and walked towards him, looking even older, even smaller than at the start of the interview.

* * *

They began gathering at the front of the police station at four p.m. that afternoon.

At first the demonstration was quiet, orderly, little more than a dozen banner-carrying protesters, complaining about police behaviour.

By six p.m. its ranks had swollen to around forty; all chanting, hurling abuse at officers entering and leaving the station.

Ken Savage ordered that they be pushed back to the other side of the road and barricades erected to keep them there. This was duly done, but several scuffles broke out before the barriers were in place.

Then the situation worsened, the crowd grew, and Savage rang for reinforcements and riot gear.

By seven thirty, groups of local youths had arrived on motorcycles. They rode with arrogant disregard around the police side of the barriers, taunting those inside the station.

With the situation becoming volatile, all personnel were ordered to remain within the building and the doors were locked.

When the mob had swelled to over a hundred, Savage made another desperate request for riot gear and reinforcements. They arrived at eight fifteen, immediately incurring the wrath of the protesters who hurled stones and other missiles at their police vans.

As the officers from neighbouring counties poured out of the vehicles and into the station, apprehension showed on their young faces; although they had been trained for riot situations, this would be the first time they faced the real thing.

The first petrol bomb was thrown at nine p.m. It exploded on the station steps in a spreading sheet of flame, blistering the paint on the doors.

Savage now had no option; he must order his men to disperse the crowd. They surged from the building to be met with a hail of paving stones prised from the pavements, and many more petrol bombs.

Crouching behind their riot shields, they edged forward, yard by painstaking yard. The mob, sensing they could not break the line or halt its advance, began to fall back and break up.

That was the moment the police charged. With shields raised, batons drawn, they picked their way through burning patches of petrol, chunks of stone, lashing out at anyone who stood in their way.

The crowd dispersed, panic spreading through its ranks, as the police fought back.

A group of around twenty-five youths formed a rear guard action, hurling petrol bombs and stones, hampering police progress, while the main mob of well over a hundred poured across the stone bridge spanning the River Thane.

Ashworth watched all of this through the glass walls of CID.

Once over the bridge, the mob split into groups to attack the police from all sides.

Already the still April air smelt of smoke, but Ashworth knew there would be more to come before this long night was over.

After a while the battle moved from his view but its sounds still rent the air.

The horrific thought that his actions had caused the riot weighed heavily upon him; and it did not escape his notice that, as a senior officer, he was not consulted as to ways in which the fighting could be contained and brought to an end. It appeared he had been frozen out.

The telephone rang. He grabbed the receiver. 'Ashworth.'

'What the hell's happening, Jim?' It was Gwen Anthony; she sounded frightened.

'We're having a spot of bother with a group of people who are opposed to violence,' he said cynically.

'A spot of bother?' Gwen echoed without humour. 'There are people all over the place. They've turned me out of the surgery.'

'Are you all right?' he asked quickly.

'Yes . . . a bit shook up,' she said. 'They just told me to go, it wasn't my fight. They didn't touch me, but, well, let's just say I'm not constipated.'

'Where are you now?'

'I'm back at the hotel. Jim, they were going through the drugs cupboard as I left.'

Ashworth sighed, rubbed his tired eyes.

Gwen said, 'I've got some news on the post-mortem of Mrs Fox. I gather that's what this is all about?'

'You've guessed right,' Ashworth said dully. 'What's the verdict?'

'I don't know if this helps but she didn't die of natural causes. It was sleeping tablets.'

All at once Ashworth's brain was alert. 'That does help. Can you remember the scene of crime, Gwen? Was there a note?'

'Of course not, Jim. I carried out the post-mortem because Josh said you wanted me to. If there'd been a suicide note, that process would have been automatic.'

'Oh, yes,' he said absently. He was thinking fast.

'Does this get us out of trouble? Does it clear Nigel of any involvement in the murders?'

'Far from it,' he said.

Gwen's question brought the worries tumbling back into Ashworth's mind. He told her the results of his interview with Gladys Smart.

'Oh my God,' she said, momentarily stunned. 'So you think it's possible Nigel actually encouraged the woman to kill her husband?'

'I'm sure of it,' Ashworth said. 'And if he's capable of that, he could easily have killed the two women for the same reason . . . to cause me a lot of trouble.'

'What are you going to do about it?'

Suddenly the darkened office was vividly illuminated. Ashworth forgot Gwen for a moment and anxiously looked out over the town.

Several thatched roofs were on fire. As he watched the orange/red flames shoot skywards, the wail of fire-engine sirens began.

With utter dejection he returned to the telephone. 'Sorry, Gwen, things are hotting up here,' he said, failing to notice the pun. 'I'll go and see Anthony tomorrow evening. I'd have gone tonight but . . .'

'Make it about eight, at the cottage. I'm going to see him then, try to talk him out of naming you in the divorce.'

'Bye, Gwen,' Ashworth said, watching the flames dancing on the walls of his office; and without waiting for her reply he replaced the receiver.

For most of the night Ashworth watched Bridgetown burn. By four a.m. that morning, some semblance of order had been brought to the streets.

Ashworth's heart was heavy. Was he the cause of this carnage? Was it his reluctance to pursue Nigel Anthony

and, as if saddened by the sight of Bridgetown, it vanished behind a bank of cloud.

No one spoke to him as he wandered through the battle-weary troops in reception. Ken Savage gesticulated for him to approach the desk. Ashworth shouldered his way through the crowd to reach the Chief Constable who smelt strongly of whisky.

'It's bad, Jim . . .'

The statement was so obvious, Ashworth did not bother with a reply.

'Come up to my office,' Savage ordered curtly.

The quietness in the corridor contrasted harshly with the mêlée of reception. Both men walked slowly, a weariness in their steps.

'I've got twenty men down,' Savage informed him gravely. 'Thank God none of them is badly hurt; mostly cuts and bruises. Three firemen are in hospital, one of them critical.'

They reached the office. 'Feelings are running high, Jim. We'll have this again tonight if we don't take some action.'

'Did we arrest any of the rioters?' Ashworth asked, opening the door and stepping aside for Savage to enter.

'Five . . . just five,' Savage muttered.

Ashworth noted the half-empty bottle of scotch on the blotter in the middle of the Chief Constable's desk, the white plastic cup: Savage's companions throughout the night.

'Fox isn't among them, is he?' Ashworth asked.

'No. Why should he be?'

Savage poured scotch into the cup, held up the bottle. 'You want one?'

Ashworth declined. 'I want to talk to him, Ken.'

'What about?' Savage asked, alarm in his voice.

'His mother's death caused that riot, and according to the post-mortem results, it wasn't natural causes but an overdose of sleeping pills.' He waited for some reaction.

'Suicide then,' Savage shrugged. 'What difference does it make now? You pushed that woman too far.'

'That's the drink talking,' Ashworth said quietly.

Savage lowered himself into his chair. 'No, it's not. The whole nick's saying it.'

'If they say it to me, they'll have to go into hiding,' Ashworth declared.

'Oh, sit down, Jim.'

'I don't want to sit down. Look, everybody's saying I'm the cause of what's happened tonight—'

'It was a result of your actions,' Savage said stonily.

'No,' Ashworth argued, 'it wasn't.'

'This is no longer an internal matter,' Savage said, dismissing the whole affair. 'There'll be an enquiry into it.'

'That's why it's necessary to establish the facts,' Ashworth pressed.

Savage drained his cup and looked up slowly. 'What are the facts as you see them then?'

'Fox fabricated a story that I was harassing his mother to stop me seeing her. He was frightened of what she might tell me. When that didn't work, he killed her to stop her talking.'

'Prove it,' Savage demanded.

'Mrs Fox told me that because she'd been a mental patient, her son was in total control of her medication. You can't overdose if someone else is handing you the tablets.'

'You want Fox brought in on that evidence?' Savage scoffed.

'Yes,' Ashworth replied stubbornly.

'No, you can't do it. All you've got is the word of a woman who was a mental patient and who is now dead.'

'You're just going to leave Mrs Fox's death where it is?'

'I've got something that looks like suicide, and I'm ordering you to leave it there.' He shot Ashworth a warning look, adding pointedly, 'If we have another riot we could end up with fatalities.'

Ashworth was about to remonstrate, but Savage's adamant expression stopped him.

Instead he said, 'I see. Thanks very much, Ken,' then turned on his heel and left the office.

* * *

Ashworth stayed away from the station for the rest of the day. During his telephone call to Sarah he played down the happenings in Bridgetown, not wanting to worry her unnecessarily.

Although his body was tired, his mind refused to switch off, but he managed to doze now and again in his favourite armchair, waking up each time with a dry mouth and aching limbs.

At seven thirty he set off for the Anthonys' cottage. The Sierra jolted along the uneven track and finally he pulled into the large clearing in front of the property. Gwen's Land Rover and Nigel Anthony's Jaguar were already there.

The front door was opened by Gwen before he reached it.

'Jim, no trouble . . . please,' she cautioned, catching his determined expression.

But Ashworth, his patience exhausted, said, 'Gwen, just about everybody at the station — in the whole of the town for that matter — has ended up despising me, so I think it's about time we got this matter sorted. Don't you?'

She followed him in trepidation and closed the door. 'Lounge,' she said, pointing to where it was. 'And he's half-drunk already.'

Ashworth entered the room to see Anthony sprawled in an armchair, a glass of brandy in his hand.

'Ashworth.' His expression mocked, as did his voice. 'I've just been reading about you in the local paper.'

He leant over and picked it up from the floor. With a flourish he held it out and began to read:

"Sinclair Harris, the Civil Liberties campaigner, said he holds Chief Inspector Ashworth of Bridgetown CID responsible for the town riots last night. Ashworth's total mishandling of Mrs Sophie Fox, a one-time mental patient, led directly to her death, for it is now believed that his behaviour caused her suicide. Mr Harris dismissed claims that the riots were orchestrated. He said they were a spontaneous reaction to heavy-handed police tactics used to break up a peaceful demonstration."

Anthony looked up with glee. 'You're not a popular man, are you?'

'I'm not here to discuss my popularity,' Ashworth retorted.

'But there's more,' Anthony told him with alcohol-induced exaggeration.

He returned his attention to the newspaper. "Ashworth must be removed, Harris warned, or there will be further trouble."

Gwen, sensing Ashworth's rising anger, stepped in. 'Sit down, Jim.'

Ashworth shook his head violently. 'No, Gwen, I don't want to sit down. I want this sorted out.'

'There's nothing to sort out,' Anthony smiled. 'You're going to lose your job.'

'That pleases you, does it?'

Anthony began to laugh.

'Yes, I can see it does,' Ashworth sneered. 'Makes you feel like a man, does it?'

Anthony was stung by the words. 'You shouldn't go around screwing other men's wives and then denying it,' he said angrily.

'Have I denied it? Have I?' Ashworth challenged.

Anthony sprang back. 'Yes, you have.'

'Well, I'm not now.'

Anthony's mouth fell open at the admission. 'I knew it. I knew it,' he scowled.

Gwen gasped. 'Oh God, Jim.'

'I've just about had enough, Gwen,' he said. Then to Anthony, 'And now you know, what are you going to do about it?'

Anthony finished his drink, and calmly said, 'I've done all I need to do.'

But then his anger boiled over. 'You filthy whore,' he yelled at Gwen, throwing his glass across the room. It hit the wall, shattered, and tiny droplets of brandy trickled down the plaster.

Coolly, Ashworth took a chair from around the dining table and sat in front of the man. He said, 'Let's talk about what you've done, shall we?'

'I've destroyed you, just as you've destroyed me,' he said as tears of self-pity weaved down his face.

'No, you haven't destroyed me,' Ashworth said firmly. 'But did you kill two women? Attack two more?'

Anthony said nothing, so Ashworth went on, 'I know you're an accessory to the murder of an old man.'

Anthony's dark mood changed abruptly. He gave an evil grin. 'Wait till that's in the papers,' he said triumphantly. 'How you persecuted an old woman, sent her to prison. The people of this town are going to be sick of the sight of you by then.'

'Why, in God's name, did you do it?'

'To get at you.' He stared hard into Ashworth's eyes. 'You've got to charge her now. You've no choice.'

Pushing himself unsteadily from the armchair, Anthony mumbled, 'I need a drink.'

Ashworth leapt up and caught his arm.

'Let go of me,' he spat.

'You'd do that?' Ashworth asked with incredulity. 'Put a seventy-six-year-old woman through an experience that could kill her, just to get at me?'

'I don't care how many people are killed,' Anthony slurred. 'The stupid old cow doesn't matter.'

Ashworth pulled back his hand to strike him, and Gwen cried, 'No, Jim.' She held onto his arm as tightly as she could. 'Don't. It won't help.'

'Yes, go on, hit me,' Anthony goaded. 'Just think how that would look in the press.'

An angry red mist descended in front of Ashworth's eyes. 'I wouldn't dignify you with a fist,' he said, wrenching his arm from Gwen's grasp.

Then he struck Anthony's face with the flat of his hand, sending the doctor flying. The sound of the slap reverberated around the quiet room.

Gwen screamed as her husband smashed into the dining table, coming to rest amidst overturned chairs. A thin trickle of blood showed from his left nostril.

'I'll get you for this, Ashworth,' Anthony whimpered. 'I'll see my solicitor.'

'I think you'd better go, Jim,' Gwen advised, taking his arm and leading him to the door. 'This is only making matters worse.'

Outside, he said, 'I'm sorry, Gwen, I should have stayed away. I realize that now.'

'Do you really believe he killed those women?'

Ashworth turned to face her. 'Do you?'

'His mind's gone, I do know that,' she admitted sombrely. 'So anything is possible.'

'I noticed he didn't deny it when I put it to him.'

Gwen shivered.

'What are you going to do, Gwen?'

'Stay with him,' she said resignedly. 'It hasn't escaped my notice that whatever's wrong with him, or whatever he's done, I'm at least partly responsible for it.'

'We are, I think you mean.'

'Yes,' she said, 'I suppose that is what I mean.' She studied Ashworth's face. 'What's going to happen to him, Jim?'

'I've one other suspect who's growing more unlikely by the minute. If I can get to him and rule him out completely,' he glanced back towards the cottage, 'then I'll have to take your husband in and start the investigation.'

'Can't you just leave it?' Gwen asked eagerly. 'If I'm looking after him, I'll make sure he doesn't do anything like this again.'

'I'm tempted, Gwen,' he said frankly, 'very tempted. But what about the divorce?'

Gwen's smile was bitter. 'I was hoping to talk him out of that, but I don't think you helped matters on that front.'

'No.' He exhaled sharply. 'Everything I do of late seems to be a disaster.'

They could hear Anthony cursing in the lounge, then came the sound of glass on glass.

'Drop the investigation, Jim,' Gwen implored. 'I'll take him away.'

'And I'll be left with my conscience,' he said miserably.

The implications of such action caused his stomach to turn; he held grave misgivings but nevertheless he said, 'Get him to drop the divorce and I'll think about it.'

'I'll do my best.' She smiled, but there was little warmth in it.

As he drove home, Ashworth's misgivings grew; he knew the man was a time bomb. And if Anthony was responsible for the murders, sooner or later his mind would snap again, and Ashworth felt sure that reported deaths in another part of the country would come to haunt him.

Another thing: it was far from certain that the man would withdraw from the divorce, and if he did not, then Ashworth would go after him with everything he had.

As the next day was Saturday, he reasoned it would be Monday before Anthony could visit a solicitor; but as the riot had disrupted the postal service Ashworth might have to wait a week before hearing anything.

And if a letter did not turn up, his crisis of conscience would really begin, because then the choice would be a stark one: he could either let a suspected murderer walk away . . . or start an investigation which would wreck his marriage.

As he neared the end of the track, Ashworth silently cursed Gwen Anthony. Firstly, for tempting him at the outset; and secondly, for offering a solution which would never bring him peace.

* * *

Ashworth drove along the High Street in despair. Most of the shop fronts had been repaired, and scaffolding erected to support the shell of the old post office.

Crowds of youths gathered on street corners, and the numerous policemen on the beat were doing their best to disperse them before the groups became too large.

The forces of law and order did seem to be in control, but it was a tenuous authority.

CHAPTER 25

Next morning, Ashworth was not looking forward to his fourth interview with Gladys Smart. He was not in any particular hurry to see Holly Bedford either. So, for those reasons he hung around reception for a while.

Approaching Sergeant Dutton at the desk, he said a cheery, 'Morning, Martin.'

Dutton nodded an acknowledgement.

'I take it I'm not too popular at the moment,' Ashworth remarked.

'You're not flavour of the month,' Dutton said candidly. 'A lot of the lads were injured in that little bust-up the night before last.'

'And they're blaming me?'

'Well, of course they are, Jim. What else do you expect?'

'Offers of support?' Ashworth suggested.

'Jim, I've known you for fifteen years now, and you've been a good friend, I'll grant you that,' Dutton conceded, 'but I do think there's something that needs to be said here. In all the time I've known you, I've never seen you handle a case this badly. You're upsetting everybody . . .'

'It seems you're taking everybody's word but mine,' Ashworth stated coldly.

'We're seeing it at first hand,' Dutton retorted. 'If your handling of that Polish woman was anything like the way you dealt with Mrs Smart, I don't wonder there were riots. Whatever possessed you to tear into a woman of that age?'

Ashworth stared at Dutton with dismay. 'Thanks a lot, Martin,' he said brusquely, before turning and heading for the stairs.

In the office, he found Holly and Josh at their desks.

'I want Gladys Smart here at two p.m.,' he announced.

'Right,' Holly said shortly.

She grabbed her shoulder bag, her coat, and careered out of the room, leaving the door swinging open behind her.

Josh stared at the door, at Ashworth, then took his jacket from the back of the chair. 'I'll go and get you a cup of tea,' he said, his smile disconcerting.

Ashworth knew this situation could not be allowed to continue, but a sudden weariness overtook him. He sank into his chair and sat motionless, gazing through the glass at the destruction of his town.

* * *

Holly manoeuvred her car through the heavy Saturday traffic. Gladys, dressed in her best things, sat silent in the back.

Holly saw little point in counselling the woman any further. Ashworth seemed determined to prosecute, but Holly felt certain she would get a sympathetic hearing in court. Whether her advanced age and failing health would stand up to the strain was another matter.

She pulled into the station car park. A group of teenagers stood in the road, jeering, shouting insults as she helped Gladys from the car.

A uniformed constable came out of the station's back door.

'Hello, Holly,' he said, studying the gathering youths. 'It's like a tinder-box out there, likely to go up at any time.'

'I know.'

'And do you know what our orders are? We're not to upset them, just jolly them along and keep them moving.'

His look was scornful as he moved away, calling, 'Give our regards to your guvnor.'

'Will do,' Holly said pleasantly. Then, turning to Mrs Smart, 'Come on, Gladys, let's go inside, shall we?'

In the interview room, Ashworth was seated at the table and Josh was standing by the door.

Ashworth's tone was formal as he said, 'Mrs Smart, would you like to sit down?'

Gladys settled herself in the chair, nerves making her breathless.

'Now, Mrs Smart, you understand that you're being asked to make a formal statement about the events leading up to your husband's death, yes?'

Gladys gave an imperceptible nod. 'Yes, sir.'

Ashworth added, 'By formal, I mean it will be taped.'

Holly wanted to scream: Get on with it. Why prolong the woman's agony?

'Yes, sir,' Gladys stammered.

Holly pressed the record button on the tape recorder.

Ashworth waved an impatient hand. 'Not yet,' he said.

Holly hit the stop button with some force.

'Mrs Smart, I'm a police officer, and at times that means I'm under a good deal of strain,' Ashworth explained softly. 'Now that can make me abrupt, ill-mannered. Would you say I've been heavy-handed with you?'

Gladys hesitated, then said, 'Not heavy-handed as such, sir, no, but you did frighten me a bit, though I don't think you meant to.'

'I see, and because you were frightened, you panicked, said things you didn't mean because you felt under pressure.'

Holly looked across at Josh who gave a puzzled shrug.

'Yes, that's right, sir,' Gladys said in her reedy voice. 'I can't take pressure now. There was a time, mind—'

'There's no need to go into that,' Ashworth cut in. 'If I frightened you, I apologize, it was not intentional. Would you like to make a complaint against me?'

'Oh no, sir,' Gladys said immediately, 'that won't be necessary.'

He nodded towards Holly. She turned on the tape, gave time, date, name of person to be interviewed.

Ashworth said, 'Tell me in your own words what happened on the day your husband died.'

'I done a terrible thing, sir,' Gladys declared loudly for the benefit of the tape recorder. 'I know you could say my actions led to Cliff dying on that day.'

Holly raised her eyes to the heavens in despair.

'What did you do, Mrs Smart?' Ashworth asked gently.

'I went out in the morning . . .'

'How did that affect your husband's death?'

'Well, I shouldn't have gone, sir. See, I had to leave him on his own, but I had to get out of the house or I'd have gone mad.'

'I can understand that . . . we all can. Now tell us what happened,' Ashworth prompted.

'I went into town, see. I used my bus pass and just walked round and round the shops. The I went home again. Cliff was in agony when I got back. About an hour after that the doctor came to give him an injection and that quietened him down. But about four in the afternoon the pain came back and he was asking for his tablets.'

'And how many did you give him?'

Gladys looked into Ashworth's rugged face. 'Two, sir.' Then she shook her head. 'No, that's not true. He was begging, sir, pleading like a child. He'd been such a fine, strong man and there he was, crying like a baby.'

'How many did you give him?' Ashworth asked again.

'Four, sir, but only because he was begging.'

Ashworth sat back. 'The post-mortem revealed a lot more than four tablets, Mrs Smart. How do you think they got there?'

'I don't know, sir.'

'Think,' he said sharply, standing up to pace the room. 'What happened after you gave him the tablets?'

Gladys went blank.

'How did you feel? Think, Mrs Smart, this is very important.'

She looked up at him, as if for guidance, then comprehension lit up her watery eyes. 'Oh, yes . . . I felt tired because I'd been out in the morning. I was very tired, sir. Then just after I gave him the four tablets, I thought I heard a knock on the door, but when I got downstairs it was only a leaflet somebody had pushed through the letter-box.'

Ashworth stopped pacing and returned to his seat. 'And what did you do with the bottle of tablets?'

'I must have put it on the table next to the bed.'

'What sort of shape was your husband in at that time? Could he sit up in bed?'

'No, sir, he was weak as a kitten.'

'So he hadn't been able to move for days . . . weeks, even.'

'Only once, sir, in the last few days. He sat bolt upright in bed. Gave me a right turn, he did. God's angels are round the walls, he said.'

'What are you saying, Mrs Smart? Because you were very tired and thought there was someone at the front door, you mistakenly left the bottle of tablets beside the bed and your husband suddenly found a surge of strength, as he had done before, and took the tablets himself.'

'Yes, sir.'

'Right. Now, there's one other thing. Did you ever discuss any of this with Dr Anthony?'

Glady's brow wrinkled as she thought. 'I don't know, sir.'

'Please think hard, Mrs Smart,' Ashworth urged.

'I think I told him Cliff kept asking me to give him the tablets, but I wouldn't.'

'Good.'

Ashworth motioned for Holly to turn off the tape recorder.

He smiled. 'Now Mrs Smart . . . Gladys . . . you've given us a statement and it's my job to decide if there's a case to answer. Do you understand that?'

'Yes, sir.'

'And I don't think there is. I'm quite happy with your explanation, so you're free to go.'

'Thank you, sir.'

As she reached for her handbag, a relieved smile on her face, Gladys asked, 'Did I do all right, sir? 'Cause I forgot some of what you told me to say when you gave me that lift home the other day. I got stuck when you asked about the tablets.'

'Oh, Gladys . . .' Ashworth buried his face in his hands. 'You must never tell anyone that we talked about this . . . never.'

Gladys quickly put a hand to her mouth. 'I'm sorry, sir,' she mumbled, starting to get up.

'Hold on,' Ashworth said, 'we'll get you a cup of tea and arrange a lift home for you.'

He wanted to get out of the room before Holly, but she walked on ahead of him.

'Why?' she asked as soon as they were alone. 'I thought you did everything by the book?'

He refused to look at his sergeant, so stared at the wall behind her. 'I do things by Jim Ashworth's book,' he told her plainly. 'I made one mistake and I'm trying to get myself out of the resulting mess, hurting as few people as I can in the process.'

Holly opened her mouth to speak.

'Don't say anything,' he said gruffly. 'You've made it very plain how you feel about me. I don't know if one mistake qualifies me as a 'fucking bastard' . . .' His voice was loaded with emotion. 'But I only know I'm human, just like everyone else.'

And with that he turned and strode off.

'Guv . . .' Holly called after him.

Ashworth stopped in his tracks, but kept his back to her. 'Yes?'

'Is there anything I can do to help?'

'No,' he said, shaking his head, 'but I do thank you for the offer.'

CHAPTER 26

It was Sunday. Holly was sitting with Josh at her small kitchen table.

'There's something wrong, Josh,' she said for the umpteenth time. 'He needs help.'

'What can we do? He hardly invites offers of help, does he? We can't just rush in and ask him what he's done.'

Holly pushed the roast beef around her plate. 'That's just what we're going to do,' she said, her tone determined.

She glanced up at the kitchen clock. 'We'll leave it till this evening . . . and let me do the talking.'

'Gladly,' Josh said, giving his full attention to his Yorkshire pudding.

* * *

Ashworth rarely wasted his time on self-pity, but on this particular Sunday he was positively wallowing in it.

The first snap shots of the baby had arrived the previous day and he had so far spent hours working through them; they helped to take his mind off his troubles.

The fact that the partial destruction of Bridgetown had been attributed to his behaviour hurt him enormously, for it was the one place on God's earth which he truly loved; and the probability of more outbreaks of violence did little to ease his misery.

Ashworth's mind had thrown up a barrier against his main cause of concern, refusing to allow any thoughts on the subject until positive action could be taken.

It was nine p.m. that evening before he realized he had not eaten all day. Hastily preparing two corned beef sandwiches, he ate them with little enthusiasm, and was washing the plate when the front door bell rang.

Viewing any interruption as an inconvenience, he dried his hands with irritation and went to answer it.

An ill-at-ease Holly stood on the porch.

'Holly,' Ashworth said with some surprise.

'Guv, this is going to be awkward . . .' she began.

'If it's about that misunderstanding we had, you can forget it. You'll probably be in charge of CID soon, so—'

'No, it's not about that . . .' She stood there undecided for a few moments, then her words came tumbling out. 'I think you're in trouble and I . . . we want to help.'

Ashworth was overwhelmed by a huge surge of gratitude. 'I see.' He looked around. 'We, you said. Where's—'

'Oh, Josh's locking the car but, between you and me, I think he's keeping out of the way in case one of us explodes,' she laughed.

'Well, you'd better come in,' Ashworth said, stepping aside.

As if on cue, Josh appeared on the steps. 'Guv.'

They were settled in the lounge. Ashworth had provided a gin and tonic for Holly, and a malt and soda for himself. Josh was abstaining on the grounds that he was driving.

'Like I said, we think you're in trouble,' Holly reiterated.

'Look, I really appreciate this, but I'm not in—'

'No, guv . . .' Holly chided, sounding more like a schoolmarm every time she opened her mouth. 'There's something you're not telling us, and it's holding up this whole investigation.'

Ashworth tried a chuckle, but failed to sound like his old self.

'I had it off with the guy who sold me the car,' Holly said brightly, 'and I'll probably do it again.'

This time Ashworth's chuckle was real. 'You're a very astute person, Holly.' He studied his glass, took in a breath. 'So, it's confession time. I'll match the eloquence of your language and tell you I had it off with Gwen Anthony once, and it's never going to happen again.'

'And that's caused trouble?' Josh asked, leaning forward on the settee.

Ashworth's gaze returned to his glass. 'Yes, I'm afraid so. Anthony found out, started drinking heavily . . . and became very violent.'

'So are you saying — with the adultery theme running through the murders and attacks — that he could be a prime suspect?'

'Exactly, Josh. The man's suffered some sort of breakdown, and I believe there's enough evidence to bring him in concerning Jenny Chambers' death.'

'But if you did, you'd have to give your reasons,' Holly cleverly surmised.

'That's right, and as you know, he was also involved in Clifford Smart's death in as much as he told Gladys he wouldn't order a post-mortem, then he did. Which is why I had to push the woman so hard, to find out if she did do it.'

'What about Fox?' Josh asked.

'Sophie Fox was about to tell me something regarding her son before he burst in with his friends.'

Holly finished her drink, then said, 'Do you think Fox could be the murderer?'

'I don't know,' Ashworth said, despondent, 'but, at the moment, all roads seem to lead to Anthony.'

'Mrs Fox's death looks suspicious to me,' Josh commented. 'I've seen the post-mortem report.'

'Yes, it does,' Ashworth agreed. 'Even more so when you consider that she told me her son was in total control of her drugs. She had no access to them.'

'So he killed his mother to shut her up,' Holly ventured.

'He could have done.' Ashworth pointed to Holly's glass. 'Can I get you another?'

She nodded. He took the glass and crossed to the drinks table. 'But she was such a poor demented soul, and with her persecution complex, it's quite possible she imagined her son was in charge of the drugs.'

They were quiet for a while, the only sound being the tonic fizzing in Holly's gin.

She said, 'But we need to look into it . . .'

'That's just what we can't do,' Ashworth said, handing her the drink. 'Savage won't allow it, says it would cause more trouble in town.'

'That's ridiculous,' Holly snorted, 'we've got to look into it. Even if it's only to establish it was suicide.'

Ashworth huffed. 'Tell Savage that.'

'I will,' Holly replied with vigour. 'Perhaps it's about time our Chief Constable was reminded that we have a procedure to follow, and it doesn't just go out of the window when a few yobs take it into their heads to start throwing petrol bombs.'

Ashworth smiled down at them. 'Thank you both.'

'We'll be off then,' Josh said, getting to his feet.

'Let me finish my drink,' Holly complained.

Soon they were at the front door.

'Goodnight, guv.'

'Night, Josh,' Ashworth turned to Holly. 'I do appreciate this, you know.'

As Josh wandered off to the car, Holly smiled up at him, saying, 'I just wish you'd let me through that brick wall surrounding you more often.'

'Gwen asked me to forget all this, let her take Anthony away,' Ashworth confided with shame, 'and I was tempted, Holly . . . just to close my eyes and hope the nightmare would go away.'

'In the circumstances, anyone would have been tempted.'
'Maybe.'
Holly kissed him lightly on the cheek. 'Goodnight, guv.'

* * *

Savage banged his fist on the desk, a violent movement, and one which he immediately regretted for his head was still thumping from last night's scotch.

'No,' he said forcefully. 'Request denied.'

Holly and Josh were seated in front of him. Holly said, 'I don't see how you can deny it, sir.'

'Because I say so,' Savage said, glaring at the girl.

Savage saw it was time to re-establish his authority. It was bad enough having Ashworth forever laying down the law, but now this Bedford woman was following suit. He had been far too lax with CID of late.

'There'll have to be an inquest, sir,' Holly declared. 'We'll need to establish the facts connected with Mrs Fox's death.'

'That's been done,' Savage insisted. 'The woman was frightened to death of the police. Ashworth went too far. End of story.'

'With respect, sir, that's not how I see it.'

Savage's eyes bulged. 'You've been listening to Ashworth . . . that story about her son doling out the sleeping pills.'

'Yes,' Holly admitted.

'Ashworth's just trying to save his own skin,' Savage said dismissively.

'And he'll still be trying to save it at the inquest, don't forget,' Holly countered. 'The chief inspector will have to give evidence, and he's not likely to say he harassed the woman, is he?'

'Have you any idea how much all this is costing in overtime?' Savage exploded. 'I've got officers working sixteen hours at a stretch trying to keep the lid on things. Not to mention the cost of riot gear and deploying men from other forces.'

Holly remained staunch. 'None of that alters the situation, sir. Sooner or later we're going to have to look into the death of Mrs Fox.'

Savage, reaching for his cigarettes, gave this some thought. 'All right,' he said grudgingly, 'I'll find out if Fox is willing to see you. He'll probably insist on having those civil liberties people present though.'

'But what if we need to bring him into the station to make a formal statement?' Holly asked.

Savage lit a cigarette and smoke poured from his mouth as he said, 'Avoid that if you can, and be careful, keep it low-key. By the way, I want Ashworth to take a couple of days' leave.'

'Thank you, sir.'

They left the office, Savage's bloodshot eyes fixed on their backs. Ashworth was right, he decided, that girl does need a good kick up the backside.

Josh had hardly closed the door before Holly started fuming. 'God, this is doing my head in, Josh. He'll find out if Fox is willing to see us . . . We've got a right of entry.'

'Calm down,' Josh muttered as he followed her stomping figure.

* * *

Ashworth made it very plain that two days of enforced leave was not on his agenda.

The thought of sitting at home waiting for a letter from Nigel Anthony's solicitor to drop through the letter-box held no attraction at all. Far better to keep his mind occupied, if only with mundane paperwork in the office.

Holly was becoming more dominant by the minute, completely swamping Josh and, at times, even Ashworth; but for the moment he was willing to let it ride, although not to the point of relinquishing control of the case.

When news came through that Fox had agreed to talk to the police, Ashworth gave her a detailed list of questions to be asked.

Then they left him brooding, seething, but above all, worrying.

* * *

One thing was blatantly apparent at Fox's flat: any displays of grief were strictly reserved for the media. Away from the reporters, Fox seemed totally relaxed and at ease.

He reclined on the settee, flanked by Sinclair Harris in donkey jacket, bold checked shirt, blue jeans, and Darren Cleveland in identical uniform.

Harris's university education was evident as he took control. 'Okay, what do you want to ask Mr Fox?'

Holly ignored him, addressed herself to Fox. 'Your mother died in suspicious circumstances and we're here to try and establish what happened.'

Harris said, 'What happened is pretty plain, I would have thought, well, to anyone of average intelligence . . . but for your benefit I'll explain it.'

Fox gave an artificial laugh.

'Your chief inspector hounded Mrs Fox until she committed suicide.'

Neither Holly nor Josh had been invited to sit down, and both now felt at a disadvantage, standing awkwardly before the trio. Holly, however, steadfastly refused to allow this to show. Favouring them with a vindictive smile, she said, 'That's not how we see it.'

'I believe the people of this town gave their verdict a couple of nights ago,' Harris said smoothly.

Once again, Holly chose to ignore him. 'Mr Fox, can you show us where your mother's medication is kept?'

'It was in the bathroom,' Fox volunteered.

'But you won't find it there now, sweetheart,' Harris chortled. 'It's been thrown out.'

'You've destroyed evidence?' Holly demanded hotly.

'How did Gerald know it was evidence?' Harris countered, full of self-assurance. 'He was distraught, having found his mother dead from what he assumed to be natural causes.'

'Yes, and it looks as though he hasn't got over it yet,' Holly said with heavy cynicism.

'Now, now,' Harris cautioned.

'And how exactly did you dispose of the medication?' Holly asked.

Harris's eyes sparkled with amusement as, once again, he answered for Fox. 'He put it in a big black plastic bag and the bin men threw it into the back of their lorry where it was all crushed up before being taken to the land-fill site.'

Fox and Cleveland laughed wildly at this.

Harris smiled. 'Do you have any more questions?'

With great difficulty, Holly refrained from uttering a harsh rejoinder, saying instead, 'Not for the moment, but we'll be asking Mr Fox to make a formal statement at the police station.'

'When, pray?' Harris asked.

'This afternoon. Two p.m.,' Holly said stiffly. 'And I'll be applying for a warrant to search this flat.'

'Good, that'll give us time to destroy anything we want,' Harris mocked. Then, 'You still don't understand, do you? You're no longer in control.'

'Two p.m., Mr Fox,' Holly ordered.

She signalled sharply to Josh and turned on her heel, eager now to be out.

* * *

Bridgetown remained tense.

By the time Gerald Fox arrived at the station, accompanied by his solicitor, a crowd had gathered outside; some thirty strong, mostly local youths, doing little more than looking for trouble.

They cheered when Sinclair Harris arrived, parking his blue Ford Orion on double yellow lines in front of the station. He acknowledged their applause with a Nazi salute as he bounded up the station steps.

From his office, high up in the building, Ashworth watched. What he saw was the beginning of mob rule, and as Holly and Josh dealt with Fox he made several telephone calls.

While the rest of the force — from the Chief Constable downwards — dithered, Ashworth was taking positive action to ensure that Bridgetown would not be run by whoever could shout the loudest.

His tenancy in the rank of Chief Inspector looked as though it might be coming to an end, but while he held the position he intended to fulfil his obligations.

CHAPTER 27

The interview with Gerald Fox was short-lived. Almost every question put to him was answered by his solicitor, and after five minutes they had no more information than was gleaned at the flat.

Holly stared at Fox across the table. His eyes were shifty, his movements rapid as he nervously smoked a cigarette.

'Who was in charge of your mother's medication?' she asked.

Fox glanced at his solicitor, Mr Watkinson, a tall thin man who sniffed before he spoke.

'My client has already stated that his mother was in charge of her sleeping tablets. I'm sure those are the items of medication which interest you.'

'Yes, they are,' Holly replied, 'but what if I were to tell you that we have information which opposes what you're saying?'

'I'd say prove it at the coroner's court.' This time, Watkinson's sniff had a triumphant ring to it.

Holly sighed; it seemed that she was forever arriving back at the same infuriating cul-de-sac.

'Mr Fox, could you please tell me, one more time, what happened to your mother's medication after her death?'

'I threw it all away.'

'Why did you do that?' Holly asked, watching him closely.

It was obvious that Fox was well-rehearsed in this part of the statement.

He said without thought, 'Because I wanted to get my mother's things out of the flat. I was distressed about her death.'

'But it seems odd to me that the only things you threw away were her heart tablets and sleeping pills.'

Fox looked to Watkinson for assistance.

'Where is this line of questioning leading?' the solicitor asked.

'Well, for starters, if we found the sleeping-tablet bottle we could establish, by the fingerprints on it, whether Mrs Fox administered the tablets herself.'

Watkinson sniffed loudly. 'My client has already stated that she did. Have you any evidence which revokes that?'

Holly shook her head but did not speak.

'Then I suggest you leave that line of questioning alone,' Watkinson said. 'Your pathologist should have informed you of any suspicions at the time, allowing you to bring in Scene of Crime officers. I'm sure you're aware of that.'

'Yes,' Holly replied, close to defeat.

'My client can hardly be held responsible for your mistakes, can he?'

She glared at the solicitor, then said to Fox, 'How many tablets were in the bottle?'

The man appeared confused, as if the question was unexpected. 'I don't know. I can't remember,' he stammered.

Holly, sensing a weakness, pushed the point. 'Was it empty?'

'I don't know.'

Fox's eyes implored Watkinson to intervene.

He did, saying firmly, 'This is not relevant. My client is here to offer his assistance, but I do feel there is little more he can do to help.'

He raised his eyebrows, inviting Holly to contradict.

'All right,' she conceded. 'Thank you for coming in, Mr Fox.'

Watkinson gave a terse nod and ushered his client from the room.

Josh left his chair and looked out of the window. 'It's a dead end, Holly,' he said dismally.

'I know,' she said. 'God, that little creep gets to me.'

Unconsciously, she fingered the scar above her eye; the dressing had been removed, the stitches dissolved, leaving a livid mark where the wound had knitted together.

'Did you notice the way he kept looking at me? I'm certain it was Fox who attacked me.'

'Now, come on, Holly, you—'

'And I'll tell you something else, I think he's as confused about his mother's death as we are.'

'Holly,' Josh said softly, returning to his seat to face her. 'Look, whatever you say, I know you're fond of Ashworth, but you really are clutching at straws.'

'Maybe,' she intoned, 'but if someone else killed Mrs Fox, that would explain why he got rid of the bottles showing just his fingerprints because—'

'They would make it look as though he'd done it,' Josh finished in a derisive tone. 'Have you anyone in mind?'

'No.'

'Then I think we'd better leave it there, don't you?'

* * *

Ashworth stood at the window, watched the events taking place outside the station, as details of the Fox interview were relayed to him.

Television cameras whirred and journalists scribbled on their note pads as Sinclair Harris gave a short speech.

Then Martin Dutton read out a police statement; and although Ashworth could not hear, he knew the words off by heart for he had been given a copy:

'The Bridgetown police wish to thank Mr Gerald Fox for his wholly voluntary cooperation, and will be doing all in their power to resolve this delicate situation which is causing the public so much concern.'

'The circus,' Ashworth observed as he viewed the proceedings.

'We have to try and placate the public,' Josh pointed out.

'The public,' Ashworth snorted. 'Do you really think that band of yobs is the public? Most of them just want to thump a copper and vanish into the crowd.' He shook his head gravely. 'No, take Harris and his cronies off the streets and you wouldn't have a problem.'

* * *

The next day was one of the longest Ashworth could remember. Sarah telephoned first thing, even though they had spoken at ten p.m. the previous night. She was deeply worried by the riots and events in Bridgetown which were now receiving national television coverage.

Ashworth did his best to be reassuring, told her all was well, but knew that he sounded anything but convincing.

As they talked several envelopes tumbled through the letter-box. Ashworth's heart gave a sickening jump as he watched them fall onto the mat — one of them could be from Anthony's solicitor. Outside, the postman could be heard whistling cheerfully as he wandered back down the drive.

He told Sarah he had to go, urged her to stop worrying, said a hurried goodbye, then scooped up the envelopes. There was a gas bill; a television licence reminder; a seed catalogue; and a long white envelope addressed to himself.

Ashworth's hands were trembling as he opened it. Unfolding the letter, he stared at its contents for some moments, then laughed aloud with relief.

He had been awarded four numbers in a nationwide draw for a Honda motor car . . .

* * *

Try as they might, no one could keep from Ashworth news that the local press were baying for his blood.

In editorials pandering to public opinion, they were pushing for an enquiry into the handling of Mrs Fox; and although they did not actually come out and say it, they most certainly implied that Ashworth should be removed from his office.

Donald Gibbings, chairman of the local Chamber of Trade and Commerce, and prominent member of the police committee, was far more forthcoming during a telephone conversation with Ken Savage.

'Get rid of him, Ken.'

'Put all this into perspective, Donald' — it was only two p.m. but Savage already had cravings for a large scotch. 'It hasn't been established yet that he's actually done anything.'

'Not the point,' Gibbings insisted. 'We need something to calm the situation down. Sacrifice Ashworth and these people will think they've won, then perhaps things can return to normal.'

Even Savage balked at this. 'Hold on, I can't throw one of my people to the lions . . .'

'Never mind about your people. I'm thinking about my members, a lot of whom are facing rising insurance premiums because their businesses have been looted, plus the costs of installing metal shutters. These hooligans are likely to go on the rampage at any time.'

'Ashworth was pursuing a murder investigation,' Savage reminded him. 'What you're suggesting would only make matters worse. I refuse to pull my people out every time there's a disturbance.'

'Ashworth's always been trouble, Ken. He's heavy-handed, upsets a lot of people.'

'Yes, he does,' Savage agreed, 'but he always gets the job done.'

'Are you refusing to do anything about this?'

'Donald, our public line on this is that we deeply regret the incident and are doing all in our power to establish what happened.'

'It's not enough, Ken.'

'That's all you're getting for the moment,' Savage replied testily.

'Can't you get Ashworth to make some conciliatory noises?' Gibbings persisted. 'The man's like a bull in a china shop. There's a report in today's *Post* that says he actually threatened those civil liberties people.'

'Greatly exaggerated.'

'Ken, the fact that there's any truth in it at all is the worrying thing. You must do something.'

Savage was eager to end the discussion. 'Leave it with me, Donald,' he said. 'I'll sort it out.'

'In the next couple of days, I hope.'

When this was met with silence, Gibbings added a gruff, 'Bye, Ken.'

'Goodbye.' Savage replaced the receiver.

'Goodbye,' he repeated, opening his desk drawer and taking out a half bottle of whisky.

Unscrewing the cap, he muttered, 'What is it they say about two fingers?'

He drank deeply.

* * *

Next morning, Ashworth stayed home until well after eleven a.m. No letters arrived with the first post, so he decided to wait for second delivery. If there was no news of the impending divorce by then, he felt he could at least breathe a little more freely.

Watching from the bedroom window, Ashworth saw the postman pass the end of his drive and deliver mail to his immediate neighbour.

Then, setting off for work, he told himself it was far too early to be certain but, even so, he hummed a merry tune as he drove along.

However, Ashworth's feelings of elation were to be short-lived. Holly and Josh were waiting in reception; and something in Holly's expression told him all was not well.

'Guv . . .' she called, moving well away from the front desk.

'What's wrong?' he asked.

'Bad news, I'm afraid. The last attack victim's regained consciousness.'

'What's bad about that?'

Holly hesitated. 'We haven't been able to interview her properly, but in the minute we were allowed to see her, she told us her assailant had a posh accent.'

'Anthony,' Ashworth exhaled.

'Looking more and more like it, guv. But Josh did point out that Fox hasn't got an accent as such, and to someone brought up in the Midlands, that could sound posh.'

'How long have I got?' Ashworth asked.

'It's going to be a couple of days before we can interview her properly. The doctors are worried she'll have a relapse if we push her.'

'And you're willing to give me that time?'

'Of course.' She smiled. 'Anyway, there's nothing else we can do, you're still in charge of the investigation.'

'Huh, at the moment, Holly, I feel in charge of very little.'

'Oh, there's a letter on your desk.'

Ashworth's heart jumped. 'A letter?'

'Yes, delivered this morning.'

Without making another utterance, Ashworth clambered up the stairs. On his desk was a white envelope. The address was handwritten, but that did not mean much; many businesses using word processors for their correspondence handwrote their envelopes.

He was trembling but, at the third attempt, was able to insert the paper-knife and slice it open. Withdrawing the sheet of paper, he unfolded it slowly, spread it on the desk. Three times he read the words before returning it to the envelope.

Tucking the letter into his inside pocket, Ashworth walked over to the glass wall and gazed down at the small band of protesters who seemed to have taken up permanent residence on the opposite side of the road.

'This could be the end of your career, Jim,' he told his reflection in the glass.

CHAPTER 28

Holly studied her reflection in the rear-view mirror; the scar over her eye the focal point.

Some days it took on the same degree of importance as an ugly cold sore would to a vain eighteen-year-old, yet on others she could almost convince herself it was hardly visible. Today — mostly because of her mounting need to relieve the frustration fuelling her irritability — it was the latter.

Her thoughts turned to Gary Williams.

On the pretext of needing some petrol, Holly drove to the garage, only to be informed by the cashier on the self-service petrol pumps that Gary had taken an early lunch.

She was driving along the High Street when she saw him emerging from the newsagents, a packet of cigarettes in his hand. He looked so handsome, so athletic, the sight of him took her breath away.

Holly was about to sound the horn when a woman followed him out of the shop; a tall, blonde woman, extremely pretty . . . and around eight months pregnant.

Gary reached back a hand which the woman took with a smile, and they strolled along the busy street, talking, laughing.

Holly looked again into the rear-view mirror, and this time the scar seemed to have gained prominence in her plain face. Determined not to cry, she drove aggressively back to the station.

Once there, Holly adopted an air of feigned heartiness, smiling and winking at all those she met en route to CID.

Ashworth was preoccupied, staring at the wall behind her desk, and he hardly seemed to notice that she had taken her seat. Josh's VDU was silent as he sat gazing at the blank, lifeless screen.

'What do we do then?' Holly asked, trying to sound bright.

Ashworth glanced up, seeming surprised to see her. 'I don't know,' he admitted quietly. 'I know what we should be doing but—'

Savage's bustling entrance interrupted his flow. 'Jim . . . a word.'

The frostiness had gone from his voice, which meant the subject he wished to broach was delicate.

'I've been thinking about public relations,' he announced, perching on the edge of Ashworth's desk.

'Have you now?'

Something in Ashworth's tone prompted Holly to reach for her shoulder bag, at the same time as Josh made a grab for his jacket. This little discussion was clearly not going to be pleasant.

'No, no,' Savage said, holding up his hand, 'I'd like you all to stay. The more heads working on this, the better.'

Holly replaced her bag and flashed Josh a resigned look as he sank back into his chair.

'It's about this Fox business. I've been giving it a lot of thought,' Savage went on. 'Now, ideally, what we want from the coroner's court is suicide while the balance of the mind was disturbed, and on the facts, I think that's what we'll get. But that still leaves us with a big problem because anything less than police harassment is not going to satisfy the mob.'

'Get on with it, Ken,' Ashworth interjected bluntly.

Savage cleared his throat and took his time; this was not going to be easy. 'Well, the long and short of it is, I've devised a little public relations exercise which I think could defuse the situation. It's quite simple . . .' He cast a cautious glance in Ashworth's direction. 'I'd like you to meet with Gerald Fox, make the right noises . . . you know . . . we regret what's happened, etcetera, etcetera.'

'You want me to accept responsibility? Is that what you're saying?'

Savage was emphatic. 'No, I don't, Jim. I've made it plain to all concerned that there's no way I'm letting you carry the can for this.' He paused. 'All I want is for you to be . . . well . . . less hostile.'

'And where would I be meeting Fox?' Ashworth pressed.

'At his flat . . . and the press will be there.' Savage hesitated. 'We're not the only ones backing down, Jim. I've had a word with Fox and he realizes this whole thing's got out of hand. All he wants is for the police to leave him alone. If we do that, he'll stop making noises. The yob element won't have an excuse to riot then.'

'But surely, to make peace with Fox, we need to accept some of the blame,' Holly said with suspicion.

Savage glared at her. This was a question he had hoped would not be asked.

'Not blame,' he cajoled. 'We could get away with an error of judgement.'

Holly, sensing that Ashworth was to be offered as a sacrifice, felt compelled to speak out. 'But what if the chief inspector doesn't feel he made an error?'

'It's all right,' Ashworth said. 'I'll do it.'

'You will?' Savage asked, hardly able to believe his ears.

'What time?' Ashworth's tone was expressionless.

'Two p.m.,' Savage answered brightly.

'Right.' Ashworth stood up. 'Now, if you'll excuse me, I'll have to work out the details.'

He made for the door and Savage, pausing just long enough to fix Holly with a baleful stare, followed him out, calling, 'Jim, what I thought we'd say . . .'

'Prat,' Holly remarked as the door closed.

'Holly, you're sailing pretty close to the wind,' Josh warned.

But Holly was fuming. 'Ashworth's being set up for this. They're fitting him up.'

'I know,' Josh admitted, 'but why do you think he took it so calmly?'

'I think the fight's gone out of him,' she raged, 'and that's what's got me so bloody mad.'

Josh shot her a knowing sideways glance. 'Is that all that's wrong?'

'No, it's not,' was her vigorous reply. 'I've just seen Gary Williams in the High Street with his heavily pregnant bloody wife.'

Josh shrugged.

'Well, thanks for the sympathy.'

'I did try to tell you.' He switched on the VDU, saying, 'I just hope he hasn't got you in the same condition.'

'Josh, a fool I may be,' Holly flared, 'but at least I'm a thinking fool. I do take precautions against that.'

He began tapping the keyboard. 'Good.'

'Oh . . . balls,' she said.

* * *

It was a very preoccupied Ashworth sitting in the back of Holly's Micra.

Although it might be unfair to describe Holly's driving technique as dangerous, her lack of patience did at times lead to her taking chances.

Josh, in the passenger seat, closed his eyes as she slammed hard on the brakes, bringing the car to an abrupt halt at a roundabout.

'Come on,' she muttered, viewing the traffic crawling around the island. 'Move it.'

When the first slight gap appeared, Holly pulled into it, forcing a Fiat Uno to stop.

By the time they reached Fox's flat, Ashworth had still not uttered a word. Holly parked and glanced at him over her shoulder.

'Do you want us to help out inside, guv? I, for one' — she glared at Josh — 'don't like what's going down here.'

Ashworth, his massive frame hunched up in the rear, smiled. 'No, it's all right, I know exactly why I'm here.'

He seemed more alert, filled with a sense of purpose, as they approached Fox's flat, and the young detectives had to lengthen their stride in order to keep up with him.

His knock on the door brought an immediate response.

'Bridgetown CID,' he announced to the spotty-faced young man in the doorway.

'Yes, I know,' he replied. 'I'm Morris Harvey, *Bridgetown Post*.'

Ashworth fixed him with a stare. 'You've been misquoting me of late.'

'I just write the stories as they come in,' Harvey said, indifferently.

'Try checking the facts,' Ashworth advised, pushing past the man. Holly and Josh followed him in, but held back at the living room door.

Fox was sitting on the settee, doing his best to look pallid and exhausted. There were six others in the tiny room; their pads and pens identified them as the local press.

The flat appeared much the same as when Ashworth had last seen it, except that now a pile of rolled-up sleeping bags filled one corner.

'Mr Fox,' Ashworth nodded, joining the man on the settee.

'Hello,' Fox replied, his voice faint, repressed.

Ashworth turned to the reporters. 'Right, any questions?'

'Yes.' A girl of around twenty, black-haired, wearing jeans, trainers, a sweater two sizes too large, held up her hand. '*Bridgetown Chronicle*,' she told him. 'I'd like to ask Mr Fox if he feels the intervention of Sinclair Harris and his organization has helped his cause.'

'Yes, it has.' The words were hardly audible. 'Sinclair and his friends are staying with me,' he nodded towards the sleeping bags, 'and I feel they've safeguarded my interests.'

Then he stared down at the carpet as if in absolute misery. 'But, of course, that won't bring my mother back.'

'Chief Inspector,' the girl said, 'do you acknowledge that the police handling of this affair was far from satisfactory?'

Ashworth cleared his throat. 'I must make it plain that I was the only officer involved in this line of our investigation. None of my colleagues were dealing with Mrs Fox . . .'

Harvey from the *Bridgetown Post* cut in. 'Does that mean you're accepting responsibility for what's happened?'

Ashworth considered his answer carefully. 'No,' he said after a pause, 'I still maintain that Mrs Fox invited me here, and far from being frightened, she was very friendly towards me.'

Fox's mouth dropped open in alarm as he turned to look at Ashworth's profile.

The journalists, sensing a scoop, began scribbling furiously.

A male voice called out, 'Have you any comment to make about Mrs Fox's death?'

'Only this,' Ashworth said. 'I'm far from satisfied by the circumstances surrounding it, and I shall continue my investigation while I hold my present position, and despite any obstacles which may be put in my way.' He glanced pointedly at the sleeping bags.

In the hushed silence that followed, Josh closed his eyes in despair, saw the whole of Bridgetown burning later that day.

Holly felt a surge of emotion which could not be categorized, could not be pigeon-holed, as she watched Ashworth taking charge, behaving exactly as she would have hoped: giving no quarter and fighting his corner every inch of the way.

Ashworth stood up, played to his audience. 'Mrs Fox told me many things during our short acquaintance, about her childhood in Nazi-occupied Poland; her marriage; and, yes, a good deal about her son.'

A high colour crept over Fox's face which bore a greasy sheen as he perspired heavily.

Ashworth wandered over to the dresser. 'She also told me about her collection of dolls, all of them in Polish national costume. Now, is that the behaviour of a woman who's frightened out of her wits?'

'Nice try,' Josh whispered to Holly, 'but he's never going to win this lot over.'

Holly could only agree.

Ashworth took two of the dolls, examined them closely before returning them to the shelf.

He turned to the journalists. 'Did you know that some of these dolls have hidden compartments? The Polish people used them to conceal jewellery and other valuables from the Germans.'

He carefully lowered the largest from the top shelf and gently shook it. The doll rattled.

Ashworth, with doll in hand, returned to the settee and sat down. As he removed the costume with great care, the journalists looked on, spellbound.

With the costume discarded, a small door in the middle of the doll's back was visible. Slowly, Ashworth tugged at the minute handle and it came open.

He tipped the doll over and a small plastic container dropped onto the coffee table. Everyone in the room watched with fascination as it rolled around the tabletop before coming to a halt.

'Well . . .' Ashworth said, leaning forward to read the label, '. . . Nitrazepam tablets.' His eyes scanned the startled faces. 'In other words . . . sleeping tablets.'

Fox stared at the container, horrified.

'The vital piece of evidence relating to the death of Mrs Fox,' Ashworth expounded. 'The fingerprints on that phial will give us the name of the person who administered the fatal dose. If the prints belong to Mrs Fox, that will bear out her son's story.'

'I don't know how that got in there.' Fox's quiet tone was now replaced by a high-pitched whine. 'I didn't kill my mother.'

'Holly,' Ashworth ordered.

She moved forward, picked up the container with a handkerchief, and dropped it into a small plastic bag which she sealed.

'I didn't kill my mother,' Fox squealed, now pleading to the reporters.

'Right,' Ashworth said, standing up, 'Josh, call the station and ask them to locate Sinclair Harris and . . .' He hesitated, choosing his words carefully, '. . . his associates. Ask them to come to the station and assist us with our enquiries.'

'Right, guv.' Josh left the room.

Ashworth clapped his hands. 'That's it. I'm glad you were here to witness this, and I'm sure it will prevent me being misquoted.'

Herding the reporters towards the front door, Ashworth added, 'And another thing that might interest you . . . Mr Fox will also be asked to assist us.'

As the last of them trooped out, Holly looked across at Fox who was sitting with head in hands.

She turned to Ashworth. 'How did you know that was in there?'

'I didn't, it was pure chance. I just picked it up and . . .' His face held a private smile as he left the sentence unfinished.

Holly's look was doubtful. 'I just hope you know what you're doing, guv.'

'So do I,' Ashworth said before turning to Fox. 'Move,' he commanded.

* * *

Ashworth escorted the nonplussed Gerald Fox to Holly's car.

'Mind your head,' he advised as Fox climbed into the rear. 'Holly, stop on the way back. I need to buy a box of matches.'

'A box of matches?' Holly queried with a frown.

'Yes.'

'Right, guv,' she said, when it became obvious no further explanation was forthcoming.

* * *

Gerald Fox remained silent during the drive to the station.

Small crowds had gathered at the front and rear of the building. Youths, attired in tattered leather jackets and grubby jeans, taunted when the vehicle came into view.

As Holly turned into the car park, a smirking teenager stepped in front, forcing her to stop. Egged on by his companions, the youth placed his hand on the bonnet and struck a defiant pose.

Holly held the car on the clutch and edged forward until with some satisfaction, she felt the bumper hit bone. The startled boy cried out and leapt to one side.

'Sorry, guv, my foot slipped,' she said, driving to the first convenient space.

'Quite understandable,' Ashworth commented. 'In the circumstances, that is.'

They were getting out of the car when the first stone came over. It struck the car roof, denting it. The youth Holly had forced aside stood just beyond the gates, repeatedly waving two fingers in the air.

Holly inspected the dent. 'I'll cripple that bast—'

'Inside, Holly,' Ashworth ordered tersely, as more missiles came in their direction.

Holly hesitated, then followed as Josh helped Ashworth bundle Fox inside the building. The door had barely closed behind them when, seconds later, a heavy object hit it with a loud thud.

'Josh, take Mr Fox to interview room number 1,' Ashworth instructed. 'Make sure he gets a cup of tea and cigarettes.'

Josh nodded and escorted Gerald Fox up the back stairs.

Holly held up the plastic bag containing the sleeping-tablet phial. 'Do you want me to take this to fingerprints?'

'No, leave it with me. I want you to stay with Fox.'

He took the bag and pushed through the swing doors into reception where he found Ken Savage in heated discussion with Martin Dutton. Bobby Adams nervously looked on.

'Jim, what's happening?' Savage barked.

Behind him, Dutton winked, proving that Ashworth's stock was once again rising within the station.

'I've brought Fox in for questioning,' he said flatly.

'But why did you order Harris and his people to be brought in?'

'I want to talk to them, Ken.'

'We're going to have another riot.' Savage gesticulated wildly towards the street. 'Harris is an important man.'

'Harris is a yob with a posh accent,' Ashworth countered.

A jittery Savage said, 'I've got to overturn your orders, Jim. This situation is getting out of hand.'

'I won't allow you to do that,' Ashworth insisted. 'I can clear up the murders and attacks as well as Mrs Fox's death.'

'Not if that lot storm the station,' Savage blustered, 'and they will if we bring Harris in.'

'I've got enough on Harris and his friends to put them away for a long time, and it's my duty to see that's done,' Ashworth said, his patience running thin. 'What we've got outside are forty kids throwing stones. Without anyone to organize them, they're not capable of lighting the fuse on a petrol bomb, let alone making one.' He stabbed a finger towards the crowd, saying, 'Just shift them, Ken, and if they don't like that idea, show them the inside of a cell.'

'I just hope you're right,' Savage huffed before storming off.

As Ashworth watched him disappear around a corner, the noise from outside increased, sounds of breaking glass reached his ears, and he thought miserably: So do I, Ken . . . so do I.

'Have Harris and his people been detained?' he asked Sergeant Dutton.

'Yes, Jim, and the man's threatening to do some terrible things to you.'

Ashworth laughed. 'Where are they?'

'The lads are holding them back, rather than bring them through that lot.'

'Can you clear the mob outside?'

'No problem. We're just waiting for the order.' A mischievous gleam came to his eyes as he added, 'A lot of the lads have a few scores to settle from the other night.'

'Now you know I won't tolerate that, Martin,' Ashworth warned sternly. 'Personal feelings don't come into our job.' However, the corners of his mouth flicked up as he said, 'I'd expect a few mishaps though, but nothing that couldn't be put down to self-defence.'

Ashworth almost ran up the stairs to CID, and once there he took the plastic bag with the container inside, the box of matches purchased from an off-licence on the way, and dropped them into the top drawer of his desk.

CHAPTER 29

The door of interview room number 1 opened to reveal Gerald Fox sitting at the table, a polystyrene cup half full of tea in front of him.

Josh was standing to the left of the door, and Holly was craning her neck by the window, keeping her car in constant view.

Ashworth motioned for them to join him in the corridor.

'I'm begging a favour,' he said. 'I want to see Fox alone.'

Josh appeared troubled, but Holly immediately said, 'Okay, guv, what do you want us to do?'

'Harris and his thugs are being brought in. Go downstairs and welcome them.'

Ashworth entered the room but remained by the door to study Fox. Outside, the sounds of jeering and shouting were growing faint, fading into the distance.

'I didn't kill my mother,' Fox said, his head bowed.

Ashworth stayed silent.

Fox looked up at him. 'I didn't.'

'Your prints are on the container though, aren't they?' Ashworth said quietly. 'You were in charge of your mother's drugs.'

'Yes,' Fox admitted, 'but I didn't hide it in the doll.'

Ashworth pulled up a chair and sat facing the man. He said, 'How do you think it got there then?'

'I don't know.' He lit a cigarette, and gabbled, 'When I found out my mother had died from an overdose, I dumped all her drugs. I was frantic . . .'

Ashworth changed the subject. 'How long has Sinclair Harris been staying with you?'

'Since my mother died.'

'Did he come to your flat before that?'

'Yes, he's a friend.'

The forgotten cigarette burned steadily away between Fox's fingers, the smoke spiralling towards the ceiling.

'So why did you agree to attend the press conference with me?'

'Because I wanted them out. They'd started making petrol bombs and storing them there.' His eyes rested briefly on Ashworth's face, then he looked away, saying, 'I just don't want any trouble with the police.'

Ashworth gave a grim laugh. 'It's a bit late for that. You've already killed two women, injured two more.'

'You can't prove that,' Fox stated loudly.

Ashworth raised his eyebrows, said nothing. The cigarette burned Fox's fingers; he muttered a curse and angrily stubbed it out.

Ashworth said, 'The girl you attacked on the Barr Nature Reserve has regained consciousness. She can identify you.'

He watched the shock disfigure Fox's face before continuing. 'Your mother told me all about you.' He paused, allowing time for the meaning of those words to register. 'Was it her unhappy relationship? Was that the trigger?'

Fox stared straight ahead. 'I did not kill my mother,' he said firmly.

'I know you killed the other women, so does that matter?'

'Yes . . .'

Fox began to sob: quiet, heart-rending convulsions; and Ashworth guessed that the man had inherited his mother's mental instability.

'Everything I did was for my mother,' he cried.

'I can help you, Gerald, if you make things easy for me. That's why I asked to see you alone.'

'I don't think anyone can help me now,' Fox murmured, his tone wretched.

'I can, Gerald. Tell me about the women,' he paused, took in a deep breath, 'and I'll conceal evidence concerning your mother's death.'

'You can't do that,' Fox said warily.

'I'm the police. I can do anything . . . remember?'

'Why should I trust you?'

'Because you've no choice. Why should I lie to you? I can prove you killed those women. It'll take time, but that I have; and if I so decide, I can let you go to prison for your mother's murder.'

'Why should you help me?'

'I liked your mother. I'd rather the truth was known about her death.'

Fox considered this, but still his countenance was wary.

'It's because everyone's always let you down, Gerald, isn't it? You . . . and your mother?'

Fox's eyes glazed over as his mind reached back into the past. 'You don't know what it's like,' he said. 'Nobody does. Most people can't remember when they were babies, but I can. Lying in my cot, watching my mother and father . . . I didn't even understand what they were saying, not the words, but I knew they wanted to hurt each other.'

He cast Ashworth a desperate look. 'Can you imagine what it's like for a boy growing up, to know that any moment his mother could start running around the house, smashing things . . . the furniture, windows . . . screaming at the top of her voice?'

Ashworth could only shake his head.

'No, of course you can't. Then they'd come and fetch her away. I'd have to stay with foster parents.' Fox sank back in his chair. 'Loony Sophie, they used to call her . . . the kids I went to school with.

'At first she told me father was dead. He just went out one day and died. I really think she believed it. But that left me with no one to hate for what had happened to us . . . so I started to hate everyone.'

'Did you kill those women, Gerald?' Ashworth pressed.

Fox brought up a hand to cover his eyes and nodded. 'Yes.'

Ashworth exhaled with relief; for the first time in this tangled web of deceit, he knew for certain that Fox was the murderer.

'I hear these voices inside my head. Sometimes I think my skull's going to split open. They scream at me until I can't stand it.'

Ashworth reached forward and touched his arm. 'Are you willing to make a statement to my officers admitting the murders and the two attacks?'

'Yes.' He looked at Ashworth and almost smiled. 'I'm glad you've caught me.' Then, 'Did my mother really tell you all that?'

'Every word,' Ashworth answered.

'I didn't think she'd turn me in . . . not when it came to it.'

'She did it because she loved you, Gerald,' Ashworth said, rising to his feet. 'No other reason. She just wanted you to get help.'

'You promise I won't be charged with her murder?'

'You have my word . . .' He crossed to the door. '. . . but don't mention it to anyone else.'

Holly and Josh were waiting at the end of the corridor.

'Fox has admitted to the murders and attacks,' Ashworth informed them as they approached, 'and he's ready to make a statement. Now, I led him to believe that his mother told me he'd committed the crimes and I don't want him disillusioned.'

'What about his mother's murder?' Josh queried.

'He didn't do that, and don't ask him any questions about it. Where's Harris?'

'Interview 3,' Holly said. 'Screaming for your blood.'

Ashworth strode off, muttering, 'Good. Good.'

Harris jumped to his feet when Ashworth walked in. 'What the hell am I doing here?' he yelled.

'Sit down,' Ashworth said dismissively as he nodded to the uniformed constable at the door.

Harris, completely out of control, screamed, 'I'll make you grovel for this.'

Raw, pent-up emotion surfaced in Ashworth at those words; he rushed to the table, leant across. 'It'll be a long day before I ever grovel to the likes of you,' he spat. 'By the time you get out of jail I'll be quite old, so you might be in with a chance then. If there's enough of you, that is.'

Harris was a man used to getting his own way by instilling fear into others, but he shrank before Ashworth's onslaught, saying feebly, 'You haven't got anything on me.'

'Yes, I have. You're very fond of the television cameras. You like appearing in front of them, laying down the law. Well, the riot was filmed and you, together with your little band of thugs, are on tape passing petrol bombs around and enticing the crowd . . .'

The colour drained from Harris's face.

'And there's the little matter of the bombs being made in Gerald Fox's flat.'

'I want a solicitor,' Harris demanded.

'All right,' Ashworth said, 'but in the meantime . . . you're nicked.'

* * *

As he trudged back to the office, Ashworth suddenly realized how tired he was.

'Not much longer,' he assured himself.

Opening his desk drawer, he took out the plastic bag, the box of matches, and placed them on his blotter.

He carefully undid the seal on the bag and took out the tablet container, ran his thumb around it to smudge any fingerprints, then dropped it back in the bag and sat down to wait.

Half an hour later, Holly found him sitting there, shoulders slumped, staring down at the blotter.

'Guv, Fox has made a full confession and we've charged him. Bradford police have been informed in case they want to question him.'

Ashworth continued to stare at the desk.

'What do you want done about Sinclair Harris and the others?'

'Incitement to riot, and anything else in the Public Order Act. Get Uniformed to throw the book at them.' He picked up the bag. 'And take this to Forensic for fingerprints.'

Holly took it. 'Anything else, guv? Anything you want to talk about?'

Ignoring her second question, Ashworth said, 'Could I ask a second favour?' His brown eyes, usually hostile, were now pleading.

'Yes, of course.'

'Ring Gwen Anthony for me. Tell her someone's been arrested for the murders and assaults.'

Holly appeared reluctant. 'How much am I supposed to know about you two?'

'You know everything,' he said. 'I just don't want to make contact with her, that's all.'

'Okay. She'll be at the surgery, I take it?'

Ashworth consulted his wristwatch. 'Yes, that's right.'

'I know the number,' she said, making for the door.

* * *

On the way back from Forensic, Holly made the call from a pay-phone in the corridor.

With everything going so well, she could not help but wonder why Ashworth seemed so subdued. Perhaps it had something to do with the fingerprints on the bottle.

Ashworth looked up expectantly as she entered the office.

'She was very pleased, and bloody rude as she always is with me,' Holly informed him. 'She asked me how much I knew. I said, everything. Then she told me her husband's dropped the divorce petition, and they're leaving the district.'

The news cheered Ashworth a little. 'Good,' he smiled.

Holly sat on the edge of his desk. 'Guv, something's bothering you about this and I can't understand why. Fox is in custody. Anthony's out of the picture, and I presume Fox'll be charged with his mother's murder—'

'No,' Ashworth whispered, almost to himself. 'Sophie Fox's death was the key that unlocked this whole thing, but no one will be charged with her murder.'

'I'm not following this.'

'It's far better that you don't. It's enough that it'll be on my conscience, without involving you.'

'I think I'm entitled to an explanation.'

Ashworth smiled. 'You're becoming very direct. All I will tell you is that if I disclosed the circumstances surrounding her death, questions would be asked as to why I hadn't acted sooner, and I think you know the answer to that.'

'You still couldn't be sure it wasn't Anthony, and until you were, there was no way you could act freely.'

'Yes.'

'I've a feeling this is all I'm going to get to know.'

'Yes, it is, and if it's any consolation, it's more than any other living soul is likely to.'

'What now?'

'Leave me for ten minutes, will you? There's someone I want to make my peace with.'

Dusk was creeping into the office. He heard the door close softly behind Holly and looked towards the telephone. Then, shaking his head, he stood up and walked over to look out at the town through the glass wall.

At least the threat of divorce which had loomed large in his thoughts these last few days had receded; and, to his knowledge, there was no other trace of his misdemeanours to be unearthed for scrutiny.

Ashworth took the white envelope from his inside pocket and, withdrawing the letter, went back to his desk for the matches.

The handwriting was an untidy scrawl.

Dear Jim Ashworth,

I know you just a short time, but I trust you. I have done terrible wrong. I was so frightened of the mental hospitals — they remind me of the camps. I know my son has harmed women, here and in Bradford, but I keep my mouth closed. Even when I see him burning the clothes soaked with blood, I say nothing. I do not want to be locked up. Whichever way I turn there is no way out. If I tell the police, would you believe a crazy old woman? My son is too clever. You will never catch him. So now I throw myself at the wire fence. When he gives me sleeping tablets I do not take them — I store them until I have enough. When he throws away empty bottle, I rescue it from the rubbish, careful not to get my fingerprints on it. I hide it in the large Polish doll on my dresser. Then I sit down and write you this letter.

I am going to kill myself, Jim Ashworth, and you must charge Gerald with my murder. Please God, you must put my son where he can be safe.

And me, I hope for peace now.

Sophie

Ashworth reached for the large ashtray stored on top of the filing cabinet since its redundancy, struck a match and lit a corner of the letter. The flames danced and flickered on the glass walls.

'I'm sorry, Sophie,' he said softly. 'I suppose you know all about me by now. All I can say in my defence is that I could no more let your son go to prison for a crime he had not committed, than I could send Gladys Smart there for something she *had* done.'

He dropped the blazing letter into the ashtray.

'In the end we all take our decisions and have to stand by them.'

Looking towards the darkening sky, Ashworth whispered, 'Peace, Sophie,' half hoping for some sign that his message had been received in another world.

But none was forthcoming.

THE END

ALSO BY BRIAN BATTISON

DETECTIVE JIM ASHWORTH SERIES
Book 1: TIED TO MURDER
Book 2: THE PRICE OF MURDER
Book 3: FLIRTING WITH MURDER

MORE BOOKS IN THE SERIES COMING SOON!

Printed in Great Britain
by Amazon

66977242R00180